# Good Bones

## by

## L. A. Kelley

**Good Bones**

Cover Art by *Debbie Taylor*

The Wild Rose Press, Inc.
PO Box 708
Adams Basin, NY 14410-0708
Visit us at www.thewildrosepress.com

Publishing History
First Fantasy Rose Edition, 2017
Print ISBN 978-1-5092-1430-3
Digital ISBN 978-1-5092-1431-0

Published in the United States of America

## Without warning,

the temperature plummeted. Katherine shivered, hugging her arms to her chest. "Why is it so cold?"

Jake's lips pressed together in a thin, tight line, his gaze fixed on the mirror.

*Click...click...click...click.*

The lamp flicked on and off. Katherine's pulse soared. "Detective?"

Jake glowered at the lamp, his face red with anger. He grabbed Katherine's arm. "I'm sorry. I was wrong. I shouldn't have brought you here—"

The French doors slammed shut. From outside came a muted thud as the front door closed as well.

Katherine shrugged off Jake's grip. "W-what are you doing? This isn't funny."

"It's not me." He peered at the mirror. "I'm sorry, Dr. Fleming. This is a bad idea. We should go now."

*Don't leave me.*

"W-who said that?" Katherine turned around to face the mirror. Her eyes widened in horror as the black splotches slid toward the center of the glass. "Trick." Katherine clutched at her shirt. "It must be a trick."

The blotches whirled together. A misty shape formed. Arms...legs...now torso...now head...an image of a person appeared from inside the gilded frame. Facial features blurred beyond recognition, but the body was definitely female.

Katherine's legs refused to move, a scream died on her lips. Shaking, she raised a trembling arm. Instead of mimicking her movement, the reflection remained rooted in place. "T-that's not me."

## Dedication

To my family

Chapter 1

The irony of living on a dead-end street didn't hit Katherine Fleming until days later. For the moment, only morning coffee called. She reached for the pantry door and her hand froze halfway. Didn't she finish the last drop yesterday? Her eyes went to the shopping list on the refrigerator. The big red letters of *BUY COFFEE* mocked her. Running low on caffeine first thing in the morning usually resulted in a snarly growl or two, but not today. Today was Saturday—all hers. Forget the budget and celebrate. "Treat yourself at the coffee shop downtown."

"Darn right, I will."

Katherine snatched her key, stuffed the shopping list and charge card in her pocket, and bounded down the stairs from the second floor to the lobby. She paused outside the entrance in the shallow recess with the intercom buttons for each apartment. Although the calendar technically said winter, her nose caught the faint scent of budding greenery. A smile played around her lips. The past few years of frigid Chicago cold suffered during graduate school were now only an unpleasant memory.

Up north, folks still shivered. Spring was weeks away and always arrived with a burst of pastels, soft gentle tones to ease Earth back to life after winter dormancy. Not in north Florida. Floral fireworks of azaleas and crepe myrtles would explode open any day in neon shades of hot pink, coral, and brilliant crimson. Within a few weeks, the hibiscus at the corner would transform into a riot of sunny orange blossoms lasting through summer. Katherine heaved a contented sigh. She couldn't wait.

When Katherine arrived at the Sandy Shoals Counseling Center in mid-January, her boss, Dr. Jeremy Ingalls, teased about her eagerness for warm weather. "Wait until July," he warned with a grin. "I was born here. The short walk across the parking lot will leave you drenched in sweat and misty-eyed for six-foot snow drifts. The air is so humid it's like breathing through a hot, wet sponge."

Diana Weller, the office manager, shook a playful finger at him. "Don't scare her away on the first day. You're trying to grow the center, remember? Besides, you returned from New York to practice here, so how bad can it be?"

"Bad." Jeremy winked. "Why do you think I escaped for fifteen years?"

Katherine gave a mental shrug. *Who cares what the summer will bring?* Today, cotton ball clouds dotted brilliant blue skies while a gentle breeze wafted through bare tree branches speckled with tiny lime green buds. Spring beckoned.

She turned the corner and ambled toward the shopping district. Finding the apartment had been pure luck. It was a perfect location. Close enough to the city center for walking, far enough down the street to muffle all the traffic noise, and, most importantly, within her limited budget.

Strolling along the sidewalk, memories of weekend

walks with her grandfather returned. Katherine's mind began the familiar back and forth as echoes of his gentle prodding rang in her head.

*Play the game with me, Kathy.*

*I'm going for coffee.*

*Aw c'mon, kiddo, humor Grampa. You know you can't resist.*

Her lips twitched in an unconscious smile. He was right. She never could. *Okay, but just once.*

*Atta girl. Who do you see?*

Katherine peered down the street. A man in his mid-twenties lounged against the bus stop sign on the corner. A young woman speaking on her cell phone strolled up and stopped next to him. She wore a snug low-cut t-shirt. The tattoo of a dolphin peeked out above her left breast. A gold dolphin pendent hung low around her neck, drawing anyone's eye to her ample cleavage, including the man. His gaze flicked to her. His stance straightened as he squared his shoulders.

The woman ended the call and dropped the phone in her purse. She glanced at him. Her gaze met his for an instant and then she turned away, but her head inclined slightly in his direction. She tugged at the hem of her shirt, flattening the material over her breasts. Her posture eased, a hip jutted out as she angled her body toward him.

Grampa's mental voice nudged gently. *Well?*

*The placement of the dolphin tattoo draws immediate attention to her breasts. Her dress and body language suggests inflated value placed on physical attributes which can mask deeply rooted feelings of intellectual inferiority. The man will make his intentions known before he gets off the bus. He's not looking for deep commitment, but she'll accept. I predict a short passionate relationship followed by an equally passionate breakup. She'll blame him for the reason it ended badly. In truth, she's blinded by appearances and isn't mature enough to see past them at this point.*

A bus arrived at the stop. The man stepped aside for the woman to enter first. She smiled at him and casually flipped back her hair. He followed and took the seat next to her.

*Not bad, kiddo.*

"Thanks, Grampa," Katherine murmured, brushing aside a tinge of melancholy. Although he had passed away several years ago, his absence was still deeply felt. The imaginary talks in her head proved only a pale substitute.

Katherine strolled past the bus, fighting the temptation to jump onboard and offer the woman her card. The well-meant gesture was sure to prove pointless. People wouldn't accept counseling help unless they first recognized a problem. She wasn't there yet.

Pity. Katherine stifled a sigh. Another client would be nice. Diana booked her calendar with anyone who called for an appointment and didn't specifically request Jeremy, but Katherine was a new counselor. It took time to build a reputation and get those important referrals. The inheritance from her grandfather had funded her education, but she had plenty of open slots, and regular living expenses now. Fortunately, enough money remained in the budget for the occasional indulgence.

The Saturday morning crowd had thinned by the time Katherine entered the coffee shop. She paused at the door and recognized a familiar face at the pick-up counter. April Ortiz waited for her order behind a man in a gray t-shirt. She was one of Katherine's first clients, but she hesitated to approach. April had made excellent progress, but canceled her last appointment two weeks ago and hadn't rescheduled yet. A patient might find it awkward to run into her counselor in a social setting.

April looked from the counter and spotted Katherine at the door. Instead of dismay, she brightened and motioned her over with an excited wave of the hand. "I did it," April blurted even before Katherine said hello.

Katherine's eyes widened. "I thought you weren't going until next month."

"I meant to call and tell you, but I've been so busy. He phoned two weeks ago after an unexpected opening and I said to myself I'm ready to do this. Can you believe it?" April gave an excited hop on her toes. "I'll buy you a mocha latte to celebrate. With whip and extra sprinkles."

"Thanks, but that's not necessary—"

April leaned around the man and called over the counter to the server. "Add another mocha latte to the order, please. Both to go."

Katherine bit back a smile. The experience certainly hadn't changed April's take charge attitude. No wonder she had sought help. "I'm so proud of you. I know how hard it was to let another person assume control."

"I didn't expect him to be so gentle and finish so quickly," April crowed, "especially with my history. We were done before I knew it." She beamed at

Katherine. "You wouldn't believe the total satisfaction when he touched me deep inside and I didn't flinch."

The shoulders of the man in the gray t-shirt stiffened. His head which had faced front toward the counter angled slightly in their direction.

"Nervousness is expected," said Katherine, "after such a long time and considering he was a stranger."

"No kidding, but I never felt anything more than a few butterflies. I kept reminding myself I had your recommendation and you'd only send me to a caring man who was a real pro and had a lot of experience. Still, I can't say it wasn't awkward. He was so nice though, and helped me feel comfortable. Before I knew it, I was flat on my back and staring at the ceiling."

"So, spill it," said Katherine. "I'm dying to hear the details."

"He asked me to open. I did. No hesitation. No screaming. Then he slipped in a finger. At least, that's what he said, but I didn't feel a thing. To be honest, by that time I had my eyes closed."

The man in the t-shirt shuffled on his feet, edging a fraction closer.

"Number 27 order up!" The man startled at the barista's call. He snagged a cup of coffee and a plate with a bagel and cream cheese, but instead of taking a seat he lingered at the counter fiddling with the napkin dispenser.

"He began with only the slightest bit of pressure," continued April, "but something inside me definitely moved. I kept thinking, 'This is so weird. I can't tell if he has his whole hand in there or just poking round with his long pointy doo-dad.' "

The man's hand jerked and pulled out a fist-load of

napkins.

"Was there any pain?" asked Katherine.

April snorted. "With all the drugs he slipped me? I was flying high. I was sore for a few days afterward, but he gave me a bunch of painkillers. I tell you, the whole experience was amazing." She sighed. "He was awesome. Is it weird to have a crush on your dentist?"

The man's lips twitched in a smile. He tossed the napkins on top of the bagel.

"Yes," said Katherine with a straight face. "Particularly since he's four inches shorter than you, gay, and nearly old enough to be your grandfather."

April grinned and jabbed her in the shoulder. "What do you mean, yes? You're a psychologist. You're not supposed to tell anyone they're weird. I knew a gal my age was too young to have a real degree. Where'd you get it? Off the internet?"

"Yup, got a two-for-one special. I'm also High Priestess in the Awesomely Enlightened Temple of Awesomeness. Besides, I didn't say *you* were weird, but it's definitely unexpected to have warm-and-fuzzy vibes for a dentist coming from a person with a dental phobia a few short weeks ago. Not to mention, working up the courage to have an impacted wisdom tooth pulled. It proves how far you've come."

April hugged her. "I couldn't have done it without you, Doctor Fleming. You're one helluva psychologist."

Katherine flushed with pride at the heartfelt praise. There was no better feeling than helping a person in need. "Call me Katherine. You walked the walk. I only showed you the path."

April's phone chimed with an incoming text. She

glanced at the display. "It's from Parker at the station." April worked at GAB-TV, a local cable access channel. "Aw, crap, a guest canceled. I need a last minute replacement pronto for *Chit Chat with Parker Pratt*. We tape today for tomorrow morning's broadcast." She grimaced. "God, I hate that title."

"Have you suggested he change it?"

"I can't, Parker owns the station and his wife, Connie, is the business manager. I'm only a glorified go-fer. Also, they're both sweethearts and Parker is an institution. He knows everybody and all the gossip in this town. He used to have his own talk radio show before they bought the cable station. Parker still does a daily podcast, too; mostly local news and community service plugs. Man, finding a new and interesting guest Parker hasn't already interviewed is a pain. Viewers are getting sick of the Goat Lady gushing over her artisanal cheeses."

Katherine chuckled. "Come back for more counseling. I'll help you work up the courage to quit."

April regarded her with shocked disbelief. "And leave show biz?" She drew in a sharp breath. "I have a brainstorm. God, I'm a genius. Are you free this afternoon?"

Katherine's eyes narrowed. "Why?"

"To do a guest spot. You'll be perfect."

"Me?"

"Sure—the interview only lasts half an hour. Talk about counseling. You'll follow Miss Harmony, the pet psychic. Parker tapes after her call-in show."

"Pet psychic?"

April clasped her hands together in prayer. "Please, please, pleeeese. Imagine all the good you can do. A sufferer with that thing…what's the thing you mentioned once?" Her brows knitted together. "You remember, that thing where a person is too afraid to leave the house."

"Agoraphobia."

"Yeah, talk about that. A poor tortured soul may finally work up the courage to get help all because Dr. Katherine Fleming happened to appear on Parker's show. Keep in mind," she added out of the side of her mouth, "this all comes with a boatload of free advertising."

Katherine regarded her askance. "You're good."

"I gotta be. This is a local cable access program airing at seven on Sunday mornings; interesting guests are hard to book. At that time of day, our entire viewer demographic is nut jobs, shut-ins, and people in tinfoil helmets afraid to surf the web because the government will infiltrate their minds—right up your alley."

Katherine chuckled. "You win, April. I'll do it. It sounds fun."

"Bless you," she gushed.

"Number 28 order up!"

The man in the t-shirt moved away from the counter, and they grabbed their coffees. "Thanks for the latte," said Katherine.

"No problem. The studio is on 12th Street. You can't miss it. Be there at 3:30. I'll give you a tour and run you through the procedure. We tape the spot at 4:00. See you then, Katherine."

April dashed to the door while Katherine lingered to put the appointment on her phone calendar. She headed to the exit with her mocha latte and spotted the man in the t-shirt at a seat near the front window.

Katherine leaned over and whispered in his ear, "You have a very dirty mind." She scampered out the door, but not before noticing the flash of a dimpled grin in her direction.

**\*\*\*\***

Jake Sumner froze at the woman's whisper. He swallowed a mouthful of coffee and turned around with a grin, but she was gone before the thought occurred to apologize for eavesdropping. Pity, Dr. Katherine Fleming certainly was cute. He could have asked her to join him…Jake shook his head.

*Forget it, buddy. You're about to get rid of one shrink. You sure as hell don't need another probing parts of your life that need to stay buried.*

He craned his neck, catching the last sight of her as she rounded the corner. Not a bad view from the rear angle either. Despite the mental words of warning, his interest had definitely been piqued.

*Chit Chat with Parker Pratt, eh? Maybe I'll catch the show.*

Chapter 2

At 3:30 on the dot, Katherine turned off 12$^{th}$ Street and parked in front of GAB-TV studios, located downtown between a Chinese restaurant and an insurance company. April waited in the lobby.

Katherine glanced around. "This building is a lot bigger than I thought. Don't tell me it's all for *Chit Chat with Parker Pratt*."

"Oh, hell no," laughed April. "We mostly produce commercial shows for business owners—ergo Miss Harmony. The rest aren't as whack-a-doodle though." She ticked a list off on her fingers. "A realtor has a regular spot to show video tours of her new listings. We have a chef that cooks the special of the week on the menu from his restaurant. The Chamber of Commerce promotes new businesses, a financial planner talks investment strategy, stuff like that. Parker and Connie are big on community service, too, so we cover local high school sports and produce occasional specials or host performing artists. Good publicity for them, good community mojo for us. Follow me, I'll give you a tour."

April showed Katherine the production facilities. They peeked into the business office. Parker's wife, Connie, was on the phone and waved hello. April paused at the entrance to Studio B. The ON AIR sign was lit. She put a finger to her lips. "Parker and Miss

Harmony are doing the show," she whispered, easing open the door.

On a raised dais were two leather armchairs in front of a library backdrop. A man with a gray thatch of hair sat in one and a woman in the other. On her lap was a shorthair white cat wearing a sparkly rhinestone collar. Little blue gems inserted among the diamond-like ones spelled out WHISKERS. Set between the two chairs was an end table with a speakerphone.

"Is Whiskers ready, Miss Harmony?" asked Parker.

"He is," she said. The cat yawned.

Katherine raised an eyebrow.

"Didn't I mention?" whispered April dryly. "Whiskers is the psychic. Miss Harmony only channels his responses."

"Then we'll take our next caller," said Parker.

Katherine's stomach gave a nervous flutter. "The show is live? I thought you said it was taped."

"Parker's show is taped," murmured April, "but a month ago Miss Harmony and Whiskers began a live call-in show on Saturday afternoon. She hired Parker as co-host to lend authenticity, but all he does is answer the phone and try hard not to roll his eyes."

"H-hello?" A nervous woman's voice came through the speakerphone.

"Hello, caller," said Parker in a soothing tone, "you're on the air. What is your first name?"

"Janelle."

"Janelle, do you have a question for Miss Harmony?"

"Yes, well, not a question really."

Janelle's voice strained to get out the words. Her emotional distress tugged at Katherine's heart.

"M-my mother died recently..." Janelle paused to draw a shuddering breath.

Miss Harmony leaned forward. "I'm so sorry, my dear. Her death must have been very difficult for you. Whiskers senses she was sick."

"Yes, it was sudden."

"I understand," Miss Harmony cooed. "Whiskers says it took you by surprise."

Janelle drew in a sharp breath. "Why, that's right."

"Oh brother," murmured Katherine. "Miss Harmony is echoing—rephrasing and telling the caller exactly what she just stated."

"Whiskers," continued Miss Harmony, "feels the sudden loss has been terribly hard for you."

"Duh," muttered Katherine with growing disgust. "Of course, it's hard. She lost her mother and is plainly grieving."

Janelle's voice trembled. "It all happened so fast; her death, the funeral. Now, I have to sell the house, go through her belongings." She paused as if to force her emotions under control. "I-I can't shake the feeling Mom wants me do something else. Something I've forgotten."

Katherine whispered to April, "A sudden death often brings a lack of closure. Deep down, Janelle needs to not only hear her mother approves of her actions, but also receive assurance everything will be okay."

Miss Harmony lifted Whiskers so they were face to face. The cat hung limply as she peered into his eyes. She nodded once and returned him to her lap. Whiskers yawned again, lifted his rear leg, and licked his genitals.

"Whiskers wants you to know your mother said

you're a good daughter. Her love is still with you even though her spirit is in a better place. The little chores can wait. Don't stress over any of them. Things will sort themselves out in the proper time, but take care of your own needs first."

April nudged Katherine. "You're good."

Janelle gushed her thanks to Miss Harmony. "That sounds just like Mom." This time she spoke without a tremble.

The calls continued, each speaker mourning a recently departed loved one. Miss Harmony, or rather Whiskers, started with trite phrases of assurance the deceased was at peace. Besides echoing, Katherine discerned a general casting technique as Miss Harmony threw out multiple questions to zero in on details. "Did the loved one's name have an *S*? No? Wait, it's difficult to hear Whiskers. He says an *E* or is it an *A*? An *A*. Of course, I hear quite clearly now. That's exactly what Whiskers tried to tell me." Mawkish clichés oozing sympathy coupled with Miss Harmony's impressive ability to wheedle information from the caller made for slick patter.

The show came to an end. Whiskers appeared to have fallen asleep. With a flick of the hand, Miss Harmony summoned April. "Fetch Whiskers' cat carrier. I hate to budge him. Psychic exertions can be so exhausting." She peered at Katherine. "I don't believe we've met." April handed Miss Harmony a worn, soft-sided cat carrier and made introductions.

Miss Harmony beamed at Katherine. "Lovely to meet you. I also do private readings." Leaning in, she pressed a business card into her hand. "Has anyone ever mentioned your aura is positively transcendent?"

"Yes, all the time," said Katherine with a straight face. "It itches, too. Can you get rid of it?"

Miss Harmony blinked and stepped back. "No...I...uh, must be going...clients to see..." She shoved Whiskers into the carrier and zipped up the side. As she hurried toward the door, the cat shifted position and pressed his nose against the mesh. His unblinking stare fixed on Katherine.

April snickered. "You're a bad person."

Katherine grinned and slipped the card into her jacket pocket.

Despite Parker Pratt's gray hair, he bounded off the dais with a spring in his step and shook Katherine's hand with a firm grip. "Welcome. I'm eager for our talk." His eyes twinkled. "What did you think of Miss Harmony?"

Katherine cleared her throat. "She's skilled at telling people exactly what they want to hear."

He chuckled. "How politically correct of you. I think she spouts a giant load of horse manure."

Katherine raised an eyebrow. "Then why—"

Parker had a devilish look on his face. "It's a giant load of horse manure, but the commercial breaks include plugs for my own talk show. Ratings are on the rise since I started with Miss Harmony."

April scowled. "How can anyone swallow her line of crap?"

"I heard that." Connie entered the studio, her expression displayed undisguised amusement. "Good thing Miss Harmony left the building. It seems April isn't a true believer in the supernatural, Katherine. How about you? What do you believe in?"

"I believe people in emotional distress should get

help from a certified counselor and not a phony with a bejeweled cat."

"Here, here," Connie crowed.

Parker chuckled. "Connie hasn't forgiven me for adding Miss Harmony's show to the schedule."

His wife sniffed. "The only positive aspect of Miss Harmony's character is she pays her bill on time."

With a grin, Parker took Katherine by the elbow. "Let's see if we can convince my audience of the greater benefit in using proven therapeutic techniques."

He escorted her to a seat on the dais. For the next thirty minutes, they had a pleasant discussion on the positive effects of mental health counseling. Parker was a warm, knowledgeable host with an interesting question ready any time the conversation lagged. He quickly put Katherine's nerves at ease. As they neared the end of the interview, he asked what a new patient should expect at the first appointment.

"A comfortable atmosphere is key. The counselor must make a personal connection and offer assurance the individual's issue is treatable, and they can work through the healing process together. This is especially important with phobias."

"How so?" asked Parker.

"Although phobias are irrational fears, the physical sensations are real. People experience sweaty palms, dry mouth, racing heart—all the normal responses to imminent danger. Even if the mind recognizes the illogic of the situation, the body's reaction overwhelms common sense and adds fuel to the emotional disturbance. 'I have no reason to be afraid, but I am afraid, so I must be crazy.' A sufferer can get stuck in a vicious cycle, so it's important for a counselor to project confidence. No matter the depth of the fear, help is available."

The half hour flew by and taping ended. "Not too horrible?" said Parker with a grin.

Katherine chuckled. "To my surprise, it was fun. Thanks for having me."

"I'm glad to hear that. You were a wonderful guest. I wish we had more time to discuss phobias. Fascinating topic," he mused. "Perhaps in a few weeks, we can schedule another interview."

"I'd like that."

Connie and April had watched from the sidelines and ambled over to join them. Connie nodded at April. "She said you worked at the Sandy Shoals Counseling Center. How are you getting along with Jeremy Ingalls?"

"He made me very welcome. Do you know him?"

"Only socially. We've met at functions hosted by the Ingalls Trust."

"His father, Prentiss," said Parker, "amassed quite a fortune in real estate and was very active in the community. His path and ours crossed often. Prentiss died a few years ago and left a tidy sum to charity. Connie and I serve on the board for several nonprofits that received generous donations from the Ingalls Trust."

Connie winked at Katherine. "Keep a sharp eye on Jeremy Ingalls. Rumer is he's quite the player. Has he made a pass yet?"

"We're strictly business," Katherine assured her with a smile, "not to mention he's too old for me. Or it could be that Diana, the office manager, warned him away. She's a bit of a mother hen. Besides any man that keeps pictures of his sports car and speedboat in his office is not my type. Jeremy certainly loves his toys."

"So introduce me," said April. "I like toys."

"Not a chance in hell," scolded Connie. "He's too old for you, too. Your mother would have a fit."

April made a face. "A word of advice, Katherine—don't accept a job from people who attend the same church as your family." She grabbed her arm. "Come on. Let's get something to eat and I'll tell you who else to avoid around here to keep a social life secret from my mother."

"Is it that bad?" Katherine chuckled as April ushered her out the door.

"You have no idea," April grumbled. "Mama has spies all over town. I swear CIA operatives come to her for training."

"Why don't you be my date on Friday? I make a great chaperone. Jeremy is having a party at his house, and I don't have anyone to take. You can be my plus one."

April's eyes lit up. "Thanks, I'd love to. Everyone knows the big Ingalls' house on the bay. I'm dying to see inside. So how come you haven't met anyone special yet and need me as a date?"

"Haven't been here long, super busy, ended my last relationship a few months before I left Chicago, not ready to jump into another."

April tsked. "Totally lame excuses. You need to get out more. No one down here caught your eye?"

A faint smile twitched at Katherine's lips. "I noticed a cute guy in the coffee shop this morning, so I'm not dead yet."

April stopped next to a car and took out her keys.

"Let's go. He may still be there and have a Catholic friend for me—" A voice squawked inside the car.

"What's that?" asked Katherine.

"Police scanner. I'm a stringer for the local news station. I'm trying to get on full-time as an on-air reporter, but I don't have any experience, so I phone in the story." She grimaced. "Then they send the *real* reporter to do the follow up."

The dispatcher gave the address of a possible break-in. She regarded Katherine with a hesitant expression. "Do you mind if I beg off? It could be important…"

"Go. Report."

"Thanks." April hopped in the car. "See you Friday!"

Since Katherine never sprung for the latte that morning, her budget granted permission to stop at the Chinese restaurant next to the station for takeout on the way home. She hurried back to her apartment, propped both feet on the coffee table, and opened the carton of cashew chicken. After a few bites, Katherine shifted in the cushions, vaguely ill-at-ease, and turned on the TV. She had enjoyed the peaceful solitude of her own place since arriving from Chicago. Now, for the first time, the quiet seemed oppressive. Maybe April had a point. The time had come to get out more.

At bedtime, Katherine tossed the empty containers in the overflowing garbage can. She sniffed and wrinkled her nose. *Nope, don't want this mess hanging around until morning.* She grabbed the bag and ambled outside. The trash bin sat behind the building at the back of the renters' private parking lot, in a corner bathed in deep shadows. Katherine heaved the bag inside and it landed with a thump.

The bushes rustled.

Heart pounding, Katherine licked her lips and took a step back. "Hello? Anyone there?"

A white cat darted from the brush past her legs. Katherine squealed and hopped aside. It bounded across the lot and paused in a faint pool of light spilling from a window on the first floor. Glittery sparkles reflected from an object around its neck.

"W-Whiskers?" Katherine clutched her shirt. "What the hell are you doing here—other than giving me a heart attack?"

The cat's eyes reflected an amber glow and seemed to regard her with veiled expectation.

"What?" Katherine snapped, irrationally irritated at the prospect of being judged by a feline.

Without a sound, the cat bolted away and disappeared into the shadows.

****

*Jake.*

Jake's eyes shot open. "Wha—?" He bolted upright, momentarily disoriented in the dark. This wasn't his bedroom. He reached to his shoulder an instant before remembering the gun in its holster wouldn't be there. His hand dropped to the side. Jake blew out a breath and relaxed. He wasn't in the apartment. He had laid down on the couch at the house for a few minutes to rest and must have fallen asleep and had a weird dream. Someone calling his name…?

Jake shook his head to clear the cobwebs. He reached over to the end table to turn on the lamp. His hand froze. Instincts whispered an alert.

*I'm not alone.*

"Who's there?" he demanded.

At the very edge of hearing came the soft *whoosh* of an exhaled sigh. The hair rose on the back of his neck. Jake tensed, jumping to his feet. He snapped on the light. The room was empty, and one window open a crack. The gauzy curtain fluttering in the breeze made hushed sounds.

Almost like words.

Out of the corner of one eye, he caught movement. Jake spun on his heel to see his own wide-eyed reflection gazing back from the antique gilded mirror on the wall. He rubbed the back of his neck. "You have to cut back on the coffee before bedtime." Jake slammed the window shut and strode to the French door. He grabbed the knob and pulled back his hand in surprise. It was icy cold to the touch.

"Please," he growled, "don't tell me the air conditioning is on the fritz, too."

Jake checked the hall thermostat—68 degrees. The temperature was fine, nothing to worry about. He poked a tentative finger at the doorknob again and relaxed. This time it felt perfectly normal. No need for another expensive visit from the electrician after all. He scratched his head. "Seriously, you really need to cut back on the coffee."

Chapter 3

Katherine rose early. She settled into the couch with a cup of coffee to watch Parker's show and caught the last few minutes of *Answers from Beyond with Miss Harmony*. As each second ticked by, the level on her internal disgust-meter cranked a notch higher. She sneered at the screen. "Oh, brother, I swear to God even Whiskers has you pegged. If a cat could roll his eyes, his would orbit the eye sockets."

*What is she, Kathy?* prodded her grandfather's mental voice.

"Skilled at reading people. The trite phrases and platitudes offer enough comfort for desperate individuals to believe in her so-called psychic powers. The question remains whether she's harmlessly deluded or aware her behavior is a giant crock."

Katherine cocked her head and regarded Whiskers with sharp intent. Could he really have been in the parking lot last night? Her disdain for Miss Harmony soared. Allowing a pet to roam free begged for trouble. Whiskers could get into a catfight or hit by a car. Miss Harmony was not only a nut bag, but a callous pet owner, too. As Katherine sipped the coffee, her resentment cooled. Miss Harmony surely took better care of her meal ticket. Whiskers can't be the only white cat in Sandy Shoals with a rhinestone collar.

Miss Harmony's show ended and Katherine's

interview with Parker aired. After a few minutes, her lips formed a contented smile. Unlike Miss Harmony, she came across as mentally competent and thoroughly professional. Not to mention, she looked damn good in that red suit. She might get a few more clients after all.

Katherine's optimism proved correct. When she arrived at work the next day, Diana greeted her with a twinkle in her eye. "So what have you been up to this weekend? I made two new appointments from people who specifically requested Dr. Fleming." Katherine described the interview with Parker.

"A TV spot is excellent publicity," said Jeremy, "but don't discount word-of-mouth to build clientele. I counseled at the women's correctional center when I came back to town. I only had a short contract, but the time there allowed me to connect with the local police department. Now, I'm on retainer with the force. Anytime an officer has a referral for counseling, I get the call."

"Are referrals common?" asked Katherine. "Police work is stressful."

"Not that many. I have one person now seeing me who was involved in a shooting. Counseling is mandatory anytime an officer fires a gun."

Katherine met with her first new client that morning, pleased to note she arrived without a tinfoil helmet. April called at lunchtime. "Did you see the interview?" she blurted in a rush. "Of course, you did. The whole crew thought you came off great, especially Parker. He wants you back again a week from Saturday for a conversation on phobias so it's all set. Not this week because we have The B Guy. Can't wait until Dr. Ingalls' party on Friday. Gotta go, I have a call on the other line. Bye!"

Katherine stared at the phone in her hand wondering exactly when during the conversation she actually agreed to the second interview and who the heck was The B Guy? "Well, why not?" she murmured. "Maybe I can snag two more clients after the next show."

****

By the time Katherine and April arrived at Jeremy's house on Friday, the party was in full swing. April eyeballed the luxury sedans parked outside and whispered out of the corner of her mouth, "I'm way out of my league."

"Me, too," said Katherine lightly. "I only came for the food."

Steps led up to mahogany double doors and an elaborate two-story entrance with marble foyer. "Nice digs," muttered Katherine under her breath. She shot April a teasing look. "Mind your manners."

April grinned. "At least until we've eaten."

They wandered toward the back of the house where a wall of glass fronted the bay. A crowd gathered around a bar in the kitchen/family room. Other guests wandered outside to a large deck. Caterers had set up an extensive buffet, and the tables had a breathtaking view of the water.

Jeremy waved a greeting from across the room. They joined him, and Katherine introduced April. "You have a beautiful home," she said.

"Thanks. Credit goes to my father though. I just had the good fortune to inherit."

Katherine motioned at the crowd. "Nice turnout."

"Business associates, mostly," said Jeremy,

"members of the board of the Ingalls Trust, and anyone else I want to schmooze." He nodded toward a dark-haired man and his eyes twinkled. "The police chief. Never know when you'll need a parking ticket fixed."

Diana waltzed over to Jeremy's side. "Several members of the board need to speak with you."

He grinned. "Even off-duty, Diana watches out for me."

"Humph," said Diana. "I'd like to see anyone else do a better job."

"Not a chance." Jeremy called over his shoulder as Diana led him away. "Enjoy yourselves. Food is outside."

Katherine and April wandered through the sliding patio doors to the deck. Across the lawn was a long pier into the bay, and tied at the end was a flashy speedboat. As Katherine gazed in appreciation at the view of the water, April sighed. "Is this what it feels like to have money?"

"No. This is what it feels like to inherit from a daddy who had money."

April snickered. "Another thing I'll never experience."

"Let's eat then. I'm starved." Katherine motioned to the buffet line. "They have shrimp and prime rib."

April's voice dropped to a conspiratorial whisper, "I brought the big purse. You distract the server and I'll stuff enough inside for three meals."

They loaded their plates and sat at a table to eat. The large glass windows fronting the patio offered a clear view of the massive family room anchoring the kitchen. Jeremy stood next to the bar talking with an attractive blonde woman who appeared barely out of her teens. He offered a drink. She took it with a flirtatious smile. Katherine eyed the scene with interest. Jeremy's stance clearly signaled approval of her.

Katherine's attention drifted to Diana. She stood in the middle of a group of people. Her gaze lingered on Jeremy and the blonde. Jeremy bent his head low and said something in the young woman's ear. She threw back her head and laughed. The guest next to Diana appeared to ask her a question. She answered with a few words and a smile, and then returned her interest to the couple across the room.

Did Diana have a thing for Jeremy? Katherine looked away. *None of my business.* She briskly rubbed her arms.

"Cold?" asked April. "Want to go inside?"

"No, I'm fine. Got goosebumps all of a sudden."

April's eyes twinkled. "My mother would say someone just walked on your grave."

"I've heard that phrase before and it never made sense to me. How can someone walk on my grave when I'm still alive?"

April shrugged. "Beats me. Mama's also fond of saying, 'A mí la muerte me pela los dientes' which translates as 'Death peels my teeth.' "

Katherine laughed. "What does that mean?"

"She used it anytime she met one of my boyfriends, so honestly I was afraid to ask."

\*\*\*\*

*Flick...flick...flick...flick.*

"Not again," Jake growled. "What the hell is wrong with you?"

Even after switching out the lamp and bulbs twice, the light continued to flash on and off. No doubt about it now. Something must be hinky in the wiring, and he had to cough up for the electrician again. This wasn't how he planned to spend Saturday morning. Jake stifled a groan at the thought of the costly weekend service call. The last thing he needed was another unexpected expense. He should have listened to Ethan. His partner had warned him old houses were money pits.

Too late now. Jake pulled out his phone and glanced at the display. The bars faded in and out. "Perfect," he spit in disgust.

The coffeehouse always had a strong connection. As Jake snatched his jacket from the sofa, he caught his snarling refection in the old antique mirror on the far wall. "What the hell are you looking at?" As always, the mirror had no response. He yanked the lamp's plug from the outlet before storming out the door.

****

Katherine ambled to the coffee shop enjoying the perfect Saturday sunshine. The buffet at last night's party had been excellent. She experienced momentary regret at talking April out of stuffing leftovers in her purse. A prime rib sandwich today would have been tasty, but for now a latte had to suffice.

Her lips formed an unconscious smile. It had been nice to get out and socialize. The party was a fun diversion from the past few hectic months when she concentrated solely on finishing her degree and finding a permanent position. After that came all the excitement of settling in Sandy Shoals. She hadn't missed a social life…until now.

Katherine reached for the coffee shop's door handle. A man exiting with his cell phone to his ear nearly collided with her. He flashed an apologetic grin, stepped aside, and held open the door. "Sorry..."

Although wearing a blue t-shirt under his jacket instead of gray, those dimples had stuck in her mind. "No problem," said Katherine. She walked past him and entered the shop, her female radar sending an alert. The man's attention remained glued to her. Katherine paused, pretending to search for the wallet in her purse. Out of the corner of her eye, she noted his bemused expression.

He opened his mouth as if to say something, but the person on the other end of the line snagged his attention. "Yes, I'm still here... That's great. I didn't think you could squeeze me in today. Five minutes away? No problem. I'm headed back now. I'll text the address."

Katherine lingered by the window. She watched him hurry to a pickup truck at the curb, admiring his well-muscled form.

*Well?* said Grampa. *What's your impression?*

*The way he walks... I see confidence, but no arrogance. He has a position of responsibility. Nothing ordinarily throws him, but today he's distracted. An unexpected kink developed in his plans, but he has a way to handle it.* Her lips twitched in a smile. *And my-oh-my he fills out those jeans nicely.*

The man slid behind the wheel. The engine turned over. His gaze strayed to the coffee shop. Katherine's heart unexpectedly fluttered, but then he backed the truck from the curb. Stifling her disappointment, she turned from the window and went to the counter to place an order.

\*\*\*\*

Jake gaped at the electrician. "You found

nothing?"

"The wiring is all to code," he said. "The electric outlets function perfectly. I ran every test and can't find a thing wrong. Sorry, I had to bill you for the time."

Jake handed over his charge card. "I understand. I'm happy the house is okay." As if mocking Jake, the bulb in the lamp continued to burn steady and bright.

The electrician gave him the receipt. "Old houses can have crazy quirks."

Jake shut the front door behind him. He returned to the parlor and sank into the couch. What a lousy morning. He even blew the chance to talk to Katherine Fleming for the second time. Unexpectedly, Jake had found her image popping into his thoughts more than once during the past week.

*Fancy running into her like that.* Jake's curiosity had been piqued by their first encounter. Enough for him to catch the end of Miss Harmony's ridiculous talk show last Sunday and then *Chit Chat with Parker Pratt.* For a shrink, she looked really hot in that red suit.

Jake voiced internal approval. Smart, too. The type of person anyone could go to in trouble. She probably gave great advice.

The lamp flicked off.

Jake leaned his head back against the cushions and moaned at the ceiling, "Aw, c'mon."

\*\*\*\*

Katherine rose early Sunday morning. Curious about The B Guy, she tuned into GAB-TV for *Chit Chat with Parker Pratt* and watched the last few minutes of Miss Harmony's show. She was as nauseatingly effusive with callers as ever. Whiskers sprawled limply in her lap with his eyes closed.

Katherine hoped he wasn't dead.

The B Guy was really a bee guy; a beekeeper who sold his honey at the local farmer's market. He exuded such enthusiasm that Katherine walked over in the afternoon and bought a jar. They had a pleasant conversation and he took one of her cards to pass to a cousin who recently left a bad marriage and needed a little help to get her life on track.

On Monday morning, the cousin called the office for an appointment. Diana said the new client mentioned she had actually seen her guest appearance on the previous week's show. Katherine was now definitely a fan of Parker.

By Friday, Katherine's thoughts drifted more and more toward the weekend. Parker's second interview on Saturday afternoon certainly would be nice publicity. She should celebrate with a morning coffee at the shop around the corner. The thought of running into the man with the truck again produced a pleasant tingle in spots that hadn't tingled in a while. Her love life had been sadly lacking since the move south.

*It wasn't that great in Chicago either,* scolded her inner Grampa. Her mother's voice chimed with her often-expressed opinion. *You're too picky.*

"I'm not picky," she murmured, "just observant. Okay," she sighed, "possibly a tad too observant."

Katherine drummed her fingers on the desk. Relationships always started well, but ardor eventually cooled leaving a hole in her heart no one seemed to fill. How could she make her mother understand? Being observant was also a curse when she could spot the flaws in a romance before they became apparent to others. Lately, her love life seemed like a dead battery waiting for the jumpstart.

*You think too much,* said Grampa. *Lead with your heart next time, not your head.*

She snorted. "You taught me."

On the way home from work, Katherine detoured to the supermarket. A few steps from the entrance, she pulled up short. Miss Harmony exited the store with a tearful elderly woman at her side. The stranger was well-dressed and wore several pieces of expensive jewelry. She gazed at Miss Harmony in awe. "Can you really reach my husband?"

Miss Harmony pressed a business card into her hand. "I'm certain of it," she gushed. "Call me Monday and we'll set up an appointment."

"Thank you." The woman clutched the card to her chest. Her voice trembled. "It's been so hard... I've felt so alone."

"Put your mind at ease. You're in my hands now." With a grateful smile, the woman said goodbye. Miss Harmony's gaze followed her as she crossed the street. Her eyes narrowed slightly, the corners of her lips made a faint upward turn.

Katherine scowled. In the full light of day, the signs were so clear. "You really are a piece of work."

Startled, Miss Harmony turned around. "Why, Katherine," she gushed. "I didn't see you there."

"I thought a psychic with your powers would sense my transcendent aura. Wait..." Her voice dripped sarcasm. "I forgot, Whiskers is the psychic. You're the hustler." She motioned toward the elderly woman. "How much will you take that poor woman for?"

Miss Harmony bristled. "You needn't be insulting, and, by the way, my fees are lower than yours." She regarded her without a shred of guilt. "You and I are basically the same. We both help clients achieve peace of mind."

"We're nothing alike," Katherine snapped. "My goal is to help get people well enough to function on their own. Yours is to sucker them in and pry their wallets open."

"Grieving loved ones get comfort," Miss Harmony cooed. "They're happy and satisfied with my services." Her voice dropped to a sly whisper, "I intend to keep them that way. Now if you'll excuse me, I must be going."

Miss Harmony sauntered away calling over her shoulder, "I understand you're a guest on Parker's show tomorrow. Don't forget to touch up your makeup. The camera picks up every flaw, and you looked a little pasty last time."

Katherine scowled. "Pasty, my ass."

She finished the shopping quickly and hurried home. The encounter with Miss Harmony soured her evening. Katherine went to bed early, fighting a vague feeling of malaise. She curled under the covers and shut her eyes. "Saturday will be better. I have the show with Parker in the afternoon and in the morning I'll treat myself to a latte." Her spirits lifted once more at the possibility of running into the man with the truck again.

Chapter 4

Jake slammed the French doors to the parlor. He leaned against the wall, heart pounding a ferocious beat. Saturday morning had started so well, too. He got up early with plans to head for the coffee shop, maybe run into Katherine Fleming...

His gaze went to the parlor door. *It can't be. It can't be. It can't be.* No matter how many times his mind desperately repeated the words, the simple mantra didn't erase any of the last few minutes from memory. He drew a deep steadying breath, and the mantra changed.

*You saw it. You saw it. You saw it.*

"Okay! I saw it. It's real. Now what the hell do I do?"

Ideas barreled through him, each one considered in a flash and then rapidly discarded. Finally, a face appeared. "No, no, no," he groaned. "I can't."

*Have you completely lost your mind? It's crazy. You're crazy for even considering the idea.*

Jake bolted from the house, slammed the front door, and got in his truck. He gripped the steering wheel, staring out the windshield at the windows of the parlor where the light continued to flick on and off. Jaw set, he whipped the phone from his pocket. He had a signal now. He placed the call, and made an appointment to meet right away. Jake hung up with a sickening feeling he just made the biggest mistake of his life.

**\*\*\*\***

Katherine walked to the coffee shop Saturday morning, an image of the mystery man in the t-shirt occupying her thoughts. She lingered at a table, reading a book on her tablet for two hours, and keeping a watchful eye on the parking lot for the pickup truck. Casual conversation starters played over in her mind, but her careful advance planning was to no avail. He never showed.

Despite the sunshine, Katherine trudged home in gloom. She kicked at a pebble on the sidewalk. What was the big deal? It's not as if they planned a rendezvous. He was a total stranger for heaven's sake. She didn't even know his name. Katherine cut through the parking lot to the back entrance of the apartment building, so sunk in wistful melancholy her surroundings barely registered.

"M'row?"

"What the—" Katherine jumped, heart in her mouth, as a white cat pounced from the bushes and playfully batted at her ankle. "You again?"

The cat rubbed his face against her leg. In the bright sunlight, the name on the rhinestone collar was clearly visible.

Katherine knelt down and patted his head. "Well, I'll be damned, Whiskers. What are you doing here? Miss Harmony films today and she can't work her little scam alone."

Without warning, Whiskers jumped into her arms. Katherine cradled him with a chuckle. "Wow, you're a lot more active out of the studio. Does she dope you up before air time to keep you quiet?" She stroked his paw and cooed, "I'll bet she does, poor thing."

Her finger brushed against something sticky and instinctively pulled away. Red glistening droplets clung to her skin. "What did you step in? Miss Harmony will definitely not be pleased. The camera picks up every flaw..." Katherine's eyes widened and she sucked in a breath. "Is that blood? Are you hurt?" She gave Whiskers a quick once-over, but to her relief the cat appeared unharmed. "I hope you didn't kill a bird. If so, Miss Harmony shoulders the blame for letting you run free."

Katherine stood up with Whiskers. "I'll call and tell her you wandered over to my apartment. Meanwhile, come inside with me." She made a face. "Of course, seeing as you and Miss Harmony are psychically joined, she must already have a clue."

Miss Harmony's business card remained in the pocket of Katherine's red suit, but the call went directly to voicemail. She left a message and sent a text as good measure. Hours passed without any response, so Katherine phoned April.

"No problem," she said. "I'll pass the word about Whiskers. Miss Harmony will pick up for me."

Two o'clock came and went without a response, and Katherine's irritation escalated. The time neared for her to go to the studio for Parker's interview. What was the deal with that woman? Did she really expect her to transport Whiskers in a car without a cat carrier? Forget it.

Katherine peered at her lap. For the past half hour, Whiskers had been curled in a contented ball, the perfect houseguest. Once released into the apartment, he took a short tour, poked his nose under all the furniture, and then jumped on an end table next to a window to fix his attention at the street below. After tiring of that, he apparently decided Katherine's lap was the perfect spot for a nap.

She scratched his ears. "I have to go to the studio for the taping, and I won't leave you outside. In exchange for water and tuna, will you agree not to scratch the furniture or use my carpet as a litter box?" His throat vibrated in a low-pitched purr.

Katherine chuckled. "We've barely met, and I like you so much better than Miss Harmony."

She changed clothes and left a bowl of water and a plate of tuna on the floor before heading out. Whiskers shoved his face in the food as if he hadn't eaten in a while.

The studio inside GAB-TV was quiet. Katherine found Parker on the dais thumbing through a sheaf of papers with April. Miss Harmony was nowhere to be seen.

"She never showed," said April with a disgusted snort. "I called all day. When airtime neared, I got pissed and left a final message. I told her I'd send the cops to check on her if she didn't answer. That got her attention. Seconds later, the phone rang. Miss Harmony said she was off the air permanently, and hung up before I could get a word in."

Katherine's mouth dropped open. "She quit her own show?"

"Seems so," said Parker. "We substituted an infomercial." He chuckled. "As if anyone could spot the difference."

"The mention of the cops did it," April jeered. "My

theory is Miss Harmony's shady past finally caught up with her and she went on the lam."

"What should I do with Whiskers? He's still at my house."

"Connie has Miss Harmony's address in the files," said Parker. "You can drop by her place after the taping and remind her you aren't a damn pet sitter." He took her by the elbow. "Meanwhile, let's get started on more pleasant discussion—our interview awaits."

Katherine was relaxed the second time around. The conversation soon turned toward phobias, especially after Parker mentioned with a twinkle in his eye he had an aversion to cats.

"An aversion isn't a phobia," said Katherine lightly. "It only becomes a problem when irrational fear interferes with life. For instance, an individual can be content to stay at home and rarely leave the house, but will readily do so to shop, meet friends, or go to a doctor's appointment. That person isn't agoraphobic. A true agoraphobic deals with trauma, battles real physical aversions, and may not be able to even open the front door."

"What sort of treatment is there?" Parker asked.

"In many cases, a counselor must come to the patient. Recovery may be a slow process because the root of the issue is hidden. Trauma triggers the initial response, but once the cause is isolated, a therapeutic course of treatment can be developed."

"So you're saying counseling sessions can help even the worst agoraphobic out the door?"

"Actually, my goal would be to get the patient well enough to take the initiative and decide the time has come to move forward and leave the life of a shut-in behind. No matter how complex or usual the case, help is at hand for any troubled soul." Not a shred of doubt tinged Katherine's words. "All anyone has to do is reach out and ask."

After the show ended, Connie dropped by the studio and handed Katherine the address for Miss Harmony. Katherine glanced at the paper with a puzzled frown. "Strange…I could have sworn Miss Harmony would never willingly cancel the call-in show. Not only did it bring new clients, but she sucked up attention like a vacuum on high."

"It came as a big surprise to everybody here," said Connie, "but when you see Miss Harmony today, please don't talk her into returning. The station doesn't need ad revenue badly enough to sit through more of her idiotic drivel."

"No worries," said Katherine, amused. "I'm not a fan."

Katherine drove to Miss Harmony's house and parked behind a van with the logo of a storage company on the side panel. As she got out of the car, two men in coveralls carried a sofa out the front door. Katherine walked up the driveway as they loaded the van and closed the rear gate. She passed a car with the backseat crammed full of suitcases and boxes. A woman on the lawn pounded a For Rent sign into the grass.

"Excuse me," said Katherine, "I'm looking for Miss Harmony."

"I'm the landlord. She's inside—"

The front door whipped open. Miss Harmony blew past Katherine without a sideways glance, two suitcases in hand. Her face was nearly as pale as Whiskers' fur. She stuffed the luggage in the backseat and slammed the door. "What you waiting for?" she screamed to the men in the van. "Take everything to storage. I'll send a new address later."

"I found Whiskers," said Katherine.

"Whiskers?" Miss Harmony blinked and then eyed Katherine as if seeing her for the first time. "Ungrateful bastard. He runs away whenever I open the door." Her voice hardened. "He always came back, but won't find me here. He can starve to death for all I care." She jumped into the driver's seat.

"Of all the…" Temper soaring, Katherine strode across the lawn and grabbed her arm through the window. "What the hell is your deal? When you take on the responsibility for an animal, you don't simply abandon—"

"Let go of me." Miss Harmony jerked from her grip. Long, swollen scratches ran along each arm.

Katherine's eyes narrowed in suspicion. "Are those from Whiskers? Did you try to hurt him?"

"I had to protect myself." Miss Harmony's hands tightened on the wheel, knuckles white. "It was easy money," she babbled. "The cat was friendly, put people at ease, good for business. One day, he jumped into my lap during a reading. I pretended he gave me the answers. The fools bought it. They loved him, but I can start over in a new place…get another damn cat." She turned the key in the ignition, a crazed light in her eyes. "He lied. He lured me there. He wants my soul."

Katherine gaped at her. "Why the hell does Whiskers want your soul?"

Without warning, the fear in Miss Harmony gave way to rage. The dramatic change in her attitude took Katherine by surprise and she took a stumbling step back.

"Don't be stupid," Miss Harmony snarled. "He's a cat. What would he do with my soul?"

"Then who are you talking about…" A pinprick of compassion filtered through Katherine's intense dislike. Con artist or not, Miss Harmony was in severe mental distress. Was she on medication? If so, it had certainly worn off. "Come inside with me. Is there someone I can call?"

Miss Harmony rammed the gear into reverse and burst out in maniacal laughter. "It can't get me now."

"It?"

The tires screeched down the driveway.

"Hey," yelled the realtor. "I need a forwarding address to send your security deposit."

Miss Harmony poked her head out the window. "Eat it!" Within seconds, her car was out of sight.

"Nut job," the realtor snapped. "I never should have rented to her."

Katherine gawked at the tires' skid marks on the pavement. "What set her off?"

"Damned if I know. She called out of the blue to say she was leaving today. For good. No notice, no nothing. She sounded weird so I decided to come by for the keys. She practically threw them at me." The woman snorted. "Nut job."

Katherine gazed at the house with bemusement. "Seems I'm now in possession of her soul-sucking cat. May I go inside and collect his things?"

The landlady shrugged. "Take whatever you want. Any stuff left behind will get pitched in the trash."

Katherine emptied a hamper in the bathroom full of Miss Harmony's dirty clothes and packed Whiskers' belongings including carrier and litter box. She found a few old, worn toys and tossed them inside, too. The only cat food was an unopened box on the counter in a supermarket bag. Katherine glowered at Friday's date on the receipt. No wonder Whiskers was hungry. Had she even fed him since then?

Katherine drove back to her apartment, puzzling over Miss Harmony's erratic behavior. What a turnaround from twenty-four hours ago when she was smug and self-assured, ready to scam a new client without a shred of remorse. Today, she was borderline crazy. Katherine shivered with a sudden chill. Not just crazy—afraid. What the hell happened to her?

When Katherine opened the door, Whiskers jumped down from sentry duty on the end table under the window. He greeted her with a friendly meow and brushed his cheek against her leg. The plate with tuna had been licked clean.

Cautiously, Katherine sniffed the air and then relaxed. Other than a faint fishy aroma, nothing smelled out of the ordinary. "Well, you're the perfect houseguest. I'll set up the litter box first." She placed it in an out-of-the-way corner behind the trash can. "Is here okay?" Whiskers prodded it once with his nose. His meow seemed to indicate approval.

Katherine kicked off her shoes and plopped on the couch with a sigh. Whiskers jumped into her lap. "Well, make yourself at home," she chuckled, stroking his back. "For a soul sucker, you're awfully pleasant company." Katherine leaned into the cushions, musing over her chance encounter with Miss Harmony yesterday in front of the supermarket. How did she miss any hint of a complete mental breakdown? She was good at reading people, but didn't see this coming. An uneasy sensation crawled up her spine. Had she lost her touch? Did other patients suffer because an issue that should have been easy to recognize slipped by undiagnosed?

With a shake of the head, Katherine dismissed the idea at once. "I swear nothing was wrong. Whatever happened to Miss Harmony came on suddenly between yesterday and now." Katherine ran a gentle hand from Whiskers' head to the tip of his tail. "Care to tell me what's going on?"

"Meow."

"Can't breach phony psychic cat confidentiality, eh? I totally understand." She cocked her head and peered at Whiskers. "I never had a cat. What if we try this new arrangement on a trial basis? We'll see if you can live with me and I can live with you. If it doesn't work out, no hard feelings. We'll go our separate ways, but I'll find a good home for you. No more midnight strolls," she vowed. "You're strictly a housecat now."

"Meow." Whiskers curled into a fuzzy lump of contentment; the only movement a slight twitch at the tip of his tail.

"It's a deal then." Katherine unhooked the rhinestone collar and tossed it on the coffee table. "This is cheesy and undignified and doesn't suit a cat of your discerning qualities in the least. As soon as the pet store opens on Sunday, I'll buy you a new one."

Whiskers closed his eyes and purred.

****

"M'row."

Katherine reclined on the couch and peered over the top of her computer tablet at her new roommate.

Their first full day together had gone well so far. To Katherine's eyes, the new navy blue pinstripe collar she purchased that morning was particularly dashing and much more Whiskers' style than gaudy rhinestone. The new toys Katherine brought home also met with his approval. Whiskers had enjoyed a rousing game of chase-the-laser-dot, followed by a short nap. Upon waking, he returned to his favorite spot on the end table and peered out the window.

Whiskers' muscles tensed. He held a fixed stare. "Are the birds mocking you?" said Katherine lightly. "My advice is don't take it personally. Deep down, they're jealous of your new classy appearance and cushy living conditions."

He placed his two front paws on the sill, nose nearly pressed to the glass. Something on the street definitely captured his attention.

Curiosity rising, Katherine put the tablet aside and ambled to the window. After living in noisy Chicago, the secluded area held a definite draw. The apartment building was on a dead-end with no thru traffic or random pedestrians. What did he see that so captured his attention?

She followed Whiskers' gaze and drew in a sharp breath. The sidewalk below was empty except for a single person. Directly beneath her second floor window, the man from the coffee shop paced back and forth.

He stopped in front of the recess, his attention appeared to focus on the eight intercom buttons for the different apartment units. The building's security was another aspect that met with Katherine's approval. The door to the lobby locked automatically, and a visitor had to be buzzed in by a tenant.

Katherine's heart skipped a beat as he raised his hand. Her head turned to the intercom speaker next to the door and then back to the man on the street. The buzzer remained silent.

The man's hand dropped to his side. He began the slow pace again.

Was he searching for her? How did he get her name and address?

Katherine swallowed hard. Goosebumps rose on her arms. Her last name was above the intercom button. If he knew her name, he had her apartment number now.

The man stopped again at the door, running his hand through his hair. His indecisiveness was painfully obvious. *Push the button. Don't push the button.* Katherine could almost hear the internal argument— which didn't match his physical appearance at all.

Her professional judgment took over and regarded him with a practiced eye. He had a lean, muscled form with the graceful movement of a natural athlete. The hesitance in his stance implied mixed emotions, but Katherine's odd angle kept his face from view and made it impossible to get an accurate reading on his true intent.

"Don't tell me you're shy?" Katherine murmured. She quickly dismissed the idea. This man would definitely have no problem approaching a stranger. Used to acting quickly, but for a reason now at an impasse? His inability to make a decision clearly bugged him. A lot.

What was the issue? He didn't hide in the shadows. He didn't stake out the building. He simply couldn't push the button. Interest piqued, Katherine's creepy stalker vibe faded.

"Why are you here?" she whispered. "What do you want?"

As if coming to a decision, the man turned on his heel and strode from the building's entrance.

"No, wait!" Katherine blurted, grabbing her keys. Curiosity pushed her from the apartment and down the flight of stairs. She peeked out the front door recess and caught a glimpse of the man turning the corner.

Katherine followed for several blocks dodging pedestrians out for a Sunday afternoon stroll. Suddenly, he pulled up short to gaze at a shop window, and she ducked into a doorway. He changed direction and crossed the street to an alley leading to a public parking lot. His demeanor had altered. His stride came with steady purpose, any sign of indecision erased.

Katherine crossed the street and entered the lot. She rose on her toes, scanning across the tops of the parked cars with a puzzled frown. He had disappeared.

"Hold it right there."

Katherine spun in a half-circle, pulse racing. The man from the coffee shop had moved silently behind her.

Chapter 5

He blinked. "It's you."

Katherine's heart hammered in her chest. She took a step back. "Me. What do you want?"

The tenseness in his posture vanished. His expression filled with concern. "I'm sorry. I didn't mean to frighten you. I couldn't shake the feeling I was being followed and I'm a little on edge." He shuffled his feet. "I've had a weird weekend."

Katherine's eyes narrowed. "Yeah. Me, too. Just now, I noticed this guy staking out my apartment building."

A faint smile twitched at his lips. He held up both hands in a gesture of surrender. "I swear, I am not a stalker. I'm going to take one hand and reach for my back pocket. My ID is inside." He slowly removed a thin black bi-fold, flipped it open, and handed it to her. The sunlight glinted off a gold shield.

She gaped at him. "You're a cop?"

"My name is Jake Sumner. I'm a detective on the Sandy Shoals police force." His voice softened. "I apologize for scaring you, Dr. Fleming. That was the last thing on my mind."

She eyed him warily. "You know my name."

"I overheard you in the coffeehouse after you ran into your client with the dental phobia. I watched Pratt's show the next morning, and then saw you again at the coffeehouse the next week. I would have said something then, but had an appointment to keep."

Confusion flooded through her, followed by pleasant anticipation. *Does he want a date?*

Jake cleared his throat. "Then yesterday…it was… I don't know… After it happened, I couldn't sleep much. Got up early this morning and saw you on TV again talking about phobias. I had your name, and it's not hard for a cop to get an address—although strictly against department policy to milk the system for personal reasons…." He ran his hands through his close-cropped hair and his lips formed an awkward grin. "Geez, I'm giving off a psycho vibe. I sound like one of those crazy guys girls' mothers always warn them about."

Katherine smiled at his fumbling response and returned the badge. "It's okay. I've decided to give you the benefit of the doubt."

"Good…that's good," he said with undisguised relief. "Because I really need help with a problem."

*Not a date.* Katherine stifled a pang of disappointment. Jake Sumner as a patient meant no Jake Sumner as a potential romantic interest. "You need my services as a counselor? Dr. Ingalls is the police department psychologist on call—"

"No," Jake flustered. "I mean, I can't go to him. Let's just say, I understand patient privilege, but prefer that no one with any connection to the precinct learns of this."

Katherine nodded in understanding. "You think it'll hurt your career if word got out."

Jake grunted. "You have no idea."

A person needs her help. Katherine dismissed her

lingering regrets. "Okay. I have openings on Monday—"

"No!"

She jumped at his sudden response.

"Sorry," he said in a rush. "I mean we can't go to the office."

"We?"

Jake glanced away as if holding Katherine's gaze made him uneasy. "I bought this house...and it has a tenant...and she won't leave."

*He's not the patient.* Although the pleasant tingle returned, it came with niggling doubts. "Isn't this a problem for a lawyer?"

An indefinable emotion flickered across his face. "Trust me. Serving an eviction notice is useless. I...uh, think she's afraid to leave."

"You don't want to drag her through the courts." Her voice softened. "That's kind of you."

Jake brushed aside her response. "I couldn't sleep last night. I heard you this morning on TV talking about people who can't go outside. They get stuck from a traumatic experience. You said ways exist to convince a troubled soul to leave the house. You can help them."

Katherine regarded him with doubt. "Possibly, but I must warn you severe cases of agoraphobia may require anti-depression or anxiety medication. I'm only a psychologist and can't prescribe drugs, but I can refer you to a psychiatrist."

"My tenant isn't the kind to take drugs." He fixed Katherine with a pleading gaze. "Will you come with me now and talk to her? Find out why she won't go?"

Her mouth dropped open. "Now? I don't know what magic tricks you think I can perform, but treating agoraphobia is often a time-consuming process."

"But it doesn't have to be. She may open up to you right away. Please," Jake begged. "A few minutes. I'm desperate. I'll pay for the session."

"She must agree to counseling," stammered Katherine, "I can't just—"

"I'm sure you'll talk her into it. My truck is over there." Jake pulled a key chain from his pocket.

Katherine froze in place, paralyzed with indecision.

Jake motioned to a camera mounted on the wall. "Wave."

"Huh?"

"Wave. This parking lot is covered by security cameras. They have a great view of me, you, and my truck's license plate." Jake held out his cell phone. "Send an email to your work, personal account, or anyone else that you left here with me."

Katherine hesitated for a moment, then took the phone and sent emails to all her accounts. "Getting in Detective Jake Sumner's car at Third Avenue parking lot. License plate SFX-53A. He's acting strangely. If my body turns up later, he's the prime suspect."

Jake grinned. "Nice."

She shot him a wicked look and added a P.S. "Avenge my death." His grin widened.

Jake insisted Katherine hold onto his phone. They got into the truck and he lowered the windows. "We're only a few blocks away. I'll drive slow. No funny business, I swear. You can jump out anytime."

Katherine considered the earnestness in his expression. *No one can fake that much sincerity.* She relaxed into the seat. "That's okay. All of a sudden, I'm eager to meet a person who throws Detective Jake

Sumner for a loop. You don't strike me as a man who rattles easily."

"I'm not," he muttered. "At least, I haven't been, but this chick is different."

"What can you tell me about her?"

"Nothing."

"Age? Occupation? Name?" He stared out the windshield in silence, and she eyed him in disbelief. "Do you even have her name? What kind of landlord are you?" she sputtered. "What kind of cop are you? Aren't police officers trained to be especially observant?"

"I recently bought the house and it's an unusual situation. I prefer you meet her first. I don't want my opinion to affect your judgment."

"How could having her name affect my judgment?"

"Oh," he said brightly. "We're here. Told you it wasn't far." Jake parked in front of a two-story bungalow with a wide front porch. The house was old and needed work; the paint cracked and peeling, the bushes overgrown, yet it exuded an indefinable charm. Good bones—like her grandparents' old house. All it needed was a little TLC.

"It's lovely," said Katherine.

He scowled. "It will be if I ever get her to leave."

As they walked up the flagstone sidewalk, Katherine shot a sideways glance at Jake. The tenseness in his stance had returned. His jaw muscles were noticeably tighter. Katherine's stomach held a nervous flutter as he unlocked the door.

"I'll leave it open," Jake said. He led Katherine into the foyer and then stopped and called out, "Hello?

It's me. I'm back."

Beyond the foyer was a stairway to the second floor while a hall went to the rear of the house. To the right was a large living room. Katherine glimpsed a formal dining room beyond that. The kitchen must overlook the backyard. The French doors to her left appeared to close off a parlor.

Jake called again. "I brought someone to meet you. Her name is Katherine. She wants to help."

The silence lengthened. "I don't think she heard you," said Katherine.

"Oh, she heard, all right," Jake muttered. "This way." He pushed open the French doors.

Katherine followed him into the room. Muted sunlight filtered through gauzy curtains on the windows. She jumped aside as her shoe crunched over the remains of a shattered mug in a puddle of coffee on the hardwood floor. The room was sparsely furnished with only an old couch and an end table holding a lamp.

Jake flicked on the light. Other than faded floral wallpaper, the single decoration on the walls was a large antique gilded mirror. The glass was old, dotted with hazy black splotches where the reflective silver coating had worn away. Katherine's image was blurred and barely recognizable. She ran a finger over the window sill, and it came away covered in dust. "Your tenant is a lousy housekeeper. This room doesn't seem as if anyone has been in here in years."

"Yeah," Jake murmured. "It's not her thing."

"I don't understand," said Katherine. "Where is she?"

Without warning, the temperature plummeted. Katherine shivered, hugging her arms to her chest.

"Why is it so cold?"

Jake's lips pressed together in a thin, tight line, his gaze fixed on the mirror.

*Click...click...click...click.*

The lamp flicked on and off. Katherine's pulse soared. "Detective?"

Jake glowered at the lamp, his face red with anger. He grabbed Katherine's arm. "I'm sorry. I was wrong. I shouldn't have brought you here—"

The French doors slammed shut. From outside came a muted thud as the front door closed as well.

Katherine shrugged off Jake's grip. "W-what are you doing? This isn't funny."

"It's not me." He peered at the mirror. "I'm sorry, Dr. Fleming. This is a bad idea. We should go now."

*Don't leave me.*

"W-who said that?" Katherine turned around to face the mirror. Her eyes widened in horror as the black splotches slid toward the center of the glass. "Trick." Katherine clutched at her shirt. "It must be a trick."

The blotches whirled together. A misty shape formed. Arms...legs...now torso...now head...an image of a person appeared from inside the gilded frame. Facial features blurred beyond recognition, but the body was definitely female.

Katherine's legs refused to move, a scream died on her lips. Shaking, she raised a trembling arm. Instead of mimicking her movement, the reflection remained rooted in place. "T-that's not me."

A plaintive whisper filled the air. *Help.*

A blast of frigid wind whipped the curtains and knocked Katherine into Jake. With the sound of breaking glass, a vaporous arm separated from the mirror and reached toward her.

*Help me...*

"Out now!" Jake dragged Katherine across the room. He yanked open the parlor doors and shoved her into the foyer.

*Please...* The unearthly plea followed Katherine out of the house.

*Pllleeeaaassseee...*

Jake slammed the front door shut behind them. The muted cry faded away.

## Chapter 6

*Ticka-ticka-ticka-ticka.*

The mug clattered against the tabletop. Jake gently removed the hot tea from Katherine's hands. "Wait a bit to drink. The first time I saw her, I dropped a cup of coffee and nearly burned myself."

Katherine nodded numbly. She gazed around her apartment in confusion, the last few minutes a hazy blur. "How did I...?"

"I drove you home. I am so sorry, Dr. Fleming. I should have warned you. I tried, but it all sounded so crazy and after yesterday I didn't know where else to turn..." Jake's voice suddenly softened and his tone took on a teasing note. "This is partly your fault."

She blinked. "What?"

"You followed me. You got in my car. Gutsy, curious, and smart, although tailing a stranger wasn't the best move. I thought you could handle it. I should have realized nothing prepares you for a...for a..." Jake rubbed the back of his neck. "God, I can't even say it."

"A ghost."

"Thank you."

Whiskers placed his forepaws on Katherine's thigh. She scratched his head, and he jumped into her lap. She drew a shuddering breath. "You have a ghost. I've seen a ghost. A real ghost. I-I can't seem to wrap my head around it. I didn't believe in them before."

"Me neither, and yet, there she is." Jake snorted in disgust. "I can't believe I was stupid enough to buy a haunted house. No wonder I got such a deal."

A smile played about Katherine's lips. "No ghost mentioned in the real estate listing?"

"Not hardly. Just an old empty house. I saw it needed work, but as soon as I stepped inside I fell in love with the bones..." He shot an I-can't-believe-I-said-that glance at her. They both chuckled.

Katherine stopped shaking. She wrapped her hands around the mug and let the comforting heat filter in. "So who is she?"

"Haven't the slightest idea."

"Previous owner?"

"Elderly man, so not my current tenant. The house was empty for a while. I bought it with a sealed bid auction—low balled because I knew every room needed updating and couldn't believe how lucky I was to get it. The location is prime, and the sale generated a lot of interest. I only closed a few weeks ago and started the remodel."

Her eyes twinkled. "Bodies in the attic?"

"Nope, but I haven't had a cadaver dog check the walls yet." Jake regarded her with interest. "After our little encounter, I didn't expect you to be so together with all this."

She sipped her tea. "Trust me. I'm one step ahead of full-blown hysteria."

"You don't act it. I was right. Gutsy. That's why I got the crazy idea you'd be okay..." Jake shook his head. "I'm sorry I dragged you into this. There's no way anyone can be prepared to face what I have in that house." He glared into his cup. "Even the so-called psychic couldn't hold it together."

A terrible suspicion formed in Katherine's mind. Her eyes widened. "No. Tell me you didn't…You wouldn't…" A flush crept into Jake's cheeks. She pointed an accusing finger. "You did! You hired Miss Harmony. How could you use that phony? What were you thinking?"

"I wasn't," Jake flustered. "In my defense, I was at the end of my rope. You may be surprised to hear that when you search *paranormal housecleaners* online, you don't get any sane hits—hey, wait a minute." He squinted at Whiskers. "Is that her cat? How'd he get here?"

Katherine gave him a withering glare. "You first. You owe me that much."

Jake chuckled. "Okay, but try not to think of me as a complete ass."

"I promise to withhold judgment until the end."

"Far enough." Jake leaned back his seat. "As soon as I closed on the house, I hired an electrician to redo the wiring. Everything was up to date, and then the problems began."

"Let me guess," said Katherine, deadpan, "flickering lights."

"Yup and weird temperature shifts as if the thermostat was out of whack. I had a hard time getting a signal on my phone, too, and every so often heard strange noises. Kind of whispery, but I couldn't make out any words. I even thought someone called my name. The second time I saw you in the coffee shop I was speaking with the electrician. He came to the house again, but didn't find any problems. Then yesterday morning, I was in the parlor when the lights flickered once more. The temperature dropped. This time, I had a prickly sensation up my spine as if someone looked over my shoulder. I turned around and saw the blotches in the mirror move. I thought my eyes played tricks until they made a shape—a blurry woman's shape."

Katherine's grip tightened on the mug. "Did she say anything?"

Jake grimaced. "Frankly, I didn't hang around long enough to find out." He narrowed his eyes. "Did she talk to you?"

"A few words like 'Don't leave' and 'Help me.' "

He blinked. "I didn't hear anything."

"Get back to the story," Katherine urged.

"I made a beeline for my truck and sat inside with the keys in my hand trying to figure out what the hell to do. I couldn't tell anyone in the police department I had a ghost in my house. They'd laugh me off the force." Jake shifted in his seat. "I watched Miss Harmony's show last week before your interview came on. I knew she fed people a line of crap, but thought there was a slim chance she had run across something similar to this. To be honest, a part of me needed confirmation I wasn't crazy. I phoned her and she hurried over." He wrinkled his nose in disgust. "Probably because I offered to pay cash."

"I take it the meeting didn't go well," said Katherine. "Let me guess, Whiskers scratched her."

He eyed Katherine with a quizzical expression. "How did you—never mind. Miss Harmony had Whiskers in her arms and freaked at the first sight of the ghost in the mirror. She held him out and screamed, 'Take him instead.' "

"Did she mean you or the cat?" said Katherine

lightly.

Jake's eyes twinkled. "At that moment, it didn't appear Miss Harmony had a preference. Whiskers squirmed around in her arms trying to get free and scratched her. That's when she threw him at the mirror."

Katherine scowled. "She threw Whiskers? What a jerk."

"Yeah, he landed okay, though. He didn't even seem upset. I picked him up and ran after her. Now that I think about it, Whiskers was the calmest one of us, not a bit rattled. By the time I reached the front door, Miss Harmony was gone. I put Whiskers on the porch so I could fish the keys from my pocket, and he bolted. I checked around the house, but couldn't find him. I hoped he went home."

"He didn't," said Katherine. She described finding Whiskers and her visit to Miss Harmony. The story ended with a snicker. "I understand her reaction now. She thought you wanted to suck up her soul."

"If I was collecting souls, I'd have much higher standards than Miss Harmony." Jake cocked his head. "So, what's your professional judgment? Am I a complete ass?"

"Not complete," Katherine said with the hint of a smile.

"I accept that." Jake placed a gentle hand on her wrist. "Are you okay?"

"I'm fine now," said Katherine. The tea cup had cooled, but the slight pressure of his fingers sent unexpected warmth up her arm.

Jake opened his mouth as if to say something, his manner hesitant. Then he pulled his hand away and scooted the chair from the table. "I should get going. I've taken enough of your time. Again, my apologies for ruining your day."

"What will you do about the house?"

"At the moment, I'm clueless. I have no desire to share spaces with the current tenant, but can't put a haunted house on the market. Plus, I don't want word to get out. I like my privacy. Imagine the freaks lined up around the block fighting to get a look at a real ghost." His eyes took on a faraway gaze. "I was drawn to this house from the beginning. The first time I saw it, I pictured a future there. I can't abandon that plan easily."

Katherine set Whiskers on the floor. "You're not a man who runs from difficult situations."

An undefined emotion passed over his face. "No, I prefer to face them head-on, but can't continue to pay mortgage and rent, either. Maybe, she'll eventually go away." Jake rose to his feet. "It's not your problem. I'll figure it out."

Katherine walked him to the door.

Jake paused on the threshold. "Lock the deadbolt—"

Their eyes met, and they both grinned. "Can't believe I said that, too." Jake stepped into the hall and then turned back to Katherine. "If you're not comfortable alone, I can call someone for you."

The offhanded comment caused a prickle of irritation. *Does he think I'll collapse in a sobbing heap as soon as he leaves?* Katherine drew herself up. "Thanks, but I'm fine." As soon as she locked the door behind him, an anxious feeling settled in the pit of her stomach. The apartment chosen for silence now seemed infused with unnatural quiet. For a moment, she considered calling Jake back.

"Oh, hell, no," she snapped. "A grown woman doesn't need a babysitter."

She made dinner, but only picked at her food. Heavy lethargy settled on Katherine's shoulders. Her head pounded with the effort to think straight. *What a day. Go to bed. Everything will make more sense in the morning.*

Despite the brave words, Katherine's heart fluttered when she entered the bathroom. She forced her gaze to the mirror over the sink. Nothing but her reflection peered back; wide-eyed, face pale. Katherine fought a rising swell of fear. "Stop it. You're safe. Don't be a big baby. Ghosts don't make random house calls." She swallowed hard. "Do they?"

Katherine changed for bed and crawled under the covers, echoes of the unearthly cry ringing in her ears. She turned off the lamp on the end table and the dark instantly pressed down on her like a heavy quilt. The air was stifling. She could barely breathe. She jumped out of bed, switched on the hall light, and left the door ajar.

A comforting glow filtered through the crack. Her grandfather's voice chided gently. *Is this a picture of your life from now on?*

"I saw a ghost," she argued. "Being jittery is a perfectly normal reaction. I-I'll be fine in the morning."

*Are you sure?*

Katherine shuddered. "No." What would happen tomorrow night, and then the next, and the next? How long would she sleep with the light on, tremble when approaching a mirror? A window? Any reflective surface? How long until fear infiltrated every part of her life?

How could she help anyone else if she couldn't help herself?

Katherine's voice hardened. "I will overcome this. I refuse to spend the rest of my life cowering under the covers—"

The bedroom door opened wide. Katherine's mouth went dry.

Whiskers jumped on the bed, and she let out a squeak. He nuzzled her hand. With a shaky chuckle, she stroked his fur. "You sure don't act as if you went through a traumatic experience. Miss Harmony went berserk, but you're perfectly fine. Why didn't the ghost scare you?"

Katherine stared mindlessly at the ceiling. "You tell all your patients to face their fears. Can't take your own good advice?"

Return to a haunted house? Maybe, not yet. Okay, then, no confrontation with a ghost until the problem was thought through. Strip away the supernatural stuff. Take a clinical approach. What did you see? The light flickered. The temperature dropped. Doors closed by themselves and curtains moved. The ghost had a certain amount of control over inanimate objects, but nothing slammed into her. She hadn't been hurt—not physically anyway. Then the image of the woman formed in the mirror and her arm reached out.

*Help me.*

Now safe in her apartment, with no apparitions crawling from the wall, the phrasing of the plea struck Katherine as pitiful rather than menacing. "Not one word threatening to suck out my soul despite Miss Harmony's insistence," she murmured, scratching

Whiskers behind an ear. "Did you sense she wasn't a danger, too? Is that why you weren't afraid?"

It's big step for a human to reach out for help. Where does a ghost turn if not to the people it haunts? Had a desperate soul from beyond cried out and her first reaction had been a panicked bolt for freedom? Guilt pricked her conscience.

With fierce determination, Katherine threw back the covers and darted into the hall. In one unhesitating flick of her finger, she turned off the light and returned to bed. Whiskers curled into a ball next to her and purred.

****

On Monday, Katherine's last appointment ended at three o'clock, but she stayed to surf the internet. She tried one website after another and grimaced. No wonder Jake had been frustrated. Suggestions for removing a ghost ranged from silly mumbled incantations to waving burning incense over a dead chicken.

"Katherine?"

Startled, she looked up from the computer. Jeremy stood at the door. "I said goodnight. You seem distracted today. Need help with anything?"

"No. I'm making notes on a client." She clicked off a website entitled Proven Methods of Spectral Cleansing.

"Interesting case?"

"Yes. A bit of anxiety." Katherine cleared her throat. "She's hesitant to leave the house."

"I can recommend a psychiatrist for a drug regimen..."

"That won't be necessary," she said in rush. "I

believe she'll respond well to counseling."

"All right, then. See you tomorrow."

Katherine logged off the computer. A hazy idea formed, solidifying into a plan of action. The trouble was Detective Sumner made it clear he didn't know the ghost's identity. The previous owner had been an elderly man. Perhaps she was a friend or relative? How much digging had he actually done? She pushed back from the desk. Only one person held the answers…

\*\*\*\*

Jake stared blankly at the computer screen vaguely aware he read the same paragraph three times. Or was it four? Either way, his concentration was shot. *That's what you get for staring at a computer for ten hours.* He had come in early to do research on his house, searching for any mention of the address in crime reports going back to construction in the 1920s. He scoured the files and discovered nothing. Prior occupants had been annoyingly law-abiding citizens.

He scowled. Man, he really blew it yesterday. Totally screwed the whole situation. Barreling headlong toward bankruptcy, he managed to creep out the most interesting woman he'd met in a long time.

*Shake it off, Sumner. You can fix this. You always do. Every problem offers different options for solution, so what's the next step?*

Jake peered at the screen, waiting for inspiration, but his mind remained blank.

"Hey."

Jake startled at the finger jab in the shoulder. His partner, Ethan Reardon, leaned in with a smirk. "Must have been one hot date last night. What's with you today? You're out of it and look like hell. My love life should be so good."

"Oh, I—no date. Just, uh, another late night at the house."

Ethan shook his head. "I told you that place was a money pit." He motioned to the computer. "What are you working on?"

Jake minimized the screen. "Nothing new. Checking reports on the cold case files the lieutenant left."

"Any leads?"

"No, but I haven't finished yet."

"Shout, if you need another set of eyes..." Ethan ambled to his desk.

Jake's attention returned to the screen. "Fifth time's the charm," he muttered.

****

The police department was downtown, only a short walk from her apartment. Katherine asked for Detective Jake Sumner at the front desk. She got a visitor's ID and directions to homicide.

*Homicide?* A nervous flutter rippled through Katherine. She hadn't realized Jake was a homicide detective.

As she entered the office, a man strode up to her with a welcoming grin. "I'm Detective Ethan Reardon. Can I help you?"

"I'd like to speak with Detective Sumner."

"He's my partner." Ethan shouted toward the back. "Jake! You have a visitor."

Jake rose from his chair, surprise on his face at the sight of Katherine. He hurried across the room. Dark circles rimmed his eyes, hinting at a lack of sleep. Unlike Detective Reardon, he wore jeans and a t-shirt instead of a suit, and no shoulder holster.

Ethan flashed a wicked grin. "I'm available for consultation, Detective Sumner."

"No thanks, I got this." He grabbed Katherine's elbow, ushering her to a chair next to his desk. "I didn't expect to see you again." His expression filled with concern and his voice dropped to a whisper, "Did something *unexpected* happen?"

"No, I'm fine, but I need to talk to you." Katherine's face flushed. Her plan sounded so logical until she sat face to face with Jake Sumner again. "No, wait. That's a lie. I'm not fine. I'm sorry to bother you at work," she stammered, "but didn't have your number. I suppose I could have phoned you at the precinct, but—"

"Just come out and say it," said Jake kindly.

"I've decided to take the ghost as my new client."

## Chapter 7

Jake blinked. "Say what?"

"It's not as crazy as it sounds—"

"Hell, yeah, it is."

"No, really," said Katherine. "I thought this over. I'm not a flake or phony psychic. I'm trained to help people."

"Breathing people," Jake sputtered "People with actual heartbeats, not monsters who try to suck you into a mirror."

"That's just it," insisted Katherine. "I don't think her intent was to harm us. The only person injured so far was Miss Harmony and she caused the scratches from Whiskers herself. I'm not saying the experience wasn't a whole new level of terrifying, but I've had a chance to calm down and reflect."

"I appreciate what you're trying to do," he said in a tone that brooked no argument, "but absolutely not. You may choose to believe this thing isn't dangerous, but I don't. I'm sorry, but the answer is no."

Katherine stiffened in her seat. "You misunderstand. I'm not here to ask permission only to gather information. I've decided to help her, and you have no say in the matter."

Jake's shoulders stiffened. "Excuse me. This is my house we're talking about."

"What?" she scoffed. "You claim ownership of a

ghost? Don't want to share the astral plane?"

"I don't even know what the hell that means," he hissed, "but I have a responsibility for your safety inside those walls, and I can't protect you from something like this. So listen up, Dr. Fleming when I say back off. I won't let you inside my house."

Her temper flared. "Not a chance. I'll break in if I have to. I'll…I'll…" The anger died. Katherine slumped in her seat, despair weighing her down. "A woman cried out to me in a voice filled with pain. I wish you heard her anguish. I'm convinced now she didn't intend to scare us. She wanted help."

Jake's hard edge softened. "Did you get any sleep last night?"

"About as much as you," said Katherine with a faint smile. She drew herself up. "I ran from her, Detective. I ran from someone who pleaded for help. I've never done that before."

His fingers clenched. "It's not a good feeling."

Katherine's gaze sought his. "I have to help her. At least, I have to try. I can't walk away. I won't." She leaned across the desk, regarding him sharply. "I don't think you can either. Wasn't it guilt rather than fear that really kept you up last night?"

Jake glanced away. "Is that your official diagnosis?"

"More of an observation. When the ghost appeared, I was frightened, but you showed anger because your actions may have led me into a possibly dangerous situation. Deep down you have the need to help her, too, and are frustrated by the inability to act." Katherine sat back in the chair and folded her arms. "That's my professional judgment."

Inner turmoil played out across his face and then Jake's sober features lightened with a wry grin. "I have an idea you're going to be a big pain in my rear—and that's my professional opinion, Dr. Fleming."

She grinned. "Katherine."

"Jake. So, what now, Katherine? Do we buy a crystal ball?"

"I'm not planning a séance. They're a giant load of crap. So are Ouija boards, tea leaves, tarot cards, and the other worthless junk used by scam artists such as Miss Harmony. I plan to call on my training and adopt a therapeutic approach. That means one-on-one sessions with the client."

Jake raised an eyebrow. "Going to talk the ghost onto the couch? This I gotta see."

She shook her finger at him. "The couch is not a requirement. Don't you understand anything about therapy?"

He hesitated slightly, and she regarded him with surprise. "You've seen a therapist?"

"Yeah," he said slowly, "well, not exactly. I mean, I was involved in a shooting a little while ago. A sign-off from a counselor is mandatory."

Katherine opened her mouth to ask a question and he waved her aside. "It was a man, not my current houseguest, so no connection there. You want to head back to the parlor?"

"I hope to have more information first. I'm sure you researched the house. What did you find about the previous occupants?"

"Nothing useful. As I told you yesterday, the last owner was an elderly widower. His wife died fifteen years ago out of state and he moved to Sandy Shoals to be closer to his kids."

"How old was the wife when she died?"

"Seventy-two, and she died in the hospital, not at home."

Katherine wrinkled her brow. "Not her then. I didn't get a clear image of the woman in the mirror, but I can't shake the impression she was much younger."

"How do you know she didn't run into a cosmetic surgeon after death," said Jake with a droll tone, "and get a supernatural facelift? We're walking uncharted territory here."

"I don't, but we have to start with a few assumptions. No ghost story I recall ever mentioned the spirit of a dead person coming back older than in real life. Let's assume, then, no plastic surgery in the mystic beyond, and her appearance is the same as the time of death."

Jake shot her a sharp look. "Her life may also have ended abruptly, unpleasantly, and possibly by human hands."

"She was murdered?" Katherine drew in a breath. "I-I didn't think of that. I assumed she just had unfinished emotional business that tied her here."

"We have to consider the possibility."

"Of course…shouldn't there be a record?"

"Not if the body was never found. It's possible she died in the house, but her body was moved. Or the death ruled natural or an accident."

"Oh," said Katherine softly. "This could be more complicated than I thought. What else did you discover?"

"The house was owned by a succession of families dating from construction in the early 1920s. Funny thing, I didn't find a single police report for that address, including missing persons. You'd have thought if the previous occupants experienced weird going's-on, they'd have called the cops at least once. This ghost thing is new."

"You accessed files going back that far?" asked Katherine in surprise.

"Yeah, after the first incident I poked around. Not all the paperwork is computerized." Jake motioned to a stack of old ledgers. "I dragged these call logs from storage. Luckily, the lieutenant assigned me to go through a few cold cases while I'm stuck on the desk."

Katherine raised an eyebrow "You're not on full duty?"

Jake shifted in his seat. "Restricted status because of the shooting. I'll be reinstated any day now. Meanwhile, since I pulled old case files anyway nobody had any suspicions when I dug into a particular address on Culpepper Lane."

Katherine motioned to a second pile of papers on the corner of the desk. "The cold cases?"

His gaze followed hers. "No statute of limitations exists on murder. Cases stay open until solved. Family members of the deceased may wait a long time for answers. Some may never get any at all."

A pang of remorse hit Katherine. "Maybe our ghost's family is waiting, too."

Jake grinned. "Our ghost? Getting a little possessive there, Fleming." He regarded her with interest. "Still want to go back to the parlor even though we have a big pile of squat?"

"Yes, now more than ever." Katherine chuckled. "But the sooner the better, before I chicken out."

Jake stood up. "Then let's go."

Detective Reardon stood at a bulletin board near the door tacking up a notice. He eyed them with undisguised curiosity. "Found a lead on one of the cold cases, Jake?"

"No," said Jake. "We were talking about someone else…that is, a person we both know…" He cleared his throat and glanced at Katherine, a hint of desperation in his eyes.

"I'm a psychologist," she said cheerfully. "Detective Sumner and I were discussing a new client of mine. They're acquainted, and the client gave permission to discuss her therapy with him." She smiled benignly. "It's part of the treatment."

"Hope it's nothing serious," said Reardon.

"Therapy is a process," she added quickly. "I can't say more. You understand—doctor-patient privilege and all."

"Uh-huh." Nothing in his quizzical expression said *I buy this.*

"I'm headed home," said Jake. "I'll see you tomorrow." Jake hurried Katherine out the door before Ethan could ask another question. "I'll have to come up with a more convincing lie by tomorrow," he murmured in her ear.

They got into Jake's truck. Although her determination remained steady, Katherine's stomach muscles clenched as they turned the corner onto Culpepper Lane. Jake parked in the driveway. "Ready?" he asked. "Last chance to run."

She swallowed hard and managed a weak grin. "Not really, but I'll go anyway."

They walked up the steps to the porch, and Jake

unlocked the door. The house was dark with no discernable movement from within.

Katherine licked her lips. "Seems quiet."

"Oh, yeah." Jake did a quick survey as they stepped into the foyer. "It's always real quiet before the fun begins. So, what's your plan?"

"Talk to her the same as any patient. Try to get her to discuss the problem and determine what's holding her here."

"Find out her name. I can work with that. I'll go first." Jake grasped the parlor door handle and paused. "I don't care if she's a client. I'm hanging by your side and if I think you're in danger, I'll pull you out of there."

Katherine followed him into the parlor, nerves stretched thin. She shot an anxious glance at Jake. His body tensed as he switched on the lamp. He nodded at Katherine.

She swallowed hard and stepped in front of the mirror. "Hello? Are you there? My name is Katherine. Jake is with me. We came back because you asked for help. I realize you only tried to make contact and didn't mean us any harm. I'm sorry I ran—we ran. Jake and I got a little freaked out, but we're here now."

The only sound in the room was her quick anxious breaths. "Please talk to me," Katherine pleaded. "I understand if you're afraid, but I have ways to help people feel safe again. Never tried them on a ghost," she added with a shaky laugh. "I'm game, but you must trust me and show yourself."

Not a single blotch in the glass altered position. "Please...at least give me a name. I can't help if I don't have any information."

The lamplight held steady, so did the temperature.

Jake stepped to Katherine's side. "Well, that was totally anticlimactic."

The built-up tension in Katherine's body evaporated. Her shoulders sagged. She gazed at him, bemused. "I don't know whether to be disappointed or relieved."

"Could be she went out to grab a bite to eat," Jake added dryly. "We should have called for an appointment first."

She grinned. "Perfectly understandable, after all it's dinnertime."

"I'm hungry myself. I didn't have much appetite over the weekend. Big surprise, but I'm starving now." Jake cleared his throat. "I'll order a pizza if you care to hang around for a while. She might show, but I get it if you don't want to eat in a haunted house."

A pleasantly warm sensation fluttered through Katherine. A haunted house had never been her ideal location for a first date, but now surprisingly acceptable. "It's not haunted at the moment, and I'm starved, too."

Jake phoned in the order. "I'll give you a tour while we wait." They walked through the dining room and into a dated kitchen decorated with rooster-print wallpaper. Gasping, Katherine closed her eyes and held two hands against her forehead. "Oh my God, this so weird. I'm getting a psychic flash."

Jake tensed. "What is it?"

"I sense…I sense…a complete kitchen remodel in your near future."

He relaxed with a grin. "You have a warped sense of humor, Fleming."

Katherine motioned to a framed cross-stitch hanging on the wall: Ice Scream, You Scream, The Police Arrive, How Awkward. Tiny ice cream cones made up the border. "I didn't realize you were so artsy. What skill—I'm in awe at how expertly you tied the French knots."

Jake made a face. "It was a gift from my mom when I graduated from the police academy. You'd hit it off with her. I suspect she needs counseling, too." He took Katherine by the elbow and led her away. "Come on, I'll show you the upstairs."

The second floor had four good-sized bedrooms and one large bath. The last one they toured was the biggest. Katherine glanced around. "Master bedroom with no attached bath?"

"Most houses of this era didn't have them. I plan to steal space from here and the room next door to build one—that is, if I can come to terms with the current tenant."

"I've had reluctant patients before," said Katherine, lightly. "Give me time. She must need a little coaxing to talk."

Jake gazed around the room, his expression filled with pride. "I appreciate the help. I've grown attached to this house. I don't want to sell."

"I can see why. It has tons of charm."

"A good place to settle down," he murmured. "I never thought much along those lines before I bought this place. People get lonely. Maybe houses do, too." He turned his gaze on her and Katherine felt the heat rise to her cheeks. The doorbell rang, breaking the awkward silence.

Jake coughed. "Pizza guy is here."

They hurried to the front door. Jake paid the deliveryman and took the order to the kitchen. Katherine ran her hand across the top of an old wooden farm table. "Did the furniture come with the house? This is nice stuff."

"My folks gave me a few pieces when they moved out of state. The couch in the parlor is theirs, too. It's been sitting in storage until recently."

"I don't suppose you found the mirror buried in the grave of a dead gypsy."

Jake cracked a grin. "Nope. It hung in the living room of my parents' unexceptional ranch-style suburban tract home the entire time I was growing up. Mom bought it at a yard sale from an elderly neighbor. She was a spinster Sunday school teacher famous for her complete lack of a sense of humor. As far as I can determine, the mirror never served as a portal into the afterlife. That's another reason I think the ghost is a recent tenant. I probably shouldn't have dragged this stuff over here so soon, but I expected to give up the lease on my apartment by now and wanted to spend money on remodeling, not storage rental."

Jake leaned back in his seat, regarding her intently. "So what's your story, Katherine? How'd you end up in Sandy Shoals as a part-time ghost hunter? You're not a local."

"No. I was born and raised in Chicago, but spent summer vacations here as a child. My grandparents always rented a house at the beach and I visited. After my grandmother died, Grampa stayed in Chicago and stopped coming. He passed away a few years ago. When I heard of a job listing at a brand new counseling center, I jumped at it."

Jake glanced away. "You work with Jeremy Ingalls."

"Yes. Do you know him?"

"We've met."

Katherine's eyes widened. "Of course. He has a contract with the police department. Jeremy is your counselor."

"Yeah. I'm required to see him after the shooting until he signs off."

"I haven't seen you at his office."

"Ingalls and I meet at the precinct." Jake paused abruptly. He motioned with his hand as if to brush aside the subject. "You must have collected plenty of good memories during summers in Sandy Shoals to want to return."

*That was a sudden change of topic.* "I did." Unconsciously, Katherine smiled. "My grandfather and I used to play this game on the beach."

"Perform spontaneous exorcisms for sunbathers?" he joshed.

"Nope. Grampa called it *What Do You See?* Before he retired, Grampa was a top salesman and the best I ever met at reading people. He taught me to observe body language. We'd stroll along the beach and then he'd point and say, 'What do you see?' and I'd say 'Two people under an umbrella.' And then he'd explain although they didn't raise their voices, they were having an argument. The man leaned away from the woman, shoulders stiff. The woman peered at a book in her lap, lips pressed tight together."

Jake chuckled. "Your grandfather would have made a hell of a criminal profiler."

"No kidding. He's the reason I got interested in

psychology. He taught me although people have complexities, everyone gives off unconscious signals. If I learn to read them, I can discover their inner truth." Her voice deepened in imitation of her grandfather. " 'Salesman or psychologist, Kathy, that's the only way to determine what a person really needs.' "

Jake cocked an eyebrow. "He called you Kathy?"

"I know, so retro. Drove me crazy as a teenager. I couldn't get him to switch to a cooler nickname like Kate or Kat."

"Retro's cool," he said with a grin. "Like this house."

Katherine returned the smile. Dinner in a haunted house was turning out to be quite pleasant. "Okay, now it's your turn. How'd you end up on the police force in Sandy Shoals?"

"Haven't you figured me out by now?" Jake said with an innocent look. "You're not very good at this shrink stuff, are you?"

"Oh, I've got you pegged," she teased. "You're a local."

"Not a stretch in deductive reasoning." Jake yawned. "That's the best you got?"

Katherine leaned forward studying his placid expression. "You became a police officer because you want to help people."

"Obvious. Not impressed."

"You're not a man to run from trouble. You need to help."

Jake glanced away. The words hit a nerve.

"But not always?" she added. Jake's gaze returned to her and this time held steady.

Understanding flooded Katherine. "Something

77

happened to change you."

Jake slammed the lid of the empty pizza box and pushed back from the table. "It's late. The ghost isn't going to show."

Katherine placed a hand on his arm. "If you want to talk…"

"There's nothing to talk about," he said stiffly. "I'll take you home."

Jake tossed the box in the garbage can. Katherine followed in silence to the front door, fighting the desire to give herself a swift kick in the pants. Jake wasn't a patient. He had issues in his life he plainly didn't want to share. Why didn't she back off and keep her mouth shut? Dinner had been going so well…

The hall light flickered.

"Jake?"

He had his hand on the front door knob and shot a wary look around. "So, she decided to show after all."

The light went out, plunging the foyer in darkness. The lamp switched on in the parlor.

Katherine's heart thumped. She stepped past the French doors into the room.

"Wait!" Jake reached out his hand. "Let me go first—"

The parlor doors slammed in his face.

Chapter 8

"Katherine...Kathy!" Jake pulled frantically at the doorknob. "It won't open."

Katherine touched the brass knob and pulled back with a start. The metal was icy cold to the touch. "It's frozen."

"Stand back, I'll break down the door."

*Please...*

The whispery plea sent Katherine's heart racing. She turned to the mirror. A shadowy face with features blurred flickered in the glass.

"Wait, Jake!" Katherine yelled. "I-I think she wants to see me alone."

"Katherine—"

"Give me the chance. I'm all right. The door startled me, but I'm not hurt. Give me time to talk to her."

Jake pressed his palms flat against the door. He peered through the glass panel at her with an anxious, indecisive expression and then dropped his hands to his side. "I'll give you five minutes, but at the first sign of trouble..."

"I'll scream like a banshee."

"And I'll come running."

Katherine stepped in front of the mirror. She swallowed hard. "I'm here."

The whispery voice deepened and took on a

masculine tone. *You're a good girl.*

"Okay…" Katherine muttered to herself. "That's creepy." She drew in a breath. "I'm sure you're a good girl, too, and don't mean me any harm. My name is Katherine. I only want to help. Please tell me your name."

*Don't let him trick you.* The voice trembled.

"Do you mean Jake?" said Katherine, confused. "He's a good man—a police officer. He wants to help, too."

*Stay a good girl. If he has doubts, you'll be sorry. Don't tell him what you know. Don't…* The image in the mirror faded.

"Wait!" Katherine yelled. "What if I promise our talks will be confidential? I swear whatever you say to me won't leave this room." Her hand reached out and touched the glass.

*See…*

The whisper filled her head, and the parlor vanished. Katherine stood outside; dusk cast long thin shadows across the ground from a metal structure— bleachers on the edge of a playing field surrounded by trees and bushes. She inhaled. The air was thick and steamy, humidity left a glistening sheen on Katherine's skin. No mistaking the weather for anything but the dog days of a Florida summer.

A nearby trashcan overflowed with plastic water bottles and power bar wrappings. Katherine wiped a hand across her brow. How could anyone play sports is this heat? She glanced around. At one end was a scoreboard with SSHS on top. Sandy Shoals High School? No scores were posted. If there had been a game, it was long over.

The field was empty. No…not quite. A teenage girl with glasses sat on the end of the playing field under the shade of the bleachers, her head buried in a book. She wore a t-shirt, shorts, and calf-length athletic socks with sneakers. Next to her was a backpack with a pair of cleated sports shoes tied around the straps. Leaves rustled within a thick clump of trees and shrubbery next to the bleachers. The girl's head jerked up from the pages. "Hello?"

Katherine's instincts fired off a warning. She made a move to approach the girl, but her legs locked in place. "Hey!" she shouted. "You need to go home now."

The girl's gaze drifted to the wooded area. Nothing in her relaxed stance indicated she heard Katherine. "Is anyone there?" After a moment of silence, she returned to her book.

Katherine's inner warning now bleated a screeching alarm. With rising panic, she struggled to move, but her body refused to obey. "Run!" she cried out. "You're in danger."

With a quizzical expression, the girl peered once more at the bushes. She shut her book, grabbed the backpack and slung it over her shoulder. She crawled out from the bleachers and turned to leave.

A man in a black ski mask stepped from behind a tree.

"Behind you," Katherine yelled.

Paralyzed in place, Katherine watched with sick horror as he crept silently behind the girl. He grabbed her around the neck. She dropped the backpack. He slammed her to the ground, rolled her over, and sat on her chest.

L. A. Kelley

"No! Leave her alone!" Katherine struggled in vain against the mystical bonds. "Help!" she screamed at the top of her lungs. "Somebody please help her."

The man pinned the girl's arms in the dirt with his legs, one hand over her mouth. With the other, he ripped a gold cross from her neck and tucked it in his pocket. The terror-stricken girl couldn't move. The heavy weight on her chest pressed down, squeezing the air from her lungs. Each breath struggled to escape the fingers covering her mouth. The man's head bent next to her ear, his voice no more than a raspy whisper. One hand brushed along the side of her face. "That's my good girl." His hands went to her throat.

"Fight!" Katherine screamed. "Don't give in."

The vision shattered into fragmented pieces. Katherine staggered back from the wall. The wavy image of the woman in the mirror faded away.

*Tina...*

An echo of the ghostly voice reverberated through the room.

"Katherine!" Jake grabbed her by the shoulders. "Are you okay?" He gave her a shake. "Kathy, talk to me."

"I-I'm fine." Katherine blinked. "How'd you get in?"

"The door opened by itself just now." Jake put his arm around her shoulder. "Let's get out of here. You could pass for a ghost yourself." He led her to the front porch and locked the door behind them. "I take it she spoke to you again?"

"Yes."

"What does she want?"

Katherine ran a shaky hand through her hair. "I

believe she wants me to find out who killed her."

Jake gawked at her. "The ghost told you she was murdered?"

"Not exactly. I inferred it from a vision."

"What did you see?"

Katherine opened her mouth and then gave a helpless shrug. "I-I'm sorry," she stammered. "I promised not to tell you."

Jake regarded her in stunned disbelief. "You made a promise to a ghost?"

"It was the only way to get her to open up. She has trust issues, and I had to swear our sessions are confidential. I shouldn't even have mentioned the murder, but you caught me off-guard and I wasn't thinking straight." Katherine drew herself up. "I'm okay now."

"Damn right you're not thinking," Jake sputtered. "She's not a person. It's a thing in my house—a thing I want to get rid of."

"At the present, she's simply someone in pain, and this is the only way to help her."

"You said she was murdered. I'm a homicide detective. You have to give me a name. I can check out the case—"

"No."

Jake grabbed her arm. "Katherine, I'm serious. A murder is no joke. Keep the details of the woo-woo psychic hand-holding sessions to yourself," he snapped, "but tell me who she is."

Katherine bristled and shook off his grip. "First of all, I don't understand what the hell woo-woo psychic hand-holding even means. I will treat her the same as any other patient and to make progress she needs to trust me. I can't break her confidence. All I can do is try to get her to allow you with me next time or at least give permission to tell her story. That's final."

Jake's face flushed. "I tell you what's final. I won't let you inside again."

Katherine stiffened. "You're not serious."

"Believe it. I'll deal with her on my own."

"The ghost won't talk to you."

"Who said I have to talk? What if I just burn the damn house down? It's my house. I can burn it down if I want. Let's see if a ghost can haunt a pile of ashes."

Katherine regarded him with a withering look. "You're angry and talking nonsense."

"I'm talking nonsense?" Jake gritted his teeth and pointed to the driveway. "Get in the damn truck. I'm taking you home."

She stiffened. "I'd rather walk."

"Have it your way," he said airily, "but it's late, so either hop in the truck or I'll follow behind on the sidewalk to make sure you get home safe."

Katherine pressed her lips together. She slid into the passenger seat and simmered in silence on the short ride to her apartment. The truck idled at the curb and she opened the door, anger boiling over. "You have to let me back inside."

"I don't have to do anything," Jake said smoothly. "She's my ghost, not yours, but spill what you discovered on this murder and I'll reconsider." Katherine slammed the door shut and stormed into the recess.

Jake lowered the window. "You are the most pigheaded, unreasonable—I won't let you poke your nose into a murder without me and that's final. You're not coming back to the house, Kathy, until you change your mind."

"Then I'll find another way without your help," Katherine shouted. "And don't call me Kathy." She shut the front door behind her with a bang.

\*\*\*\*

Jake rammed the gearshift to drive. He mashed his foot down on the accelerator, and the truck jumped from the curb, tires squealing. He gritted his teeth. "Stubborn…pigheaded." Every instinct of his screamed out that Katherine wasn't the type to give up easily. She'd keep digging until she found answers. What if she stumbled on a secret meant to stay buried?

He glowered into the rearview mirror. "I plan to keep my eyes on you, Dr. Fleming."

\*\*\*\*

Whiskers brushed against Katherine's legs. She picked him up to cradle against her shoulder. "Well, I had an interesting evening. How was yours?" Katherine plopped on the couch, kicked off her shoes, and propped her feet on the coffee table. Whiskers settled into her lap.

Katherine leaned back in the cushions and glowered at the ceiling. "Men."

Whiskers lifted his head. "Meow?"

"Not you." She patted his head, anger fading. "No offense, but sitting alone with a cat on my lap is not how I hoped the evening would end. Jake and I hit it off so well, too. I really like him. More than I expected, but that protective streak is a pain in the rear." She made a wry face. "Some psychologist I am. I should have seen that coming."

Katherine brushed aside a pang of remorse. "Since

I'm currently locked out, I'll investigate on my own. Perhaps once I discover more information on Tina, I can convince Jake to let me into the house again."

*Tina...* Rage, helplessness, horror, all the emotions from witnessing the vicious attack bubbled up inside Katherine again. No way in hell would she let a crime against that poor girl go unpunished.

*Girl?*

Katherine frowned. Funny... Even though the face in the mirror had been shrouded in mist, she could have sworn Jake's ghost was older than a teenage girl.

She lifted Whiskers to the side, went to the desk, and opened a new patient file on her laptop.

"Tina No Last Name," Katherine murmured. "Not a lot to go on."

Her fingers hovered over the keyboard. That's not exactly true.

*What did you see, Kathy?* prodded her grandfather's voice.

She typed her notes. The new patient was a teenager named Tina. She sat under the bleachers on the Sandy Shoals High School playing field. She wore sports clothes and had shoes with cleats—soccer or baseball. "No mitt or bat," she muttered, "so soccer." Her attacker also took her gold cross necklace. Was it a simple theft or more symbolic?

Katherine shivered. What happened to Tina? Was her body ever found? Was a family still wrapped in grief over her tragic disappearance? If not, a missing person's report on a student from Sandy Shoals High must exist. If only she had Jake's help...

Well, she didn't. Katherine drummed her fingers on the table. A missing or dead girl named

Tina...attended Sandy Shoals High School...attack occurred during the summer on school grounds.

"It's a start," she murmured.

An internet search for missing girls named Tina from Sandy Shoals didn't yield a single hit. Next, she tried obituaries for Sandy Shoals High School students with equally disappointing results. Since the school had been built, a few teenage girls died from natural causes or accidents, but no one named Tina.

Katherine stretched the kinks from her shoulders and checked the time—nearly midnight. She had a calendar of living clients tomorrow and they deserved a clear-headed, wide-awake therapist as much as a ghost. She shut down the computer and went to bed.

\*\*\*\*

Between patients, Katherine considered the problem of Tina's identity. Occasionally, her thoughts also drifted to Jake, but she shoved them roughly away. If he was mad, so be it. She made a promise, and that was that. At the end of the day, Katherine had a flash of inspiration and headed to the public library. Her excitement rose when the librarian informed her they had copies of all the Sandy Shoals High School yearbooks in the reference room.

Sandy Shoals had built a succession of high schools over the past century, the newest twenty years old. Katherine's glimpse of Tina's modern clothing convinced her the girl wasn't from the distant past, so she concentrated the search on students who attended since the most recent construction. Current enrollment was approximately three hundred seniors in each school year. The problem, Katherine soon realized, was Tina may not have been a senior. That meant combing pictures of underclassmen, too.

A handful of the books had girls named Tina, but the faces didn't match, so Katherine worked backward from the present, scrupulously studying the picture of every female student. She only made it through three books before the library closed. The next day after her last patient's appointment, she returned to carefully scrutinize another stack, but ended with the same frustrating results. Neither Tina's face nor name came to light.

On Friday evening, Katherine slammed the last yearbook shut with disgust and shoved it back on the shelf...nothing. Tina wasn't a student at Sandy Shoals. Why was she on the playing field? Katherine scowled. An image popped into her head of Jake Sumner with an I-told-you-so expression.

"Forget it," she muttered. "I'm not begging for your help."

She grabbed her purse, and on the way to the exit passed a teenage girl in a school uniform standing at a carrel of paperbacks. She wore a gold cross around her neck. Stitched over her shirt pocket was Saint Anne's Catholic School. Katherine stopped in her tracks. "Excuse me, but is Saint Anne's a local high school?"

"Yes, ma'am."

"In Sandy Shoals?"

"No ma'am, but it's close—in Azalea Trace just over the county line."

"A lot of local students go there?"

"Sure. Probably half my class."

With growing excitement, Katherine chose a carrel by the window and logged into a library computer. After connecting with the internet, she searched for obituaries for missing persons from Azalea Trace, but no one with the name Tina came up. "Who the hell are you?" she muttered with mounting frustration.

She had no yearbook with pictures to peruse, but a quick search yielded the website for Saint Anne's. The school printed the names of all graduating seniors by year going back to when the school was founded. Saint Anne's was as old as Sandy Shoals High, but the graduating classes smaller. Katherine had just clicked open the page with the senior class from seven years before when an announcement over the PA system reminded patrons they had fifteen minutes until closing.

Katherine yawned. *I'm beat. Call it a day.* Her stomach gurgled loud enough for a passing librarian to raise an eyebrow. Red-faced, she moved the cursor to close the webpage and head for home when one name in the list of graduates jumped out at her…April Ortiz.

With growing excitement, Katherine logged off and rushed to her car. Before getting in, she fished the phone from her purse and dialed April's number. "Hi, April. It's Katherine. Want to have lunch tomorrow?"

"You must be psychic," said April. "I was about to call you for the same thing. I'm lusting for a bacon cheeseburger from O'Brien's Bistro. God, that's pathetic. I need a man in my life. Twelve o'clock?"

"Twelve o'clock at O'Brien's. Perfect, see you then." Katherine hung up with a light heart. She didn't have Tina's identity yet, but may have taken one step closer to the truth.

\*\*\*\*

With mounting exhilaration, Jake slipped from his hiding place behind a tree as the headlights from Katherine's car disappeared. Camping outside her office after work on Tuesday had finally yielded results. Curious after their argument, he had followed her to the library. He snuck in and spied from the stacks as she diligently searched yearbooks.

*Well, well.*

Katherine must have a reason to think the ghost had attended Sandy Shoals, so she was not only female, but young. On Wednesday morning, Jake searched past and present police files for murder victims or missing children at the high school, but came up empty. On a chance the ghost was older, he double-checked teachers and administrators—nothing.

Jake drove past the library that evening and spotted Katherine's car. He parked his truck on the other side of the lot and peeked through a window as she scoured more Sandy Shoals yearbooks. "She's at it again," he muttered. "How long you gonna stick with a dead end, Kathy?"

Apparently, Jake soon realized, until she got results because on Thursday her car parked in the same place. He debated whether to stop and tell Katherine the truth, but decided against it. Surely, she would get discouraged and give up the hunt soon.

*Sure she will.*

Doubt ate at Jake all day Friday. He arrived first at the library, parked the truck far from the building, and waited. A few minutes later, Katherine arrived. Man, she was stubborn. His fingers gripped the door handle. He should tell her she wasted her time. No Sandy Shoals students or staff had been murdered. The hand dropped to his lap. No. Wasting her time kept her out of danger—and the world was a dangerous place.

Jake crept to a window to spy on her. Katherine

slammed the last book shut in obvious frustration. His lips twitched in a knowing smile. She just came to the same conclusion he reached days ago—Sandy Shoals High School was a bust. Katherine headed to the exit. She stopped short to speak to a girl in a Saint Anne's shirt and then immediately sat back down at a public computer. Fortunately, the seat she chose was near another window.

Jake changed position and glimpsed enough of the screen to deduce where Katherine's investigation led. As she rose to leave, he ran across the parking lot and hid behind a tree near her car. From there, eavesdropping on the phone conversation was simple. As Katherine's car pulled away, Jake stepped from the shadows.

An uneasy thought crept into his mind. *Katherine may be one step closer to the truth.*

Chapter 9

Katherine waited at the entrance to O'Brien's. At twelve on the dot, April jogged across the street, out of breath. "Don't tell me I'm late. I'm never late for a meal."

"Right on time," Katherine said cheerfully. They took a booth in the back. "How are things at the station?"

"I have news," said April. "Parker toyed with changes to his show and opted for a call-in format. He figured it worked for Miss Harmony, so it'll work for him. He wants to keep the first part of *Chit Chat* as conversation and then take questions from listeners for the second half."

Katherine raised an eyebrow. "At 7:00 on Sunday morning?"

April snorted a laugh. "Yeah, I can hear it now. A frantic caller asks if anyone out there saw what he did after downing a dozen tequila shots Saturday night, where he left his pants, or who is the strange tattooed man in his bed? Actually, Parker's show will move to Miss Harmony's old Saturday time slot. I'm sure a few of your fans with tinfoil hats will follow."

"Mine?" said Katherine, puzzled.

"Oh, didn't I mention? Parker wants you as the first guest." April nudged her in the side. "Can turn into a steady gig if you cure the nut jobs on the spot. After all, it worked for Miss Harmony."

"Sorry, I don't work as fast as a scam artist. Parker really wants me?"

"Yeah, but the show isn't a done deal, yet. He still has to wrangle sponsors and stuff like that. I wasn't supposed to blab his plans, but what the hell. Is it okay if I tell Parker you're interested?"

"Sure, why not?" Katherine cleared her throat. "I have a question for you, too. Did you graduate from Saint Anne's Catholic School?"

"Yup." April winked. "Sorry to say, not many of Sister Angelica's lessons in proper behavior for a young lady stuck. How did you know?"

"I saw your picture in a yearbook." Katherine launched the fabrication she practiced all morning. "I have a new patient around your age. I can't go into detail, of course, but believe an incident in the past affects her current mental health. A traumatic event may have happened to a girl at Saint Anne's. I can't get the patient to discuss specifics, so decided to dig up more information from a graduate."

"Sure," said April, "although the most traumatic thing I recall happening to anyone in my graduating class was not being asked to the prom."

"This may have happened a few years earlier. The student's name was Tina."

April sat back in her seat. "Oh my God, I haven't thought of her in years."

"You know who I'm talking about?" said Katherine with mounting excitement.

"Sure. Margaret Delaney." Her eyes held a wistful look. "We were friends."

"Margaret?"

"Tina was her nickname," said April. "She hated Margaret, said it was too old-fashioned. Her middle name was Christina, so the kids at school called her Tina. We were both on the girls' soccer team."

"Soccer team," Katherine mused. "Did you ever play on the Sandy Shoals High School field?"

"Sure, all the time. We had regular games against their girls' team during the season, but Sandy Shoals also hosted a soccer camp in the summer. All of us attended. As a matter of fact," added April with a frown, "during camp before the start of junior year everything changed with Tina."

Katherine leaned in. "What happened to her?"

"I'm not sure. Her home life was a mess. She and her mom didn't get along one bit. We all suspected her mother was a drunk, but Tina refused to talk. She kept a lot to herself."

"Her dad?"

"Never in the picture. Mom had a succession of boyfriends. Tina hated all of them." A troubled look crossed April's face.

"What is it?" asked Katherine.

"Tina stopped coming to soccer camp before it ended and she didn't show for the first few days of school. I called, but her mom said she went to live with her grandmother out of state. Frankly, I figured life got too tough at home and was glad she left. Funny, though," April mused, "Tina cut ties and never got in touch with any of us at school. Weird when I think back on it now. It's as if she wanted a clean break."

Katherine cleared her throat. "Is it possible something bad happened?"

"Like she ran away?" whispered April.

*Or was murdered.* Katherine bit her lip.

"I didn't consider that," moaned April. "Now I feel awful I didn't press harder for answers from her mother—or even tried to get Tina to open up more. She must have kept a lot of stuff bottled inside."

Katherine patted her arm. "Don't blame yourself. You can't expect a teenage girl to recognize signs of trouble."

"Poor Tina," said April with a sigh. "I hope wherever she ended up, she found a better life."

Unconsciously, Katherine hand wadded the napkin into a ball.

"What is it?" said April kindly. "You seem upset."

Katherine forced a grin. "I'm fine—here comes the food. I'm starved." As they ate, Katherine steered the conversation from any further mention of Tina Delaney.

"This was fun," said April as they walked out the door. "I'll call you. Let's have lunch again this week."

"I'd like that—" Katherine stopped short. Jake Sumner lounged against her car.

April followed her gaze and her eyes instantly narrowed. "Who's the guy? Crazy stalker patient?" She fumbled in her purse. "Say the word. I have pepper spray."

"No, he's a police detective. I'm consulting on a case for the force."

"Oh." April's eyes twinkled. "In that case, damn, he's cute."

"We're simply colleagues."

"Married?"

"No."

"Gay?"

Katherine chuckled. "My professional opinion is

hell no."

April jabbed her elbow playfully into Katherine's side. "Then make a move, girl, but if you decide he isn't a keeper toss him back in the pond and give me a shot. See ya!" April cut across the parking lot, calling out to Jake, "Be nice to my girl or you answer to me." He regarded her with bemusement.

Katherine strolled across the lot. "Detective Sumner," she said coolly. "What are you doing here?"

"Waiting for you."

"How did you know I was at O'Brien's?"

"I overheard you at the library making plans. Enjoy your lunch date?"

She gaped at him. "You spied on me?"

"Yup," he replied without a discernable smidgen of guilt. "For several evenings in fact as you scoured the library's collection of Sandy Shoals yearbooks. After you got a lead on Saint Anne's, I heard you mention April's name on the phone and remembered her from the coffee shop the day I first saw you. April had mentioned she worked at the station. It didn't take much investigation to discover her last name and the fact she was an alumna of Saint Anne's."

Katherine folded her arms. "We've already been through this. You know I can't discuss—"

"Margaret Christina Delaney."

Her mouth dropped open. "You have the ghost's name? How?"

Jake casually examined his fingernails. "I'm a detective. I detect."

Katherine glowered. "Did you come here to gloat? That's not very professional."

"Yeah, but it's fun. Actually, I thought you might

be interested in what I found. If not, I can leave…"

Katherine blew out her cheeks in exasperation. "Spill it and stop smirking."

"When I realized you expanded your search to Azalea Trace, so did I. None of the murders matched, but I found an old missing person case on a teenage girl from Saint Anne's filed by her mother. She was sixteen and a classmate of April Ortiz."

"Tina," Katherine mused, "that's what her friends called her… The ghost used the same name. Hang on, April didn't mention police involvement."

"That's because a day after her mother filed the report, she called back. Tina showed up at her grandmother's house—and yes, the detective on the case investigated. Tina was alive and well, but didn't wish to return to Azalea Trace because of ongoing family issues. Her mother decided to transfer custody."

"Tina's alive?" Katherine's mind whirled.

"I can't promise that. I couldn't find a number and haven't spoken to her, so I only know Tina was still breathing when she left Sandy Shoals. I'm checking obituaries, but haven't come up with anything yet." Jake regarded Katherine with a questioning look. "I have Tina's old file in the truck. According to the DMV, her mother lives at the same address. It's a short ride to Azalea Trace."

Katherine startled. "Are you asking for my help?"

Jake shrugged. "The conversation is bound to be delicate since it may involve the never reported disappearance of a minor. I could use psychological insight on the mother. What do you say to a road trip? Or are you still determined to do this on your own?"

Katherine flashed a grin. "I'm in."

"Good. Drop your car at the apartment and I'll meet you out front."

As soon as they were on the road, Katherine thumbed through Tina's file. "Kind of thin."

"Nothing much to report. The girl was found safe. No evidence of a crime. Case closed."

"According to the dates," Katherine murmured, "she left home in late August." Her eyes widened. "He didn't kill her."

"The ghost showed you an assault."

"Jake, I can't—"

He waved his hand. "Don't bother. Your expression says I'm right." His voice softened. "Tina didn't die that day, but there's no telling what happened later. What did you see in the parlor or do you still plan to keep quiet?"

Katherine's thoughts whirled. *Was the ghost Tina or someone else? Why give me Tina's name?* "I-I don't know. I need more information. Let me talk to Mrs. Delaney first." She leafed through the remainder of the paperwork. "I don't see any recommendation for social services follow up."

"Tina lived in another state by then. I found earlier police reports on Mrs. Delaney's address though—all domestic disturbances. No evidence of physical violence, but lots of shouting. Apparently, she had lousy taste in boyfriends."

"You think Tina's attacker was one of them?"

"I haven't come to any conclusions at the moment. Investigation requires an open mind, but that may be an avenue worth pursuing."

Katherine's gaze drifted out the window. Was Tina the victim of a sexual assault on the playing field? Did she escape only to be murdered later? Did no one try to help? Her voice dropped. "Her life was so sad."

Jake reached over and squeezed her hand. "We can find the truth, put a ghost's soul at rest. That's something, at least."

Katherine gazed at him in curiosity. "Why did you become a cop?"

He let go of her hand. "Why did you become a shrink?"

She shook her finger. "No turning questions back on themselves. That's a counselor's trick."

"A cop's, too."

"Avoiding the question…" she crooned in a sing-song voice.

Jake shot her a sideways glance. "Next time, you ride in the truck bed."

"That's illegal, and you're still avoiding."

"Sheesh, all right. Sandy Shoals is my town. I was born and raised here and wanted to help people."

"So, you always wanted to be a cop?"

Jake peered straight ahead. Seconds ticked by.

Katherine tilted her head. "That's a no?"

"I started with an architecture major in college. It didn't work for me and I switched to criminal justice. After I graduated, I signed on with the police force. I've been here ever since. End of story. Now, your turn. Why psychology?"

"Because of my grandfather, I've always had an interest in human behavior. When I found out that could be used in a career to help people, I was hooked. End of story."

"You didn't stay in Chicago after you got your degree."

"No. I hate the cold and Chicago has plenty of places for people to get help. I wasn't needed there, but always loved Sandy Shoals. When I heard of a position at a brand new counseling center, I jumped at it. Sandy Shoals is smaller than Chicago, but I can have a bigger impact." She gazed out the window. "I feel as if I owe Sandy Shoals for the good times when I was a kid. Helping its citizens in trouble is my payment."

"Whether they're dead or alive?" teased Jake.

"Doesn't a homicide detective speak for the dead? If rational people won't help, who will? Scam artists like Miss Harmony?"

"Who will?" he echoed, his expression thoughtful.

They reached Azalea Trace and turned down a county road into an older subdivision with one-story brick ranches on heavily wooded lots. Jake stopped in front of a house. A woman on the front porch chatted with a man putting a fresh coat of paint on an Adirondack chair.

Jake showed his badge and motioned to Katherine. "I'm Detective Jake Sumner from the Sandy Shoals police department, and this is Dr. Katherine Fleming, a consultant. We'd like to speak with Carlene Delaney."

"I'm Carlene." The woman eyed Jake with undisguised curiosity. "It's Franks now. This is my husband, Lamar."

Lamar wiped his hands in a rag. "What's this about?"

"We have a few questions concerning Carlene's daughter."

Her face paled. "Margaret's back in town? Is she all right?"

Katherine shot Jake a glance. "You haven't been in

touch?"

"Not in years." Carlene's voice trembled. "No reason she'd come see me."

Lamar put his hand around his wife's shoulders. "Y'all best come inside. We can talk there."

They sat at the kitchen table. Carlene drew in a shuddering breath. "Did you see her?"

"No." Jake paused as if considering his words. "I received a tip Tina may have witnessed a crime and I'm trying to locate her. When was the last time you spoke?"

"Margaret always wanted me to call her Tina." Carlene's voice came out as a choked whisper. "But I didn't. I didn't do much for her..." She rubbed her eyes. "It's been nearly eight years, and not a day goes by I don't see her face and wonder how she is." Lamar cradled his wife's hand between his, and she gave him a grateful smile.

"Why did Tina leave?" said Katherine gently.

Carlene swallowed hard. "You have to remember, I'm not the same person I was back then. I drank—a lot. Hell, I was a drunk. I couldn't see it, of course. The drunk is always the last one who does. Margaret and I fought all the time. She didn't get along with any of my boyfriends."

Jake shot Lamar a pointed look. "The police had reports of domestic disturbances."

"Weren't me," said Lamar with a wry smile. "Carlene and I met at an AA meeting a few years ago." He pulled a chip from his pocket. "Ten years sober."

"Tina took off before Lamar and I got together," said Carlene. "Can't say I ever blamed her for getting out of here. I made her life hell."

"Do you have a picture?" asked Katherine.

Carlene got up and returned with a photograph of a smiling girl with glasses in a Catholic school uniform. "Last one taken."

Katherine rubbed a thumb across the frame, and her heart gave a tug. No terror shaded Tina's eyes, merely a smiling, happy girl. "She's lovely."

Carlene's gaze dropped to her lap. "I leaned on her, took advantage. She took care of this house, her worthless mother, too. Then Margaret changed. She loved soccer, but she quit the team. Wouldn't tell me why. We had this huge fight—that's when she ran away and ended up at my mother's. I was so mad, embarrassed for having to talk to the police over nothing. Angry because Margaret made it clear she wasn't coming home. I told her good riddance. She was a burden, anyway. I even locked the door to her room."

Her voice trembled. "How can a mother say that to her daughter? A few weeks later, I was picked up on a DUI after I crashed the car. Didn't kill anyone, but it was bad." Color rose to her cheeks. "I spent three years in prison, but got sober. While I was in jail, her grandmother died. After I got out, I tried to find Margaret and beg her forgiveness, but she'd moved on, and I didn't search for her. I figured it was for the best. After all, I never did her much good, and I was putting my life together. What could I offer?" She swallowed hard. "Her bedroom door is still locked. I can't bear to go inside see all her things, and know I failed her."

"I understand this is hard," said Jake, "but is there anything else you can tell us?"

The pause was infinitesimal. "No."

His eyes narrowed. "You know something."

Carlene stiffened. "I don't."

Katherine took her hand. The skin was as cold as ice. "You didn't think clearly back then. You're a different person now. Judgment isn't clouded by alcohol; Tina's anger, quitting the soccer team, running away. They make sense. A thought you didn't dare acknowledge, a suspicion buried deep inside all these years..."

Carlene's eyes widened in horror. "I can't—I can't say it."

"Yes, you can. You did a lot of damage to Tina. Accepting the truth of those actions is the first step toward making amends. Tina deserves that from her mother."

"Honey?" said Lamar. "If you remember something to help find your daughter..."

"Help her?" Carlene choked back a sob. "I never did anything to help her. My baby," she moaned. "That last fight we had was after soccer camp. She came home. Her clothes were torn. I saw blood on her hands and fear in her eyes. I should have forced her to tell me. Instead, when she said never to speak to her again I walked away. I walked away..." Her face twisted in anguish. "Was she raped?"

"We believe a man attacked her," said Katherine.

Carlene's grip tightened on her hand. "Tell Margaret, I'm different now. I stopped drinking, went back to school, became a hairdresser." The words spilled out. "I have my own shop, and Lamar—he's a good man. We've both worked hard to make things right... If she can ever forgive me..." Her voice choked. "I-I'll call her Tina." Her shoulders heaved in wracking sobs. Lamar pulled her close.

Jake left his card. "I'm sorry, Mrs. Franks. If you recall anything else…"

Katherine placed her card on top of his. "Or if you need to talk. Call me."

"Just find her," Carlene stammered between sobs. "I don't care if she refuses see me again as long as I know she's safe."

Jake and Katherine returned to the car. She gazed at the house as they drove away; heart aching for both Tina and Carlene. So much unhappiness had been hidden behind that front door. "Is it possible," Katherine murmured, "Tina's not dead?"

"I'll make more inquiries at the department," said Jake. "I can check with the grandmother's old neighbors and see if anyone kept in touch with Tina. I really need to cross-examine the ghost." He made a wry face. "I can't believe I said that."

Katherine shifted in her seat. "She won't talk to you."

"She will if you convince her it's in everyone's best interest." Jake shot her a glance. "Which is why you're coming with me."

Katherine's eyes widened. "Now? You'll let me in the house?"

"I was in the kitchen, too. I watched how you handled Carlene. You speak comforting words, Katherine. They put people at ease and get them to face painful truths. Carlene never would have told her suspicions to me if I came alone. Hell, she probably would have continued to deny them to herself, but you saw through her." Jake's voice tightened. "This case became more complicated."

Katherine drew in a breath. "Because if the ghost

isn't Tina, we have another dead girl on our hands. Jake, what if the ghost's message to me was only a warning? Tina may be alive and headed for trouble again."

He leaned in, an eager light in his eye. "So you'll fill me in?"

"Client confidentiality goes out the window when a life is in danger." In a rush, Katherine described the vision. "If the ghost isn't Tina, who is she? Any ideas?"

He stared out the window, his lips set in a thin, tight line.

"Jake?"

"No."

His face remained impassive, not a drop of emotion colored his features. Nevertheless, suspicion pricked at Katherine that a detective with the experience of Jake Sumner would be able to tell a very convincing lie.

Chapter 10

Jake paused at the parlor door. "Ready?"

Katherine squared her shoulders. "Ready."

"We go together." He held out his hand. "If she plans to slam the door in my face, she'll have to slam it in yours, too."

Katherine placed her hand in his palm, comforted by the gentle pressure of his fingers. She forced a weak smile. "My mind says the ghost showed no signs of inflicting harm, but my primal fears are screaming to run."

Jake chuckled. "Mine, too. Don't tell Ethan."

Hand in hand, they entered the parlor. Jake stopped to switch on the lamp before they walked in front of the mirror.

Katherine drew a deep breath. "It's me. I must talk to you again. The last time I was here I promised to come alone, but the situation changed. Jake helped me find Tina Delaney's mother. I thought you were Tina, but now I'm not sure. Do you want us to find her?" Katherine took a step closer. "Is Tina still alive and headed for trouble?"

After several seconds of silence, Jake dropped her hand and crossed his arms. "Guess the ghost isn't convinced I can help."

"Please talk to me," begged Katherine. "If you're not Tina, why give me her name? Can you tell me who you are? I can't help if you won't talk to me." She motioned to Jake. "Jake is a police officer—a good man, it's his duty to help people. Mine, too. I can't withhold information from him if anyone's life is in danger, so I had to tell him what you showed me. I promise Jake and I will work together. We won't quit until we find Tina, but what you showed me before isn't enough."

The lightbulb in the lamp flickered.

*Together.* The whisper hung in the air.

"Trust us." Katherine touched the glass. "Don't be afraid."

Blotches whirled in the mirror. Shadowed eddies in the glass pulled her deeper and deeper...

Katherine blinked. She was outside, the air held a bitter chill. Summer had ended. Patchy fog softened the light from a full moon. The shimmering apparition of a woman floated a dozen feet away, her face obscured by a brilliant glow. Bright silver light pulsed from the center of her chest in time to a heartbeat. Katherine took in her surroundings at a glance. She was in the woods, no structures visible through the dense brush and scrubby pine. "Where are we?"

A breeze rustled the treetops. The wind scattered the ghost's wispy figure like a pile of dry leaves. Soon all that remained was the brilliant pulsing light.

*Follow.* The light shot into the woods leaving a faint luminous trail through the fog.

Katherine raced away, dogging the light. It zigged and zagged around the trees, until darting behind an old oak and disappearing from sight. Carved into the trunk was a crude heart. She skirted the tree and reached a small clearing. Ahead was a man in dark clothing with his back to her. He wore a jacket with the hood pulled over his head and leaned against a shovel with a red blade discolored by patches of rust. At his feet was a shallow hole, six feet in length, surrounded by piles of freshly dug soil.

Breathing hard, the man dropped the shovel and fell to his knees. As he reached into the hole, a gust of wind dispersed the fog. Moonlight illuminated the body of a woman on the ground, arms crossed over her chest, face covered by a white cloth. The man's hand slipped under the cloth. With a single clean jerk, he tore an object from the body. Gold metal sparkled in the moonlight before he crammed a necklace in his pocket.

The man rose to his feet, jabbed the shovel into the earth, and tossed a clod of dirt on top of the body. Katherine's stomach twisted in a sick knot as it landed with a dull splat.

Jab and toss. Jab and toss. With mechanical precision, the man filled the hole. He tamped down the new grave with the shovel's blade and took a step back as if to admire his handiwork.

A raspy whisper broke the quiet. "My good girl."

Breath caught in her throat, Katherine reached out to grab his shoulder, spin him around, see his face...

The vision blurred and then came into focus once more.

Katherine stood on a low mound of dirt surrounded by brushy undergrowth, the moon now a mere sliver in the night sky. The chill in the air had lessened. At the snap of a twig, she turned her head. A hooded figure finished carving a heart in the bark of an oak tree. He slipped the knife in his pocket and grabbed a red shovel resting against the trunk. Dirt caked the blade, but the metal was shiny with no patches of rust. He jogged away and Katherine hurried after him.

Brambles snatched Katherine's legs, slowing her progress as she pushed through the bushes. She stumbled, quickly regaining balance, but the man disappeared.

Her heart pounded. "Which way?" she cried.

Not far ahead a car engine turned over. Katherine pressed forward, following the sound. She exited the woods and lumbered into a muddy clearing stripped of trees and brush. Parked nearby was an assortment of construction equipment. Stakes in the ground sported plastic surveyor strips flapping in the breeze. Beyond those was a double row of headlights moving in one direction and taillights in another. The building site bordered a four-lane road.

A dark-colored sedan pulled from behind a bulldozer. Rear brake lights flared crimson as the vehicle idled at the end of the construction zone waiting for a gap in the traffic. Katherine broke into a run. As she neared the car, the driver gunned the engine and accelerated. Katherine darted into the road.

Florida license plate...most numbers covered in mud. Most, but not all...G.

*Beeeeep! Beep-Beeeeep!*

Startled, Katherine turned around. The headlights' glare blinded her as cars bore down. She raised her hands and screamed.

The vision exploded in misty fragments. Katherine staggered back from the mirror gasping for breath.

Jake grabbed her elbow. "Kathy? Are you all right?"

"I-I'm fine...did you see it?"

"No. What did she show you?"

"A dead woman." Katherine ran a shaky hand through her hair. "He buried her—somewhere in the woods."

Jake draped his arm around her shoulders. "Let's sit in the kitchen. I'll make coffee while you tell me everything. Is it too cheesy to say you look as if you've seen a ghost?"

Katherine smiled weakly. "Yes, but I won't argue."

He led her to the other room. With a grateful sigh, she sank into a chair at the kitchen table and proceeded to describe the vision.

Jake set a steaming cup of coffee in front of her. "So, we have a dead woman dumped near a construction site. You're sure she wasn't Tina?"

Katherine took a sip. "I didn't see her face, but I say no."

"That sounds more like wishful thinking."

Katherine gazed into the cup. "I guess it is. I have my heart set on Tina being alive. Maybe that's why I can't shake the impression the dead woman was young, but not a teenager."

"Any identifying marks on her? Scars? Tattoos?" Jake touched her hand. "I know this is hard."

"It's okay. I only caught a glimpse. Tight short-sleeve shirt, dark color, could be either purple or blue, hard to tell in the dark. I wish I'd gotten a better look." Katherine gazed at Jake. "He took her necklace."

"Was it a gift from the killer that linked him to the victim? Any shrinky insights?"

"A trophy," she whispered. "He took Tina's necklace, too. In my opinion, he didn't drag a stranger off the street. He knew his victim. He carefully arranged the body, her arms crossed in front. The deliberate actions implied no rush or fear of discovery."

Jake's fingers tapped absent-mindedly on the table. "The murderer didn't come upon the burial site by chance. He was familiar with the area and the construction zone."

"Weird how the moon and the shovel changed. I don't understand." Katherine sighed. "Not much to go on is there?"

"More than we had before. I've got a dark sedan with a partial license plate and a construction site near a four-lane road—I'll check recent building permits in the county." Jake pushed back from his seat. "It's late. I'll run you home. I've had enough ghosts for a while."

Katherine stood up. "I'm with you. What if we grab takeout and eat dinner at my place?"

\*\*\*\*

"Meow?" Whiskers' tail whipped back and forth. He eyed Katherine with clear expectation.

"Finish that one already?" She leaned down and plopped another shrimp in his food bowl with the chopsticks.

"You're spoiling him," said Jake. "I'll bet he's already eaten tuna from the pantry—the good stuff, not that cat glop in a can."

Katherine cleared her throat and bit her lip.

"Aha!" He shook a finger at her. "Knew it. Better watch it, Fleming. Cats are master manipulators. Don't be surprised if he starts to demand fresh lobster for dinner every night."

"An occasional treat won't hurt him. Besides," she added smugly, "Whiskers and I have an understanding."

"You're really going to keep him?" Jake's expression softened. "It's kind of you."

"I enjoy his company, more than I figured." She chuckled. "I must be a little lonely." Their gazes met. Pink rose to Katherine's cheeks.

Jake turned his head away and peered at Whiskers. "He needs tags."

"So what are you now," she teased, "the cat police?"

His eyes glittered in amusement. "The law is the law, Fleming. Don't make me come after you."

*Coming after me might be nice.* "I didn't find any tags at Miss Harmony's house. I'll make an appointment with a vet to give him a full checkup. Needless to say, I don't trust his previous owner's level of care."

Jake dumped the empty cartons in the trash. "I better get going. I plan to go in early tomorrow and see what else I can dig up on Tina Delaney and our mysterious victim in the woods."

Katherine walked him to the door. "You have my work and cell number. Promise to call me?"

"As soon as I learn something."

A nervous flutter settled in her stomach. *That's not what I meant.*

Jake lingered on the threshold. For an instant, a question lurked in his eyes and then vanished. "Goodnight, Katherine."

"Goodnight, Jake." She shut the door, brushing aside her disappointment, and plopped on the couch. Whiskers jumped next to her, and she scratched him under the chin. "For a woman who's supposed to be good at reading people, I must be piss poor at sending subliminal signals. I thought I made my interest in Jake plain. I swear, he's interested, too."

"Meow."

"Well, I'm glad you agree." She leaned back into the seat cushion. "Maybe this ghost weirdness is affecting my perceptions."

A niggling doubt pricked at the back of her mind. No, that wasn't it. Jake held back for another reason—one he clearly didn't wish to discuss.

****

Before Katherine left for work Monday morning, she pulled up a list of veterinarians on the computer. Whiskers sat in her lap, regarding the screen with an unblinking stare. "Which one meets with your approval?" she asked. "Dr. Franklin…no? Dr. Marino…no? Geez, you're picky. How about the Westside Animal Clinic? It's fairly new and Dr. Singh has great reviews."

"Meow."

"Westside it is. I'll call from the office."

Katherine snagged an appointment with Dr. Singh after her last client. She hurried home to change out of work clothes and collect Whiskers. The Westside Animal Clinic was off a main road on the outskirts of Sandy Shoals. Katherine parked on the side of the building and hefted the carrier from the car.

Whiskers stiffened. He peered through the mesh and across the parking lot into the woods as if studiously avoiding any sight of the front entrance. "Don't be nervous," Katherine crooned. "It's just a checkup and you can have fresh tuna for dinner tonight—no matter what Jake said."

The staff was warm and welcoming, and the clinic

had separate waiting areas for cats and dogs. Once in the building, Whiskers' tenseness disappeared; he now seemed more curious than apprehensive. Katherine cast an approving eye around the room. She was all for easing anxiety in any patient whether they had two legs or four.

Whiskers patiently sat through the exam, even accepting his shots and new ID chip without protest. "He's a lovely cat." Dr. Singh stroked Whiskers' back. "Healthy, but a little thin. You say, he was adopted?"

"Yes, but I don't have any records. His last owner abandoned him."

The vet shook her head. "I could shoot those people. Don't tell the cops," she added lightly.

"Actually," said Katherine with a grin, "I've met at least one cop who'd probably agree with you." She eased Whiskers inside the cat carrier, but as she pulled on the zipper it broke.

Dr. Singh offered a cardboard cat carrier as a temporary replacement to transport him safely home. Whiskers sat placidly inside, poking his nose out an air hole. He shook himself and his new tags jingled.

Katherine paid the bill and exited the clinic. As she walked to the car, Whiskers shuffled around the box, hissing. "I sorry, it's not too comfortable," said Katherine gently, "but I promise to buy a new one as soon as I drop you off at home…hey, sweetie, it's all right…calm down…you're okay."

The hiss became a low guttural growl. Katherine hugged the box tight to her chest with one hand and with the other fumbled for her keys. "Whiskers, don't—"

With a violent jerk, the box tumbled from her hand.

The lid popped open. Katherine's eyes widened in horror as a streak of white tore across the parking lot and into the woods.

"Whiskers, no!"

Katherine dashed after him in a panic, forcing herself past overgrown bushes. "Whiskers! Whiskers, where are you?"

Relief surged through her at a "meow" from up ahead. Katherine pushed through the dense foliage into a small clearing. She tripped over a tree root and steadied her footing against an old oak.

"Meow."

Whiskers sat on a low mound, placidly washing his paw. Katherine scooped him up and, with a sigh of relief, cradled him against her chest. "You nearly gave me a heart attack. You could have gotten lost in here. Do we need to talk again, young man?" she scolded. "It's not safe for a cat to roam outside, especially in the woods. You never know what kind of danger you'll run into…"

The words died in her throat. Katherine gaze drifted over the low mound at her feet and then to the oak tree. Carved in the trunk was an old crooked heart.

Chapter 11

Jake peered at the computer screen. "Tina Delaney," he muttered. "If alive, you lead a very quiet existence."

He pulled up her grandmother's obituary and called the funeral home to ask if they could shed light on Tina's current whereabouts. The mortician told him Tina's grandmother had pre-purchased a plot next to her late husband. All the arrangements had been made prior to her death and he only vaguely recalled the granddaughter.

Jake checked the grandmother's old address. The trailer park she lived in with Tina had been bought by a developer who tore it down and built a strip mall. Jake scowled at the phone. The trail ended again.

The search for a construction site next to a four-lane road had an abundance of possibilities—too many to narrow down with limited information. He ran a check with the DMV on the dark sedan's partial license plate for Sandy Shoals and Azalea Trace. The long list of potential matches yielded no one with a familiar name.

Jake drummed his fingers on the desk. Perhaps Katherine missed details. Highly-charged situations didn't produce good eyewitnesses. Question three people who saw a crime and a cop got three different stories. Why should Katherine's experience be any different?

*Because she's Katherine…*

She told him everything. Why couldn't he help her?

The image of another young woman came into his mind. *You couldn't help her either.* Jake pulled out a folder of a closed case and flipped it open. Sapphire's dead eyes stared back at him.

"You're obsessing." Ethan peered over his shoulder.

"Quit sneaking up on me." Jake shut the file with a growl. "I'm reviewing."

"Closed cases. Cases that don't need your attention. What will you gain from this? Every officer in the department along with the DA thinks the shooting was justified. Pierson shot first. You gave him multiple chances to surrender. He fired wildly and could have killed an innocent bystander. Jake Sumner fired in self-defense, protecting the citizens of Sandy Shoals. Witnesses on the street agree with your version. End of story."

"You didn't see the expression on his face. Pierson panicked. He kept shouting he didn't do it."

"They always say they didn't do it." Ethan folded his arms and regarded him sternly. "He was a junkie nut job who probably forgot he strangled her until the moment you walked in and caught him robbing the place. Sapphire was a prostitute killed by a drug dealer. It's an old sad story. Why can't you let it go?"

"She called for help."

"You came."

"Too late."

"You have too much time on your hands," said

Ethan. "When are you off the desk?"

"As soon as I pass the psyche eval for the shooting."

"Make it soon. You're no fun to be around when chained to the precinct—too moody." Ethan paused. "How's it going with you and that shrink?"

Jake shrugged. "Fine. My last session is today, and then it's back to full duty."

Ethan's eyes gleamed. "That's not the shrink I meant."

"Katherine and I are just acquaintances."

He shot an innocent glance at the ceiling. "Not the vibe I got."

"You have no vibes, only delusions."

"Since you're not interested, perhaps I should call and ask her out."

Jake stiffened in his seat.

Ethan flashed a devilish grin. "Ow—I see that hit a nerve with Detective Sumner. Such an idea doesn't sit well with him at all. Is he finally investing in a social life?"

Lieutenant Saldana walked to the cubicle. "Need more work to do, Reardon? I have plenty of cases to assign."

"Not me, Lieutenant. I'm due in court to testify in an hour."

Lt. Saldana leaned against Jake's desk. "How's it going, Sumner? The last session is today, right?"

"Yup, I'm eager to get back to work." Jake glowered at the pile of paperwork on his desk. "Real work."

Ethan grinned. "He has a definite attitude problem, Lieutenant."

A faint smile twitched at her lips. "Busy work not to your liking, Sumner? Sorry, it's the best I can do until you're cleared for duty." She cocked her head and then motioned to Ethan. "Aw, what the hell. Reardon, give him that new missing person case."

Jake raised an eyebrow. "Missing person? Not homicide?"

"The disappearance is suspicious, so we're taking a closer look."

Ethan tossed a file to Jake. "Missing Persons did the preliminary interview with her boss and landlord and checked the apartment. I didn't have a chance to go much farther, but the whole situation gives me a bad feeling." He grabbed his coat and headed for the door.

"See what you can find, Sumner," said the lieutenant. "Make follow-up calls. If you discover a lead, tell Reardon. Can't have you working a case until you're reinstated—and as far as anyone else knows, you're tackling nothing, but damn boring paperwork."

Jake's eyes lit up. "Thanks, Lieutenant." He flipped open the file and scanned Ethan's notes. Missing: Lacey Calder. Her boss made the report after she didn't show for work or answer her phone. Lacey's car was in the driveway. The landlord hadn't seen her in days. Door was locked, landlord let the investigators in. No sign of a struggle or robbery in the apartment, jewelry box in the bedroom, but purse and cell phone were gone. Mail still in the box. None of Lacey's coworkers had heard from her. Ethan checked her social media accounts. She generally posted several times a day, but nothing new had been added for days. A troubled feeling rose in Jake's gut. Just like Ethan, his warning bells rang, too.

Jake scrutinized Lacey's picture taken from the DMV; early twenties, long dark hair, brown eyes. Ethan contacted her cell phone provider and started reaching out to friends in her address book, but hadn't finished yet. Well, as the lieutenant said, make a few calls…

His phone rang. Jake glanced at the caller ID—Katherine Fleming. Unconsciously, he smiled. "Hi, Katherine. Sorry, but I didn't find anything—"

"Jake, I…I…"

Jake sat up straight. "What's wrong, Kathy? Are you okay?"

"Yes…no…" Her breath quickened. "I found the ghost's grave and she may not be alone."

****

Ten minutes later, Jake entered the parking lot of the Westside Animal Clinic. He used the siren on the squad car to run red lights all the way. The lieutenant would be pissed he left the station, but he'd deal with the fallout later. Jake breathed a sigh of relief when he spotted Katherine in her car. As he ordered, she locked the doors, windows rolled up tight. Whiskers sat on her lap and regarded him with a feline expression of interest.

Katherine got out of the car, face pale. She held Whiskers close as if comforted by his presence, and gave Jake a shaky smile. "Thanks for getting here so quickly. It was stuffy in there."

Jake's hand brushed gently against her cheek. "Stay in the car. Just point me in the right direction."

She drew herself up, determination flashed in her eyes. "No. I'll take you." Katherine placed Whiskers on the passenger seat, cracked the windows and locked the door.

They entered the woods and Jake drew Katherine behind him. His hand unconsciously went to the location of the absent shoulder holster. Scowling, he dropped it to his side. "Stay close."

Katherine directed him to an old oak tree. "Here's the heart, the same as the vision, except it's old, not freshly cut." She motioned into the clearing. "Please tell me I'm mistaken about those."

Jake's gaze swept over the two mounds. He knelt down, pulled a pair of plastic evidence gloves from his pocket, and slipped them on. "This one is the newest. I'd say the ground wasn't disturbed more than a few days ago." He gently brushed the leaves aside. His stomach twisted at the sight of freshly tamped dirt. "Katherine, go back to the car."

"No." She swallowed hard. "Keep digging."

Jake carefully scooped handfuls of dirt until his fingers hit a solid object—soft, not a rock. He carefully pushed away the soil and uncovered a white cloth. He lifted a corner.

Katherine sagged against the tree trunk and turned her head away. "Oh, God."

A young woman stared blindly at the sky—a familiar face Jake gazed on less than an hour ago. He drew in a breath. "Lacey Calder."

Katherine straightened up. "Not Tina?"

"No. A new missing person case I'm working on. She hasn't been seen for a few days. Now I know why." Jake rose to his feet. "This is an active crime scene. I have to phone it in."

Katherine swallowed hard. "Jake, I understand the appearance of the shovel now. I saw it at two different times. The second time the clinic was a construction zone, and the shovel was new. The weather and phase of the moon had changed, too. The vision must have been older. Lacey wasn't dead yet." Her gaze went to the second mound. "The killer had just finished burying someone else. Another body is here."

Jake placed a hand around her shoulders. "CSU will search the whole area. If there's another body, they'll find her. You don't need to watch, but detectives will have to take a statement. Wait at the car."

Katherine regarded him with surprise. "Isn't this your case? You said you were searching for Lacey."

*It should be me.* Jake's gaze went to the dead girl. His voice hardened. "I'm still on restricted status. Let's head back to the parking lot."

As they walked out of the woods, Jake phoned in the report. Lieutenant Saldana definitely wasn't happy to hear he was at a crime scene. Hell to pay put it mildly. He ended the call and turned to Katherine. "They'll be here soon. We need to get our stories straight."

She smiled weakly. "Should I tell them a ghost gave me a mystical vision of a woman buried in the woods?"

He snorted. "I wouldn't."

"How about my cat is really psychic? After all, he led me there."

"Not much better."

"Okay then, I'll say Whiskers escaped from the carrier and ran off. After I caught up with him, I spotted the mounds and then called my friend Detective Sumner because something about their appearance was suspicious. He found the body."

"Works for me."

Katherine gaped at Whiskers in the front seat washing his paw. "How did he know? It's like he has his own psychic hotline to the ghost."

Despite her joking manner, Katherine remained pale. Jake's voice softened. "I'm sorry you had to find her. You don't easily get over the sight of the first corpse."

Her grateful smile sent a rush of warmth through him. "Giving psychological advice? Quit stepping on my turf, Detective Sumner."

"You're the one stumbling over dead bodies. That's my turf. I say we're even."

Katherine leaned against the car. "Tell me about the shooting that put you on restricted status."

He shuffled his feet. "It's no big deal."

"It is," she said gently, "or you wouldn't be so uneasy now."

Jake blew out his cheeks in exasperation. "I don't suppose you'll drop this."

"No." Her gazed drifted to the trees. "Humor me. I need something to distract my mind from what's in there, and it will help you to talk about it."

"I already talk about it," he snorted in disgust. "Too much."

"With Jeremy. That's why you refused to come to my office when we first met. You didn't want him to see you there." Her eyes filled with sympathy. "I understand."

Her compassion reached deep inside Jake, chipping at the emotional wall he so carefully built. Without conscious thought, the words spilled out. "I was tracking a drug dealer named Danny Pierson, wanted for a murder. The victim was another dealer who shorted him on a sale. Witnesses saw Pierson pull a gun and kill the man in cold blood. Pierson had a reputation for trading sex for drugs, so I passed my card to the local girls working the streets. A prostitute named Sapphire left a message on my voicemail. She had information and wanted to see me. I was in the car on my way back to the station, so detoured to her place."

Jake's jaw tightened at the memory. "The door was open. Sapphire was on the bedroom floor—strangled. Pierson had her jewelry case and a gun. He fired and jumped out an open window. I chased him. We exchanged shots. End of story."

Katherine eyed him with obvious doubt. "I have a feeling that's only the beginning."

"The shooting was justified," he sputtered in annoyance. "There were witnesses, but anytime an officer pulls a gun, regulations call for desk duty until the shrink signs off. As a matter of fact, I was supposed to meet with Ingalls right now for our last session. He'll be pissed I missed the appointment." Jake ran his fingers through his hair. "Another delay in reinstatement."

"I can speak to Jeremy for you…"

Jake bristled. "I don't need you in my business."

Her voice tightened. "That's not what I meant."

He flushed. "Sorry, I didn't mean to snap. It's hard to be chained to a desk."

"I understand." Katherine cast him a sideways glance.

Jake narrowed his eyes. "What?"

"Your explanation of the shooting is cut and dried. It certainly sounds justified, but I suspect there's more to it than that."

"You won't let this go, will you?"

"It's my nature to see a problem and want to help. It's yours, too."

Her soothing tone lacked any of Ingalls' irritating aloofness that rubbed so hard against Jake. The harshness in his attitude softened. "Is that a professional opinion, Dr. Fleming?"

"You're not a client," said Katherine. "You're a friend, so let's call it gut instinct. What continues to bug you about the shooting?"

Jake leaned against the car next to her. "Not the shooting—Pierson. The shock on his face…"

Her eyes widened. "You don't think he killed her. Why?"

"It's crazy. All the evidence clearly points toward Pierson. He had a long criminal history and a temper. He was on the run after committing a murder. It seemed logical he needed money to get out of town. He knew Sapphire. They'd exchanged sex for drugs, so he came to her place hunting money, killed her, too, and robbed the place."

"You're a good cop," said Katherine. "It isn't crazy if you continue to have doubts."

Jake struggled for words. "As soon as Pierson saw me, he yelled he didn't do it. He had this look on his face… I can't explain, but I swear he told the truth. I tried to get him to come peacefully, tell his side of the story, but Pierson knew we had him for the other murder. Even if he didn't kill Sapphire, no chance would he walk away a free man. And with his record…well, he was never getting out of prison."

His gaze returned to the woods. "Then there's Sapphire's actions the day she died. Her message to me said Delilah told her something. Delilah sounded like a call girl, but the name didn't ring a bell with vice. She wasn't a girl I had talked to before or one of Pierson's regular customers. Who was she? What did she tell Sapphire that was so damn important?"

"Did you mention this to Jeremy?"

"He said my doubts about Pierson's involvement in Sapphire's death were due to unresolved guilt for the shooting." Jake's shoulders stiffened. "Trust me, I have no unresolved issues, but Ingalls kept poking me for details on the crime scene. He wouldn't let it go, so in the last few sessions I told him I reconsidered the case. He was right. I now believed Pierson killed Sapphire during a botched robbery, and there was nothing more to it."

Katherine tsked. "You lied."

Jake shrugged. "I gave Ingalls what he wanted to reinstate me. He seemed satisfied."

"That's not how counseling works."

"He's happy. I'm happy. What's the big deal?"

"The big deal," she scolded, "is the question of Pierson's possible innocence in Sapphire's death remains, and you won't rest easy until you have the answer."

The wail of multiple sirens approached. Jake watched the squad cars as they pulled into the parking lot. "Pierson was a scumbag loser. It's no surprise he ended up on a slab at the morgue, but he can't tell his side of the story any longer. If he didn't murder Sapphire, then Sandy Shoals has a killer on the loose—and with the case closed I helped cover his tracks."

Chapter 12

The next minutes passed in a blur. Both Lt. Saldana and Ethan spoke with Jake and Katherine and then Jake led the crime scene investigation team into the woods. Curious people gathered at the front of the clinic, peering in Katherine's direction, and talking in hushed tones. Cars along the highway slowed for drivers to gawk at the flashing lights. The commotion didn't appear to disturb Whiskers as he napped in the passenger seat.

As Katherine waited, she called April and filled her in.

"Thanks for the scoop. Are you okay?" Her voice filled with sympathy. "It must have been awful."

"Shaken up, but otherwise fine. I only got a glimpse of the body, so didn't see much beyond two mounds of dirt."

Katherine ended the call as Jake jogged out of the woods and headed toward her. "They bought the runaway cat story," he said.

"Are you in trouble?" Katherine asked with concern. "Lieutenant Saldana wasn't happy to see you here."

"She's not. I'll get another earful from her later, but so far no one suspects any other involvement from us. You'll have to go back to the station to sign a statement. I can have one of the officers drive your car."

"No, I'm fine." Katherine forced a shaky smile. "Yeah, that's a big, fat lie, but I'm capable of driving. I'll run Whiskers home first."

Ethan pushed his way through the brush with Lt. Saldana at his side and made a beckoning motion to Jake.

"Hang on, something's up," Jake murmured. "Wait here."

The tension in Katherine escalated. From the tightness around Lt. Saldana's eyes and the briskness in her and Ethan's gaits, something was most definitely up. Jake exchanged a few words with the lieutenant and then followed her and Ethan through the brush.

A car pulled into the parking lot. April jumped out and greeted Katherine with a hug. "You're still on your feet. That's good. I'd be a blubbering mess by now. Do you feel up to an interview? I want to record it for Parker's podcast and then phone it into the TV newsroom. If not, tell me to stuff it. I won't mind."

"I'm fine, but I don't have much to tell." Katherine repeated the story while April recorded.

After she finished, April squeezed her arm. "I'm so sorry this happened. You're not getting a good impression of Sandy Shoals."

"No worries," said Katherine with a slight smile. "Despite today, I love it here. Actually, it seemed silly to call 911 to report a fresh mound of dirt that seemed out of place, so I asked Jake first. He said it was worth checking and uncovered the body."

April shot her an innocent look. "Interesting how your first thought was to phone the tasty nugget. Not to mention, you're on a first-name basis now. I thought you didn't have immoral thoughts about him."

"He's a cop," answered Katherine coolly. "Who else would I call? Besides, this isn't exactly the place I'd choose for a romantic rendezvous."

Movement drew their attention to the woods. "I see Lt. Saldana," said April. "I'm going to get a statement." She turned to Katherine, her features filled with concern. "Are you sure you're okay?"

"I'm fine." As April hesitated, Katherine made a sweeping motion with her hands. "Go. Report. Do good things."

April hustled over to Lt. Saldana. Jake skirted the yellow crime scene tape and went directly to Katherine's side.

"Don't react," he said in a low voice, "in case the lieutenant's gaze wanders over here. This is an active crime scene and I'm not supposed to give out details, but they found a second woman's body under the other mound. The ME estimates from the state of decomposition, she's been in the ground over a year—it matches the time period when the vet clinic was under construction. She had cloth over her face and arms crossed the same as Lacey Calder."

Katherine's heart sank. "Tina?"

"Can't tell, yet."

She sensed a hesitation and swallowed. "But you think so?"

"I don't guess." His tone softened. "All we have is a picture of Tina at sixteen, taken about eight years ago. The dead woman seems to be in her early to mid-twenties. Because of decomposition, we can't draw a conclusion to her identity this early in the investigation. The ME will run DNA first in case she's is in the system. Also, a preliminary search of the area didn't find any other gravesites, but the lieutenant called for a cadaver dog."

Katherine shuddered. "There might be more?"

"No other mounds nearby, but we'll search the rest of the woods. This must be a killer's recent dumping ground." Jake took her hand. "Go home. You can come to the precinct tomorrow to sign the statement. I'll be busy here through the night."

Katherine's gaze drifted toward the trees. "Tell me her name as soon as you find out. I need to know..."

His fingers gave a gentle squeeze. "I promise."

\*\*\*\*

The discovery of the bodies behind the Westside Veterinary Clinic was the lead story on the local news that evening. The camera panned the area as April's interview with Katherine ran in the background. Lt. Saldana issued an official statement; more than one set of remains had been found, but the police were unable to release additional details at the present time.

As Katherine ate breakfast the next morning, Jake buzzed the intercom for entry. Her excitement at his arrival quickly turned to sympathy. His clothing was rumpled and muddy. Dark circles ringed his eyes. "You look awful—" Her face reddened. "Sorry, I didn't mean that the way it sounded."

Jake smiled wanly. "No problem. I came straight from the crime scene. I probably should have showered first."

"I'm glad you're here. I have coffee. Can I fix you something to eat?"

"Coffee is good. I'll pass on the food. I don't have much of an appetite yet."

They sat at the table and Katherine poured him a cup. "I watched the report on the news. They didn't say much."

"The remains were two young women, the most recent is Lacey Calder. Her death occurred shortly after she disappeared. The ME report is pending, but my gut tells me cause of death for both will read strangulation."

Katherine shuddered. "Any identity on the second victim yet?"

"No. DNA results will be in soon, but her height doesn't match Tina Delaney's records. She's not her. I wanted you to know."

"So Tina may still be alive..." Katherine brightened for only an instant before her mood soured. "I shouldn't be relieved when we have two more dead women."

Jake took her hand. "There's nothing we can do to help them, but it may not be too late for Tina. We'll keep searching for her."

"I don't understand," murmured Katherine. "Neither of the dead women is Tina. The ghost showed me the location of the bodies, but why give me Tina's name? What's her connection to this? What's the ghost's connection? Is she Lacey or the other victim in the woods?"

"All good questions I can't answer."

"It's so frustrating." Katherine ran a hand through her hair. "What's the next step then?"

"Old-fashioned police work. Dig into these cases and see if I can find links to Tina."

"Did you get in trouble with Lt. Saldana?"

"A royal ass-chewing, but nothing I can't handle, or haven't experienced before." Jake's lips twisted in a wry grin. "Technically, I'm just helper-boy, but now I can also be considered a material witness. I shouldn't be involved at all, but Ethan was assigned as lead detective. He'll let me discreetly peek over his shoulder when the lieutenant isn't watching."

"When do we go back to the parlor?" said Katherine eagerly. "I want to question the ghost again. Maybe she's prepared to give us the victims' links to Tina."

The humor drained from Jake's expression. He pulled his hand away. "Katherine, the situation has changed with the discovery of those bodies. Lacey Calder's murder was only a few days ago. It's not safe for you to poke around."

"Which means the police need to find the murderer as quickly as possible. The ghost can help. After all, she led us to the graves and must have more information."

"That information can be dangerous for you. Leave investigating to the police."

"I have a client. As far as I know she's not at peace, so technically I have more cause for involvement than you as this isn't your case."

Jake wrapped his hands around the coffee mug and stared into its depths. "Then I guess I'll have to keep an eye on you until this mess is over."

"I'll keep an eye on you, too," said Katherine.

"Me?" The lines of fatigue softened on his face.

"You act as if finding those bodies didn't affect you, but I know the truth. If you want to talk, I'm a good listener."

He blew out a snort. "No, you're not. I seem to recall giving tons of great advice about not getting involved. You ignored every bit."

"Then maybe it's not so great," she threw back lightly and then turned serious. "If you don't want to talk to me, there's always Jeremy Ingalls."

Jake stiffened. "No thanks." He rose to his feet with a hard set to his jaw. "I'm fine, Dr. Fleming. Save the shrinky advice for folks who need it."

Katherine jumped up, a heated flush in her cheeks. "You're the one who's pigheaded. I'm not soliciting you as a patient, but simply offering a sympathetic ear as a friend. Or don't you need one of those, either?"

Jake rubbed the back of his neck. "I'm sorry. I'm being a jerk and didn't mean to bark at you. It's been a rough night. I should go."

Katherine walked him to the door. She held him back as he crossed the threshold. "I meant what I said, Jake. Anytime you want to talk, I'm here. It doesn't have to involve the case. I-I can discuss other things…" She stammered, forcing a smile. "I'm not such a bad person to be around."

Her heart hammered as Jake placed his hand on top of hers. "You're a very good person. I'll see you soon." He walked away.

Katherine shut the door. She wandered to the kitchen and placed the cups in the sink.

*What do you see, Kathy?*

She sighed. "Not now, Grampa."

*C'mon, play the game. You know you want to.*

"That's just it, Grampa, I don't want to play games with Jake. I don't want to analyze him. I simply want to be with him."

*Do it anyway. You can't help it.*

"No, I can't." She mindlessly wiped the counter with a sponge.

*So, what is the problem?*

"Granted we didn't meet under the most normal circumstances…"

*You're dodging the question.*

"Either Jake has an issue holding him back from a relationship with me that's difficult to talk about…"

*Or.*

"He simply has no interest in pursuing one. I'm not his type."

*How will you learn the truth if you don't ask?*

"Ask? Just come out and ask?"

*You'll have an answer.*

"I know." Katherine tossed the sponge in the sink. "What if it's one I'm not ready to hear? Any advice for that, Grampa?"

Imaginary Grampa had no response.

She grimaced. "Didn't think so."

\*\*\*\*

Diana and Jeremy were at the office when Katherine arrived. Diana rushed to her with a hug. "You poor thing. It's all over the news. It must have been awful."

"I didn't see much of anything," said Katherine. "As soon as Detective Sumner determined it was a crime scene, he hustled me out of there."

Diana patted her arm. "You didn't have to come in today. I could have canceled your sessions."

"I'm fine. The shock wore off quickly. It's a police matter now."

Jeremy walked Katherine to her office. "I didn't realize you were acquainted with Detective Sumner. Did you know he's my patient?"

"He mentioned it," said Katherine offhandedly.

Jeremy raised an eyebrow. "Funny, he didn't mention you."

"We just met," said Katherine hurriedly. "I knew he was a police officer, so I called him when I stumbled over the gravesite."

"Life is full of strange coincidences, isn't it?" mused Jeremy. "If you hadn't picked that vet, if you hadn't entered the woods in exactly that spot, those women might never have been found."

"Stranger than I ever imagined."

Jeremy's eyes twinkled. "Not trying to steal my clientele, are you?"

"No." Katherine paused. "Jake also mentioned yesterday was supposed to be his last session and he missed it. I hope what happened won't delay his return to full duty. He's eager to return. I'm sure he's more than ready."

"So Detective Sumner continues to remind me at each session," Jeremy said wryly. "Are you involved with him?"

Katherine startled at the unexpected turn in the conversation. "We just met. I can't say where the relationship is headed. Why do you ask?"

"I apologize. I don't mean to be intrusive, but…" Jeremy cleared his throat. "I shouldn't say, but in my opinion Detective Sumner isn't ready for a relationship—at least, not the kind I assume you want."

A pang of regret pierced Katherine's heart. She forced a smile. "Don't worry about me, Jeremy. I'm not sure I'm ready for a relationship either."

Chapter 13

Late in the afternoon, Katherine received a phone call from April. "Lt. Saldana is having a press conference in a few hours at the precinct, and I'll record it for Parker's podcast. Afterward, I plan to catch a quick bite to eat before going back to the station. A little bar and grill around the corner serves killer hot dogs; fast, cheap, and totally bad for you. Interested?"

"Sounds great. My last patient just left. I'll meet you in homicide. I promised to come by today and make a statement."

"I planned to suggest a rendezvous at the bar and grill," April said lightly, "but now it occurs to me we're more likely to run into a certain detective at the police station. I wonder if Dr. Fleming has an ulterior motive?"

"Goodbye, April."

"Fine, I'll wheedle the truth out of you at dinner."

Katherine was pleased to note Jake was clean-shaven and appeared rested. He hustled her to his desk. "Is everything okay?"

The concern in his greeting sent a flutter through her heart. "Fine. I'm meeting April for dinner. She's at the press conference. Has it started?"

"Not yet." Jake motioned to Lt. Saldana's office. She and Ethan were visible through the glass windows, deep in conversation. "The lieutenant plans to release more information on the bodies: sex and ages, but no names." He paused with a self-satisfied air.

She placed her hands on her hips and glared. "Don't keep me in suspense, Detective."

"DNA results won't be back for a few more hours, but I'm sure of the second victim's identity."

"Already? That was fast."

He motioned to the folders on his desk. "The cold case files Lt. Saldana had me review. The other woman matches the description of Tiffani Nolan, an ex-prostitute and heroin addict."

Katherine sucked in a breath. "Our ghost has a name."

"Maybe."

Katherine regarded him with suspicion. "You don't believe either one is our ghost."

"Can't say, too many unanswered questions yet, but Tiffani vanished a year and a half ago, and her description matches the dead woman. Tiffani was on parole and her PO reported her missing when she didn't check in. Investigators didn't find signs of foul play at her apartment, and no clothes appeared to be missing, but they never located her purse or phone. Her life appeared on track. She'd been through rehab and landed a new job, so the disappearance was suspicious. Tiffani had a long history of prostitution and drug addiction so it's possible she left town to work the streets somewhere else. Anyway, the trail went cold."

Jake tapped a finger on another file folder. "I got her arrest record. She and Sapphire were once cellmates. They knew each other."

Katherine's eyes widened. "Are you saying all those murders are connected?"

Jake glowered. "I always had a funny feeling about Sapphire's death. The same man is responsible."

"Do you have any proof?"

"He did it."

"I trust your instincts," Katherine soothed, "but the lieutenant will need more. What's the story on Lacey Calder? Was she a prostitute?"

"No. She doesn't fit the pattern. Neither does Tina, and Sapphire's arms weren't crossed over her chest. Hey," Jake added in a teasing tone, "whose side are you on?"

"Yours. Lacey Calder was the most recent victim. Any ties to the other women?"

"Not yet." Jake motioned to his computer monitor. "I'm reading Lacey's file now. She worked in a clothing boutique and didn't have a criminal record, but my guess is the girl liked to party. She had a lot of parking tickets always near locations of clubs and bars. A few weeks before her disappearance, Lacey was pulled over for a DUI and got a six-month suspension on her license. That's the reason the car was still at her apartment."

Katherine glanced at the screen where Jake had retrieved the picture from Lacey's driver's license. Part of a dolphin tattoo was clearly visible under the low-cut shirt. The breath froze in Katherine's throat. "I've seen her before," she whispered.

"Where?" Jake demanded.

"At the bus stop a few weeks ago. A man was there, too, roughly the same age. He displayed definite interest in Lacey, but they weren't together."

"How do you know—never mind. You trust my instincts. I trust yours. Tell me what you saw."

Katherine described the encounter. "That must be why she was on the bus. Her license had just been suspended."

Jake rose from his seat. "Come with me. I need you to repeat the story for Ethan. He's lead on this and will add the new information to your statement."

The lieutenant's office was empty, and Ethan back at his desk. He raised a curious eyebrow at their approach. "I showed Katherine the picture of Lacey Calder," said Jake. "She's seen her before."

Katherine described the chance meeting at the bus stop as Ethan scribbled notes. "You're positive she and this man were strangers?" he said.

"Yes. Neither showed any sign of recognition, but they exchanged flirty looks. He sat next to her on the bus, ready to strike up a conversation."

"I'll take your word for it." Ethan shot an innocent glance at Jake. "Of course, certain men take forever to make a move." The statement appeared to provoke an annoyed reaction in Jake while Ethan's eyes glittered in amusement.

"He oozed confidence," said Katherine. "I'd lay money he got Lacey's name and number within three stops."

"Can you hang around for a bit and check out mug shots?" said Ethan. "We might get lucky and the guy has a record."

"Of course. I'm glad to help."

After Katherine signed the statement, Ethan set her up at a table to leaf through mug shot books. Eventually, Jake ambled over and placed a cup of coffee in front of her. "Any candidates?"

She took a sip and shoved aside the last book. "No.

I'm sorry to say Mr. Bus Stop must be a law-abiding citizen."

"Pity. We have a sketch artist on call. Can you come back tomorrow?"

"Sure, but my client meetings go until 4:00."

"No problem. I'll set it up for 4:30."

"Thought I'd find you here." April strode through the door with a smile.

"Is the press conference over already?" said Katherine.

"Yup. Lt. Saldana didn't say much." April shot a veiled glance at Ethan.

Katherine made introductions. As Ethan and April's gazes lingered on each other, Katherine bit back a smile. All signals from the two clearly blared mutual approval.

April motioned to the mug shot books. "What's with the light reading?"

"Sorry," said Ethan, "we can't discuss an open police case."

April flashed a cheeky grin. "No problem. I'll wheedle it out of Katherine over dinner...would either of you care to join us?"

Ethan certainly wasn't one to hide his feelings. His disappointment was plain. "I can't. I have a meeting. Another time?"

April's grin widened. "Sure. I'll take a raincheck." She handed him her card. "Give me a call."

"I'm afraid I've got an appointment, too," said Jake. "Katherine, I'll see you later."

\*\*\*\*

Ethan's gaze followed Katherine and April out the door. He folded his arms and peered intently at Jake.

His toe tapped the floor. The silence lengthened.

"What?" Jake barked.

"Quite a coincidence, huh?" Ethan answered smoothly. "Dr. Fleming not only stumbles onto a dead body, but also happens to have seen the deceased."

"You're suggesting Katherine is tangled up in a double homicide? Your super detective powers need fine-tuning. Maybe you require another dose of gamma radiation."

"That's a possibility, or it could be Detective Sumner's judgment is a little clouded by self-interest." Ethan jabbed him in the shoulder. "You don't want her to be involved. Perhaps our mysterious man at the bus stop wasn't the only one planning a move on someone soon."

"May I remind you, Katherine wasn't even in Sandy Shoals when our perp dumped the first victim?"

"I didn't say she actually killed anyone, but I can't shake the idea Katherine isn't sharing all she knows. Isn't your spidey sense tingling—or perhaps another body part?"

"Don't you have real police work to do?"

"I bet she'll tell April at dinner," Ethan mused. "I should call April and find out."

Jake shot him a sideways glance. "You're pathetic. That's the lamest excuse for making a date I've ever heard. Man up and ask April out. If you're lucky, her standards are extremely low and she'll accept."

His eyes gleamed in amusement. "I've got a great idea. We can double date. Or deep down, do you truly believe Katherine is a murder suspect?"

"You're not only pathetic, you're annoying."

"What's the deal, Jake? Don't tell me you're not

attracted to her."

*More than you know.* "I see enough shrinks at the moment—speaking of which, I've got to go."

"She's not Ingalls." The lightheartedness in Ethan's tone disappeared. "I think she'd be good for you. At least, give it a shot."

"One thing at a time, okay?" Jake sighed. "Let's just say Katherine deserves my full attention and I can't give it to her, yet."

"Fair enough, but don't wait too long…hey, good luck with Ingalls," he called as Jake headed for the door. "Don't say anything crazy. I want my partner back."

\*\*\*\*

"Spill it," said April. "Why were you scanning mug shots?"

Katherine swallowed a bite of hot dog and described the behavior of the man at the bus stop.

April shivered. "Totally creepy realizing you saw a girl completely oblivious death was only a few days away." She leaned forward. "Do the police consider him a suspect?"

"I'm sure they want to question him, but don't have an ID yet, and your sleeve is in the mustard."

"Damn it." April dabbed at the splotch with a napkin.

"I don't know what more I can tell you," said Katherine. "I don't want to interfere with a police investigation—and this guy may be completely innocent."

April placed a hand on her heart. "I swear whatever you pass on we'll keep between us until either you or the cops give permission." Eager light shined in her eyes. "At GAB-TV I'm a glorified go-fer, but a full-time position at the local TV news show opens soon. I want to be a reporter, but there are plenty of more qualified applicants. If I can get a scoop on this story…"

"Ethan asked me to come back tomorrow to see a sketch artist," said Katherine. "Once the police have a picture, I'm sure they'll release it to the media."

"Thanks. Anything else?"

"Nope."

"What about your detective? Did he give you any hints?"

"First of all, Jake isn't my detective."

April gazed at the ceiling with an innocent expression. "He could be, and you can't deny the eye candy factor."

A smile twitched Katherine's lips. "Granted, but Jake isn't lead on the case, Ethan Reardon is. Why don't you bother him? No wedding ring and judging from the beaming approval he gave you at the precinct, his interest includes more than maintaining good relationships with the media."

April brightened. "You think so?" A pink flush rose to her cheeks. "Believe it or not, I haven't had much luck in the romance department. I'm the only one of the kids who isn't married and my mother won't quit nagging me. She says I come on too strong and scare men away."

"I find that hard to believe," said Katherine with a straight face.

April slapped her palm on the table. "That's what I say. I refuse to settle for any man because my mother decided I'm too old to be single. Fortunately, Mama has been distracted lately since my sister-in-law announced her pregnancy—the first grandchild."

"I take it she's excited."

April rolled her eyes. "To say the least. You'd have thought the Vatican issued a press release proclaiming the second coming of Baby Jesus will occur before the end of the year in the Ortiz family."

\*\*\*\*

At 4:15 the following afternoon, Katherine arrived at the police station. To her disappointment, Jake wasn't there.

"He took the day off," said Ethan.

"Oh, I see." An uneasy sensation crept up Katherine's spine. Jake ditched in the middle of an investigation? "Something wrong?"

Ethan shot a glance toward Lt. Saldana's office. "Ingalls refused to clear him for full duty."

Katherine drew in a sharp breath. "What? Why?"

"I don't have a clue. The lieutenant called Jake into her office first thing this morning and broke the bad news. They had a shouting match and then Jake stormed out of here and told me he was taking the day off." Ethan's voice dropped to a whisper, "What gives? You know Ingalls. Why didn't he clear him?"

Katherine shook her head in disbelief. "I can't imagine any reason. I assumed Jake would be reinstated."

"So did Jake."

"Is he at home?"

"I'm not sure. He won't return my calls." Ethan eyed her sharply. "You might have better luck."

At that moment, the sketch artist, Andy Harrell, arrived. Ethan showed them to a quiet area, and

Katherine pushed concerns about Jake Sumner to the back of her mind. Andy appeared in his late twenties with a cheerful disposition that put her right at ease. "Don't worry about getting the fine points right," he said. "That's my job. You describe. I'll listen, ask questions, and then together we'll give this guy a face."

Andy's soothing voice coaxed the details from Katherine's memory. She watched in awe as under his skillful hands the mystery man's facial attributes slowly came to life. When he held up the finished product for inspection, her eyes widened in delight. "That's him. You have amazing talent, Andy. It's like artistic psychology. You get people to remember things they didn't realize they forgot."

He chuckled. "Thanks, Katherine. That's high praise."

She thumbed through his sketchbook admiring an assortment of seascapes. "Do you only work in pencil?"

"No, mostly oils and watercolors. I have a studio where I live in Bayou St. Pierre, but enjoy coming over here to help the cops, too. Someone close was a victim of a crime once. This work makes me feel as if I'm sticking it to the bad guys."

"I remember driving to Bayou St. Pierre with my grandparents as a kid and eating fried shrimp on the pier."

"It's a nice little place. Used to be a fishing village, but is now more of an artist's colony. You can still get great seafood though. I sell my work at local galleries, and my wife is the activities coordinator at the community center. If you're interested, the center hosts an art show on the pier as a fundraiser soon. I'll have several paintings for sale. Artists donate ten percent of any proceeds to a scholarship fund for regional art students."

Katherine's eyes lit up. "I'd love to come. Most of the walls of my apartment are still bare."

"Great." He handed over a business card. "Give me your email and I'll send the flyer."

Andy went in search of Ethan to deliver the drawing. Katherine headed to her car and called Jake's number, but his phone went directly to voicemail. She tapped her fingers on the steering wheel with a frown. Jeremy's decision didn't make any sense. Why didn't he reinstate Jake? What happened at yesterday's session? She dialed again, but he didn't pick up.

"You won't find the answers sitting in a parking lot," she muttered.

On a hunch, Katherine drove to Culpepper Lane. Her spirits rose at the sight of Jake's truck in the driveway. She rapped on the door. Footsteps approached and then the door swung open.

Jake's face was streaked with grime. Sweat plastered the t-shirt to his chest. His eyes narrowed and his lips set in a tight line.

Katherine's heart gave a nervous flutter. "Hi—"

"Haven't you caused me enough trouble?"

Chapter 14

Katherine blinked. "Me? What did I do?"

"You should know." Jake's voice held no warmth. "During our session, Ingalls mentioned he spoke with you at the clinic. Then he asked a lot of questions on the new case, how it affected me, that sort of thing. No big deal. The next day I go to the lieutenant's office, figuring Ingalls gave me the all-clear, but she says no. He didn't sign the release and told her we have more work to do on my *issues*." Jake scowled. "What the hell did you say to him?"

"Nothing that warranted this," said Katherine, stunned. "Jeremy and I only exchanged a few words."

"You must have said something—"

Katherine drew herself up. "As a matter of fact, I did. I told him you were eager to return to full duty." Her voice rose. "I didn't bother to bring up your snarly attitude."

The storm left Jake's face. His shoulders sagged. "Sorry. I'm just—I thought everything was settled. Now this. I don't get it."

"Me neither." Katherine's voice filled with sympathy. "I'm sorry, too, Jake. I realize how important it is for you to get reinstated."

Jake grimaced. "Oh the plus side, I discovered anger and demolition go hand in hand." He cocked his head. "Want to see?"

She grinned. "Absolutely."

Jake led the way to the back of the house. Katherine's eyes widened in surprise at the stacked boxes and suitcases shoved against the wall in the dining room. "You moved in?"

"Yeah, I was tired of paying mortgage and rent. I figured what the hell. I may as well live here. A few flickering lights and weird noises don't bother me now that I know the cause. Plus," he grunted, "I was pissed. Toting boxes kept me from heading to the clinic and shoving Ingalls through a wall—probably not a smart move considering the circumstances."

Katherine chuckled. "Probably not. The current tenant doesn't mind sharing the space?"

"So far no squawks." His gaze drifted to the hall. "Our ghost isn't dangerous. She's sad."

*Our ghost.* The admission brought a rush of pleasant sensations. "She's not. I'm sure of it. Have you seen her?"

"Nope," he admitted with a sheepish grin, "but I've been studiously avoiding the parlor."

Katherine cleared her throat. "As long as I'm here, we can say hi together. She led us to Tiffany and Lacey's bodies. Perhaps now, she'll reveal her true identity."

"Fine, but we'll visit after dinner. I can't face the astral plane on an empty stomach. I'll call for pizza."

"Sounds good to me."

They entered the kitchen, or what remained of it. The cabinets and most of the appliances had been removed. While Jake phoned in the order, Katherine's astounded gaze went from the bare walls to the sledgehammer propped against the back door. "I seriously underestimated how pissed you are."

"I couldn't afford to destroy my apartment and lose the security deposit. I need the dough. I totally recommend demo for your stressed patients and tender an invitation to host a group therapy session here to remove the wall between the kitchen and dining room." Jake's eyes twinkled as he handed her the sledgehammer. "Go ahead, give it a whack."

"I'm not exactly dressed—"

"Aw, go on. It's been a tough week for you too, Fleming. Show me what you're made of."

Katherine hefted the sledgehammer. "Well, if you insist…"

*Wham…wham…wham.* Chunks of plaster fell to the floor with each blow.

"You're definitely onto something," she said, panting. "Very therapeutic. I'll recommend it to all my clients."

Jake took back the sledgehammer and regarded her with amusement. "Hmm…someone besides me carries a load of pent-up aggression."

"Like you said, tough week." She sighed. "We don't have the murderer's name yet."

"We'll get there. We're closer than a week ago. Along with the bodies, we have another clue."

"What?"

"The partial license plate."

Katherine's brow furrowed. "I thought you didn't find anything."

"I didn't in the current DMV database, but the car you saw was at the clinic during construction."

Katherine's eyes widened. "So, you went back a few years! What did you find?"

"Nothing." Jake cleared his throat. "I haven't searched yet. I planned to run the plates again this morning, but got distracted by a temper tantrum. I'll do it first thing tomorrow."

Her voice filled with sympathy. "I know how frustrating this is."

For a few seconds, Jake appeared to wrestle with an inner dilemma. When the doorbell rang, his relief was palpable. "Pizza." He strode out of the kitchen.

"Saved by the bell, Detective Sumner," muttered Katherine. "What are you hiding?"

She followed Jake to the front door and waited while he paid for the delivery. "No place to eat in the kitchen," said Jake. "The dining room is full of boxes. We can eat on the porch…"

Katherine motioned to the parlor doors. "I'm game if you are."

Jake rolled his eyes. "Fine. Three for dinner. I hope I bought enough."

They entered the parlor, and Jake turned on the lamp. Katherine glanced around. Gauzy curtains fluttered at the window, but not from any apparition. The sash had been thrown open. The pleasant evening breeze carried a delicate floral scent. Katherine inhaled in appreciation. Roses?

Everything else in the room looked the same—well, not quite. She ran her finger across the end table and then blinked in surprise. "You dusted?"

"Yeah." Jake said, plainly flustered. "I feel she's more of a houseguest and less of an intruder. Silly, huh?"

"No, that's sweet, but you may never get rid of her now," Katherine teased. "Women can't resist a man who cleans." She stood in front of the mirror. "We're here."

Seconds ticked by. No splotches changed position. The bulb in the lamp burned steady and bright. The only movement in the room was the gentle flutter of the curtains. Jake sat on the floor and opened the box. "Well, that was a serious letdown. Let's eat. I'm starved."

Katherine nibbled at the slice. She scanned the parlor for any sign of the ghost, but nothing caught her eye. "I guess she isn't coming."

"Don't sound so disappointed," said Jake. He nodded toward the pizza box. "You didn't eat much."

"I'm not too hungry..." Her gaze turned to the mirror. "Do you think that's all she had to tell us? What if she's gone forever?" The thought unexpectedly troubled her.

Jake's voice softened. "Isn't that a good thing? Wasn't that the whole point of talking to her in the first place? If she's Tiffani or Lacey, maybe she only wanted to be found. You did that."

"Why give us Tina's name at the beginning?" Katherine argued. "She wasn't buried in the woods. We don't know what happened to her."

"She's a ghost, Kathy," Jake said gently. "You can't expect logic or understandable motives. What if she's satisfied with everything we've done? This might be the end she wanted."

"The end." A cloud of depression hovered over her. Katherine pitched the remainder of her pizza into the box and rose to her feet. "I-I better get going." On impulse, she faced the mirror. "If you're listening, thanks for the help. Jake and I found the women behind the clinic. I'm still here if you need me, and would really like your name." Seconds passed and Katherine turned away with a sigh. Jake escorted her to the front door.

Katherine paused on the threshold, emotions whirling. *I'm not ready to go. I'm not ready to leave this behind. I'm not ready to leave Jake behind.* "Well, goodbye," she stammered. "Thanks for dinner."

Jake gently plucked something from her hair. "Plaster bit. You've got quite a mean swing, Fleming. Definitely lots of pent-up aggression." He flicked the plaster to the floor. "The most frustrating thing in police work is when a cop runs out of leads and the case grows cold. I have a pile of files on my desk to prove the point."

"At least you can give partial closure to two families. They'll have a body to bury."

"True, but other unsolved cases are out there. No one may ever know why those people died. You have to learn to deal with that or the frustration eats you up."

Katherine glanced toward the parlor. "You'll call me if she shows."

"Yes, but you have to accept the possibility the ghost's own story will stay buried with her. Did you ever think that may be a good thing? Digging around in the past can be painful."

"Not to a counselor. Digging around in the past can be therapeutic." Katherine regarded him sharply. "Those are funny words from a detective. Aren't you always prying out painful secrets from unwilling subjects?"

"True, but in this case the ghost's secrets may not matter."

"A secret always matters to someone. That's why it's hidden." Katherine's heart pounded. *Please ask me to stay. Don't tell me it's over.*

Jake stepped aside to let her pass.

Katherine forced a smile. "I'll see you around." She walked to the car and drove home with a cold ache in her heart. Whiskers met her at the door. She bent down to scratch his head. "Is it true? Is the ghost done? I should be thrilled with another satisfied client. Granted this one was pro bono and won't get me any referrals, but even so, a success is a success. Right?"

"Meow."

Katherine sighed. "Yeah, you don't have to tell me. No more excuses to be with Jake."

She kicked off her shoes and sat with her laptop to add notes to the case file. "Jake thinks the ghost is done with us," Katherine muttered at the screen. "Maybe you rest in peace now, but I can't until I have the whole story. You're connected to those other women and know what happened to Tina. I'll find out how, with or without Jake's help."

**** 

Jake watched until Katherine's car was out of sight. He wandered into the parlor and picked up the pizza box. "Are you really gone?" No spectral voice whispered in his ear.

Had he finally gotten what he wanted? Had the ghost disappeared? Jake stared at the mirror, struggling with unexplained malaise. What the hell was his problem? He should be turning cartwheels.

A disconcerting notion crept into his head. Maybe a house of his own wasn't all he wanted anymore. The desire grew to share it with someone special—no more relationships that burned out after a few months. No half-hearted attempts at romance, but a woman eager to build a life at his side. A person who could help him accept the mistakes of the past and move on.

Only his scowl reflected from the glass. "I'm not ready. It's too soon."

The floral scent in the room became more pungent, unearthing a fragmented memory. A young woman's image came to Jake's mind. His face paled. It can't be. "No," Jake whispered. "Your body was found. I watched them bury you on consecrated ground. There's no reason for you to be here. Unless…"

He ran to the window, brushed aside the curtain, and peered over the sill. Relief flooded through him. No mysterious odors sent messages from the beyond, merely an overgrown gardenia bush blooming beneath the window. That it brought to mind Bethany's perfume was simply an eerie coincidence.

Jake slammed down the sash and returned to the kitchen. He pitched the pizza box in the trash and then picked up the sledgehammer. Muscles tensing, he swung with all his might at the wall. Broken lath and plaster tumbled to the floor. If only it was as easy to remove both his guilt and the last troubled image of Bethany from his thoughts. Only then could he set his sights on Katherine Fleming.

****

Katherine sipped her coffee as she watched the local morning news. The police department had released the sketch. Andy's portrait certainly was a good likeness. Someone out there had to have information on him. None of the names of the other two victims were made public, but the newscaster stated the police planned to make an announcement after notification of next-of-kin. Jake must have been right. The woman in the other grave was Tiffani Nolan.

Her phone rang with a call from April. "Guess what? Detective Studmuffin Reardon called for a date. He can't get away for long, so we're grabbing a quick lunch tomorrow. Now I have another person to pump for information besides you. Speaking of which, Parker decided he wants you to be the first guest on the new show."

"That's great," said Kathryn. "When?"

"Not for a couple of weeks, but Parker and Connie invited us both to their house for dinner on Saturday. He'll fill you in on the details and I can grill you for more information on the case. Gotta run. Have another call. I'll text you the time and address. See you then." She severed the connection.

Katherine eyed the phone with amusement. "No problem. I can make it. Bye."

Jeremy's car was already in the parking lot when Katherine arrived. She unlocked her office and logged into the computer. Instead of checking emails, her gaze drifted to the hallway. Her fingers drummed a rapid tattoo on the desk. Why didn't Jeremy sign off on Jake? What possible problem did he notice?

Footsteps coming down the hall stopped in front of her office. Jeremy poked his head in the doorway. "Good morning, Katherine."

His easy manner provoked a surge of annoyance. What was his problem with Jake? "Morning, Jeremy. You're in early."

"I had paperwork to catch up on... You seem troubled. Can I help?"

"I spoke with Jake."

"Oh?" The muscles around his eyes tensed slightly. "You saw him last night?"

"We ran into each other and had dinner together."

"It sounds as if you have a budding relationship." His demeanor remained impassive, but to Katherine's ears, the flat, even tone of voice plainly indicated disapproval.

"I wouldn't call it that," she added smoothly, "but we're friends."

His voice tightened. "I can't discuss the case."

*He's upset. More than he should be.* "I understand." Katherine forced a smile. "I only meant to say Jake wasn't happy with the decision. I have to admit, I was surprised, too."

"I expect so." Her unemotional response must have eased Jeremy's concerns. The censure in his tone disappeared. "I don't wish to interfere with your private life, Katherine, but Detective Sumner continues to have issues that need to be addressed."

Katherine carefully chose her words. "I hadn't noticed any, that's why your decision was unexpected."

"You may not want to hear this, but you could be too close."

"My only concern is for a friend's wellbeing."

"Then my advice is to step away and give Detective Sumner more distance. You fit in well here, Katherine. I'd hate to have anything interfere with that. I say this for both his benefit and yours."

A knot of apprehension tightened in her stomach. *Is that a veiled threat? Does Jeremy assume a relationship with Jake will compromise my ability to perform the job? Why?* "You really believe distance is

156

necessary for his wellbeing, then?"

"I do."

"Thank you, Jeremy. I appreciate the advice. I never want to do anything to hinder a person's recovery."

The final remnants of stiffness left Jeremy's posture. He was relaxed once more. "I'm glad to hear that."

Katherine gazed at the doorway, mind whirling, as Jeremy's footsteps faded down the hall. The knot tightened a little more. Why the warning? Why the niggling belief Jeremy's words implied a hidden meaning. Jake had issues he didn't want to discuss, but could they possibly relate to something more serious? A danger? And if so, to whom?

*Jake didn't ask for my help.*

*He doesn't want my help.*

*But maybe he needs my help.*

"You know me, Detective Sumner," muttered Katherine, "I can't walk away."

Chapter 15

Jake lumbered down the stairs rubbing his eyes. Sleep had come in fits and starts all night, interrupted by tattered remnants of dreams. They woke him leaving nothing behind but increased edginess. Each time, he grappled with the niggling sensation of an important task left undone. As dawn approached, Jake finally called it quits on any further attempt at a restful night. Now, he paused in front of the parlor on his way to the kitchen, the sense of urgency growing again. The call to action was as clear as if a person shouted his name—or left a message on his phone.

The phone...? He froze in his tracks.

Pulse racing, Jake pushed open the door and stepped inside. "Bethany? I'm here. I'm alone."

The edginess disappeared.

Jake backed from the parlor. *It can't be her.* "Coffee...I need coffee." He turned on his heel and walked briskly to the kitchen.

****

"Watcha working on?" Ethan leaned over Jake's shoulder and peered at the pile of papers on his desk. "License plates?"

"Cars registered in the tri-county area around the time of Lacey Calder's murder. I'm running down stolen one's first to see if any match the description of tips from the hotline. Could be our perp didn't want to

158

get his upholstery dirty. It's a longshot, but I figured, what the hell? It's not as if I have real police work to do."

Ethan clapped him on the shoulder. "I'm sorry, man. You got a tough break. Try sucking up to him more. Yes, Dr. Ingalls, no Dr. Ingalls, you're so brilliant Dr. Ingalls, and beautiful and charming, too. Sign the goddamned paper, Dr. Ingalls…"

Jake blew out his cheeks in disgust. "I'd glue my lips to his ass if it got me back to duty."

Ethan snorted out a laugh and then peered at a piece of paper and narrowed his eyes. "You have a license plate list here from over a year ago."

"That's when Tiffani disappeared. Thought I might find a connection. Don't you have real police work?"

He shot a glance at Lt. Saldana's office. "I got the preliminary report back from the ME on Calder. Figured you'd want to know."

"What did he find out?"

"Tox screen showed no drugs, but alcohol in Calder's system—no surprise, she already had a DUI. Cause of death is definitely strangulation. The size of the bruises on her neck indicate a man's hands—nothing unusual there either. Bruises on arms and chest, too. He must have pinned her to the floor and sat on top with his hands around her neck. DNA evidence confirms Tiffani Nolan as the second victim with COD as strangulation, too. The lieutenant will break the news to the next of kin today. We're headed out as soon as Saldana gets off the phone."

"She's coming with you?"

"Yeah, this case is a big deal, and she wants to assure the family in person the death is a top priority.

The lieutenant will hold another press conference and announce Tiffani Nolan's identity once we return." He brightened. "On a happier note, I went out with April."

"Oh? Must have gone well. You're smiling."

Ethan chuckled. "She's something. Funny, smart…she grilled me for information on the case, but in an adorable way so I kind of liked it."

Jake shook his head. "God, you're both so strange. Going to see her again?"

"The lieutenant has us working overtime on this case, but I thought I could squeeze out an hour on Saturday for dinner. April can't make it though."

"Ah, she wised up and dumped you already."

"Nope." His eyes twinkled. "She has plans with your girlfriend, Katherine Fleming."

Jake stiffened. "She's not my girlfriend."

"Aw," Ethan crooned, "that's so cute when you say things as if you expect me to believe them. Anyhow, we'll try to get together soon. How about you and Katherine double-date with us?"

"How about you get back to work?"

The lieutenant's door opened, and she signaled to Ethan. "Later, Jake," he called over his shoulder.

Jake followed Ethan and Saldana's exit with a dark look. He should be with Ethan. He should be working the case. He snatched the list of old license plate numbers from the pile. "Then find hard evidence rather than feeling sorry for yourself."

****

Even across the phone lines, Katherine read the sorrow in April's voice. "What's wrong?"

"Dinner with Parker is off. Connie had a visit from Ethan and Lt. Saldana yesterday."

Katherine drew in a breath. "One of the murder victims?"

"Tiffani Nolan was Connie's younger cousin, but had been estranged from the family. Connie's in shock, of course. She and Parker were Tiffani's closest relatives. The police released the remains, so they've arranged a burial for her on Saturday. They plan to have a short graveside service."

"I'll come," said Katherine.

April heaved a sigh. "I hoped you'd say that. I didn't want to sit alone. Do you know where Saint Anne's is?"

Katherine's mouth went dry. "She was a member of Saint Anne's parish?"

April snorted. "Frankly, I don't believe Tiffani had been near a church in years, but Connie and Parker are active members. The parish cemetery is across the street from the church. The service starts at one. I have work to do at the station in the morning, so I'll meet you there."

As soon as April clicked off, Katherine dialed Jake and passed on the news. "Thanks, Katherine," he said. "I can check into the Saint Anne's connection."

"Do you think it means anything?" she said with growing excitement.

"Hang on, Sherlock. Don't jump to conclusions. Saint Anne's is the largest Catholic church in the area. It must have thousands of members on the roster— some active, others who show up Christmas and Easter, and even more who haven't been for years. Simply because two victims have a tenuous connection is only circumstantial evidence. They may have both shopped at the same drugstore, too."

"But, yet…"

"Yeah, it's definitely interesting and I'll poke around…" Jake paused and in the background came the sound of shuffling paper. "I read Ethan's report on the family interviews. Nobody mentioned Saint Anne's."

"Ethan doesn't know about Tina, so I'm sure he didn't ask."

"Yeah, and there's no way to tell him without mentioning my current tenant situation." Jake's frustration came through loud and clear. "I need to talk to the families, but no way will Lt. Saldana allow it."

"Parker and his wife are hosting a memorial service for Tiffani at one o'clock on Saturday. I'm going. So is April. It's a normal place for people to talk about the deceased. Will the lieutenant object to you stopping by to offer condolences if a friend asks for moral support?"

Jake chuckled. "That sounds like a perfectly reasonable suggestion to me. I'll pick you up at 12:30."

"See you then." Katherine hung up the phone. She placed her hand against her cheek. The skin was unreasonably warm. "It's a funeral," she snapped in disgust. "Get a grip."

\*\*\*\*

Jake hung up the phone. A smile played over his lips, pleased to have been handed a logical reason to be with Katherine Fleming.

*She wouldn't have suggested escorting her to the service if she didn't want to see you again.*

He tapped a pencil absentmindedly against the desktop. Katherine certainly occupied more of his thoughts lately, igniting urges ignored for a while. The question was should he act on them?

*A relationship with her won't be the same as the others. Katherine is different. No way would I have a flash in the pan romance that ended as quickly as it started.*

The rhythmic tapping increased in tempo. Yesterday, his decision to distance himself from Katherine made so much sense, but each time he heard her voice, the inner wall he so painstakingly constructed crumbled a little bit more.

*What will Katherine say if it falls completely, and she learns the truth about Bethany?*

The memory of Bethany unearthed a painful jumble of emotions; shame, guilt, anger. He never bothered dealing with any of them. He didn't want to before. Another crack appeared in his internal wall. Through it came Katherine's voice. "I'm a good listener."

Jake shoved thoughts of Katherine brusquely aside and turned his attention to the list of license plates. It was a long shot, to be sure. Katherine had only noted a Florida plate on a dark sedan with G at the end. One by one, he checked each tag for a connection to any of the dead women, but came up empty.

With mounting discouragement, Jake pulled out the last sheet of paper. On a hunch, he had also run the tags substituting a "6" for a "G." Katherine's glimpse of a plate covered with mud on a dark night could easily have confused the two.

Jake ran his finger down the list. Halfway down, he stopped as one name jumped at him.

****

Katherine put the finishing touches on her makeup and then gave herself a once over in the full-length mirror. She nodded in approval. The navy blue dress had a classic cut and an appropriate hemline. The makeup muted—her whole appearance understated and suitable for a funeral.

Whiskers wove around her legs. Katherine bent over and scratched him on the head. "Sorry, can't pick you up. Navy blue dress and white cat hair don't mix."

The buzzer sounded. Katherine let Jake in the building, greeting him with a smile. His dark suit with the navy blue pinstripe tie made a perfect match to her dress. "You clean up nice, Detective Sumner."

Jake's gaze traveled from Katherine's head to her toes, displaying definite approval. "So do you. I see you got rid of all the plaster dust. Ready to go? I'm parked out front."

They hurried downstairs. As the truck pulled from the curb, Katherine cleared her throat. "Did she…?"

"Not a peep from the ghost—no creepy vibes. Maybe she's gone."

Katherine peered aimlessly out the window. "I should be happy, but can't shake the feeling I left a job half-finished. I didn't even get her name."

"That may not have been part of her plan." Jake cocked his head. "I came across something interesting in that license plate number you saw in the vision."

"Oh?"

Jake explained his idea to exchange the letter for a number. "After that, I got a hit. A blue sedan with tags ending in 6 is registered to Parker Pratt."

Katherine sat up straight. "Wait a second—you think Parker is linked to Tiffani's death?"

"You tell me. You said the murderer was a man. Remember any more details?"

"No, but Parker?" Katherine shook her head. "Not possible."

"Let's face it Katherine, what do you really know about the guy?"

"Not much," she admitted, "but I'll find out more soon. I'm the first guest on his new show. April hinted if it's successful, he'll ask again."

Jake's disapproval was plain. "You're not serious. He's a person of interest now."

"Only to you. I say he's innocent. What will you tell Ethan? The license plate came to me in a supernatural vision, and you're totally okay with that? They'll never reinstate you then. I'll find a way to ask Parker about the car and watch his reaction."

Jake scowled. "Katherine, this is no joke. Lacey Calder has only been dead a few days. This guy continues to kill. Whoever he is, you don't want to start poking around and attract his attention."

"Are the police any closer to finding him?"

Jake's grip tightened on the wheel. "No, but a few strong tips came in on the hotline concerning the man in the sketch. We'll get a name soon."

"He may not have anything to do with the murder," Katherine argued. "I'll be careful, but we can't afford to ignore any lead—and Tina Delaney is still out there. I can't shake the horrible feeling all these separate parts are connected. The answer is right in front of me. If only I could pin it down..." Her voice tightened. "I can't let this go until justice is done for those women and Tina is found. Tell me," she demanded, "would you walk away? Could you if a person asked for your help?"

"No."

Katherine gazed at Jake. His jaw tensed, eyes straight ahead, hands griped tight around the wheel.

*What do you see, Kathy?*

*I see a man in pain. I understand now.*

"But you did once." She laid a gentle hand on his arm. "Tell me."

\*\*\*\*

Jake stared in grim silence through the windshield. Katherine's hand remained on his arm. The touch on the sleeve filtered warmth to his skin, spreading through him. The gentle pressure from her fingers seemed to reach out, chipping at the wall.

*Push her away, keep the guilt locked inside. I need it.*

Did he? Jake faltered. *What good has it done me all these years? Done Bethany's memory?*

The last bit of the wall crumbled away.

Saint Anne's church was up ahead. Jake turned onto the access road leading to the cemetery and parked behind a hearse. Nearby a group of people clustered around a freshly dug grave.

Heavy weight pressed down on Jake's shoulders. "Her name was Bethany Quinn. I met her in college and fell crazy, stupid in love. It was not the healthiest relationship. She was spoiled and impulsive. She drank too much and partied too hard. She cheated. We'd fight. I'd break up. Bethany would show at my door with a tearful apology. I went crawling back. All was good again—at least until the next argument."

His lips twisted in a grim smile. "I knew we were no good for each other, but once those male hormones activate, it's like trying to kick a heroin addiction. For a while there, Bethany Quinn was my drug of choice."

The pressure of her hand on his arm increased slightly.

Jake sighed. "Eventually, I grew a pair. Bethany pushed one too many buttons, and I ended the relationship for good. A month after the final breakup, she called again." Jake's hands clenched. "This time I didn't answer. This one time I didn't pick up. I'll show her, I said to myself. Bethany won't hear from me again. The message went to voicemail, and I didn't open it. A few days later, the police showed at my door asking questions. She was missing."

"Right after the phone call?" Katherine whispered.

"Must have been. Then I remembered the voicemail. I didn't bother to delete it," he added bitterly. "I enjoyed having the constant reminder at my fingertips that Bethany and I were done. I played it for the police. Only three words. *Jake, help me.* After that, the message cut out."

His words came fast, spilling onto each other. "Bethany reached out to me and I turned my back. I swore that would never happen again. The next day, I changed my major from architecture to criminal justice."

"Did the police suspect you?" Her voice held nothing but sympathy.

"With our stormy background, how could they not? I was completely cooperative though. I gave them access to my dorm room and my car, and I had a good alibi. I was out with a bunch of people when the call came in from her and afterward had no unusual absences or suspicious behavior. The police focused their attention elsewhere, but the trail went cold. Her body turned up six months later off Route 35."

Jake leaned back in the seat, eyes staring blankly overhead. The weight was even more oppressive now, squeezing the breath from his lungs. He inhaled deeply. "They never found out who did it. Not one damn suspect. Soon after I joined the force, I pulled the case file. Bethany's purse and jewelry were gone, so they figured it a mugging gone bad."

"But you don't," said Katherine softly.

"All I know is I didn't help her. I turned my back." Jake shook off her hand. "I walked away." He slid from behind the wheel, got out of the car, and slammed the door.

Chapter 16

Katherine hurried to Jake's side. "The ghost is Bethany."

Jake slumped against the door. "Seems so clear cut now, doesn't it? I refused to believe...didn't want to. After all, her body was found. Her parents buried her, but deep inside I knew... That's why I'm the one she haunts. I've tried talking to Bethany alone, but she won't answer."

His anguish tore at her heart. "Jake—"

"What's your diagnosis, Doctor?" he spit out. "Wait, don't tell me. Bethany's death isn't my fault. It was never my fault. I suffer from psycho-social-sexual-traumatic-borderline obsessive compulsive idiotness."

Katherine leaned against the car next to him. Her lips formed a smile. "I'm sorry. I'm not familiar with that one."

"It's called Jake Sumner Syndrome," he grunted. "Didn't they teach you anything in shrink school?"

"I must have been absent that day." Katherine pressed her shoulder against his. "Besides, I'm not your psychologist. I'm your friend."

Jake glowered at the ground. "So, your opinion as a friend?"

"The emotions you experience are entirely normal. You are a man of conscience. As such, any injustice is bound to trigger an angry reaction. The unsolved

L. A. Kelley

murder of a young woman once close to you added frustration to the mix, and the desire to make things right. Throw in a dash of unnecessary guilt and you have quite the psychological cocktail." She tilted her head toward him. "Do you honestly believe you deserve condemnation?"

The tension in Jake's shoulders eased. "Maybe, a little."

Katherine's tone softened. "I don't have to state out loud you bear an unreasonable burden. Deep down, you realize that or wouldn't have told me the story."

Jake gazed at the gathering at the gravesite. "Think I'm searching for absolution?"
"You have it, Jake, but won't accept the truth. No blame in her death falls on you. In your heart, you understand, in all likelihood, Bethany's foolhardy actions alone led to her demise. The term for her type is 'accident waiting to happen.' "

"That doesn't sound too clinical," he grunted. "You can't be a very good shrink."

"Never said I was," said Katherine with a faint smile, "but I stand by the diagnosis." Her heart gave a sympathetic tug knowing the next words would be painful for him to hear. "Even if you took that phone call, you couldn't have saved Bethany. She was already in the killer's clutches. The problem is Jake Sumner will accept absolution only from a dead woman's lips and he can't get it."

"Is that why she won't talk to me? It's her punishment?"

Katherine gazed at him in sorrow. "I'm sorry, Jake. I can't say, but so far she hasn't been vindictive. She led us to those women, and if those victims were so important to her…"

"Bethany was one of them, too. Funny, how I couldn't see it before," he mused. "The truth is so clear now. They were killed by the same man."

"Yes. Maybe all she wants is to bring him to justice. Makes sense she came to a homicide detective for help."

He turned his head to face her. "Suggestions on how to live with the guilt in the meantime?"

"Well, this cop once told me either learn to accept things you can't change or the frustration eats you alive."

Jake snorted. "He must be an idiot, too."

Katherine grinned. "On occasion, but other times he's rather nice."

"Need a new patient to fill up the schedule?" Jake's voice held a teasing note. His hand slipped over hers, and their fingers entwined.

Warmth rushed up Katherine's arm. Her grin widened. "Hell, no. You'd be a terrible patient."

"Can't argue that," he said wryly. "Ingalls and I certainly don't share the love."

"Have you told him…"

"About Bethany? Nope, but he knows. I can tell. Maybe Lt. Saldana mentioned it. Back then, she was a detective and lead on the case. Ingalls keeps dancing around the subject of my past as if he's holding something from it against my reinstatement."

"Why haven't you talked about Bethany to him?"

Jake scowled. "Because he pisses me off. I don't like talking to Ingalls. I like talking to you."

"Thanks, but I'm not your shrink." She stumbled over the words. "I'd rather keep you as a friend."

Katherine's heart fluttered as Jake gave her hand a gentle squeeze. "So would I."

"Katherine!" April walked across the grass toward them. "Glad you made it... Well, hello, Jake. Nice to see you again." Her gaze went to their clasped hands and her eyes gleamed. "Kind of you to give Katherine moral support."

Katherine flushed and dropped his hand.

"Nice to see you, too," said Jake lightly. "By the way, I hear my partner survived your grilling."

April snickered. "I'll break Ethan, yet." She turned toward the gathering around the gravesite and all lightness fled from her expression. "It's awful, isn't it?"

"Yes," said Katherine softly. "We should get over there. The service is ready to begin."

They greeted Parker and Connie who thanked them for coming, and then took their seats. The cemetery was well-maintained. A row of crepe myrtles in full-bloom added a splash of bright pink color against the gray tombstones.

"It's a nice place—" April flushed. "Sorry. I guess that's not appropriate to say at a funeral."

Katherine cast an eye over the mourners. They all seemed to be peers of Parker and Connie. No one's features displayed grief except for the couple. The others must have come with the same reason as Katherine; no connection to Tiffani, but to lend support to the Pratts. "I don't see anyone Tiffani's age," she whispered in Jake's ear.

"She was a junkie hooker," he said. "Not sure she had any real friends, or if they'd be the kind to show at a funeral. Sad to say, but my guess is the only two people who may ever miss Tiffani are Parker and

Connie."

The service was brief. Katherine listened to the priest's kind words with a tinge of melancholy. There wasn't much to say about a short, young, life gone so horribly wrong. The most he offered was reassurance to the family Tiffani was in a better place.

Katherine regarded the casket, decorated with a spray of white roses. A better place? She wasn't so sure. Did Tiffani's spirit float in oblivion waiting for answers, too? A stiff breeze rustled the leaves and despite the sunshine, she shivered with a sudden chill. Jake removed his jacket and placed it over her shoulders.

The service ended, and the casket lowered into the grave. As Katherine and the others extended condolences, Parker and Connie invited them back to their house. "I'm not comfortable lying to them," said Katherine as they followed the Pratt's car. "I'm supposed to offer Parker and Connie support, and instead I'm devising subtle ways to question guests about Tiffani. I feel like a jerk."

"Don't," said Jake. "You're not a liar. Your presence will still offer comfort, and finding Tiffani's killer will bring more closure to the Pratts than a funeral where most people who attended didn't mourn the deceased."

The Pratts lived only a few minutes away. The house reminded Katherine of Parker; slightly old-fashioned, but with definite charm. Friends and neighbors had brought food and set up refreshments in the dining room. Jake poured Katherine a cup of coffee. "You work one side of the room," he whispered. "I'll work the other. See if you can find anybody who either knew or saw Tiffani around the time she disappeared."

Katherine nodded. She wandered through the house, making polite inquiries. She soon concluded her first estimation was accurate. Although a few guests remembered Tiffani, she had been out of the Pratts' lives for a while and none knew her well. They were here solely to lend support for Connie and Parker.

April caught up with Katherine and pulled her aside. "I just got off the phone with Ethan. He's at the precinct, ready for a break and asked me to meet him for coffee." She flushed. "Is it awful for me to leave now?"

"No." Katherine patted her arm. "You went to the service and have been here over an hour. You gave the Pratts your emotional support on a difficult day. Don't feel guilty, April. There's nothing more you can do for them."

"Thanks." The relief in her tone was evident. "How about you?"

"Jake and I will stay a little longer."

"Okay." April gave her a friendly nudge. "He's into you, Katherine. I don't have to be a shrink to understand no guy spends his day off escorting a girl to a funeral for funsies. Either of you ever going to make a move?"

Her gaze strayed across the room to Jake. A smile tugged at her lips. "We're working on it."

As soon as April left, Katherine wandered over to Jake. "No luck with my inquiries. You?"

"Nothing. The crowd's thinned. People are starting to leave." Jake motioned to the Pratts. "They're alone now. This is a good chance to talk to them."

Parker and Connie offered thanks to Katherine and

Jake. "It was kind of you to come," added Connie.

"I'm so sorry for your loss," said Katherine. "Were you and Tiffani close?"

"Not really," said Connie with sigh. "Tiffani's mother was my cousin. She was a single parent who doted on Tiffani. Never said no and spoiled her rotten."

"A handful?" asked Katherine kindly.

Connie smiled weakly. "You're not supposed to speak ill of the dead, but Tiffani ran wild, never disciplined at home. Eventually, she got into drugs and then prostitution to support her habit. Parker and I tried to help. We even put her up for a time after her mother passed, but then one of my necklaces went missing. I knew she'd taken it and threw her out."

Katherine shot Jake a coy look as she stifled her rising excitement. "A necklace? It must have been important to you."

"A silver filigree locket—not much value, but it belonged to my grandmother. I had planned to give it to my own granddaughter when she turned sixteen." A hopeful light shone in Connie's eyes. "Did the police find it?"

"It's an active case," Jake said kindly. "I can't discuss the details. I'm sorry."

Connie sighed. "My guess is you didn't. Tiffani must have pawned it."

"When was the last time you saw her?" asked Katherine.

"Roughly two years ago," said Parker, "Tiffani called from jail. We visited. She'd been picked up on another prostitution and possession charge and got six months. She swore this time to get clean. She said she was getting counseling and planned to continue after her release."

Jake raised his eyebrow. "Did she?"

"Honestly, I don't know. I only heard from her once right after she got out of jail." Connie's voice softened. "It's funny, now that I think of it. Tiffani called to apologize for taking the necklace. She never asked forgiveness for any of her actions before. She wanted to return it, but I told her to keep the necklace as a gesture of good faith. That's why all this is so sad. I had hoped, this time, Tiffani might turn over a new leaf." Connie motioned to her husband. "Parker even gave her his old car for transportation to find a job."

Jake and Katherine exchanged a quick glance.

"I offered to drop it off," added Parker, "but Tiffani said she'd come by. Connie and I were both working so I left it in the driveway unlocked with the keys in the glovebox. It was gone when we got home."

"Did you happen to mention the car to Detective Reardon?" asked Jake.

"No. I didn't remember until now. Is it important?"

"Don't worry," said Jake in a soothing manner. "It's probably nothing, but I'll take the information on the car and the necklace and pass it to Ethan."

Connie blinked back a tear. "I thought badly of Tiffany—I assumed she took off with the car and a new boyfriend and went back to her old ways, but she must have died soon after. Now, I feel awful I didn't make more of an effort to find her. I didn't even file a missing person's report. Frankly, at the time, I was fed up and glad she was gone from our lives."

Katherine placed an arm around Connie's shoulders. "Any guilt over Tiffani's death is misplaced. You and Parker did more than enough to help her. In the end, we must all take responsibility for our own actions. Tiffani was an adult. Her choices put her in dangerous situations. Not yours."

Connie dabbed at her eyes. "Thank you."

"Katherine and I should be going," said Jake. "Again, we're sorry for your loss." He paused and said, "By any chance did Tiffani attend Saint Anne's school?"

"No. She went to the local high school, but dropped out her senior year." Connie sighed. "She wasn't exactly a church-goer either."

Parker escorted Jake and Katherine to the door. "If Connie needs to talk," said Katherine, "have her call me. I'm not trying to drum up business," she added quickly, "strictly as a friend."

"That's kind of you. I'll tell her." Parker took Katherine's hand in his. "I knew you were a good choice for the show. I'm sorry the premiere has been pushed aside for a bit. I'll contact you when we have a shooting date."

"No rush. Whenever you're ready."

Jake and Katherine strolled to the truck. "That was productive," said Jake as he drove from the house. "Parker's car was used to move Tiffani's body to the burial site. I can run a trace on the VIN and see if it's turned up anywhere since. It might give us a lead."

"Could evidence be inside after all this time?"

"Maybe, but I'm more interested in who's behind the wheel now and how he got the car."

Her eyebrow shot up. "You can't think Parker lied?"

"We have to consider the possibility. No one witnessed Tiffani take the car. Parker didn't report it stolen."

"It wasn't stolen," sputtered Katherine. "It was a gift."

"Or it had evidence inside. Blood maybe?"

"The killer isn't Parker."

"We can't rule him out."

"I can."

"Gut instinct, Dr. Fleming?" said Jake with clear amusement.

"Call it what you will. Did you find Connie's missing necklace?"

"Not on Tiffani's body, but I'll tell Ethan."

Katherine gazed out the window. "I noticed at the bus stop Lacey Calder wore a chain with a gold dolphin pendant. Did you find one on the body?"

Jake shot her a glance. "No, and I don't recall such a necklace in the list of jewelry at her apartment." His shoulders stiffened. "Bethany had a necklace, white gold with a diamond star pendant. She wore it all the time."

"Was it on the body?"

"No, but she had been buried in a shallow grave. Several months later, a tropical storm blew through the area. Heavy rains and flooding washed the remains down a hillside. When they were finally found..." His grip tightened on the wheel. "Bones had been scattered. The necklace could easily have been lost."

"Or stolen by the killer," murmured Katherine. "Can I jump to a conclusion now and say he takes souvenirs?"

His voice hardened. "Agreed. What's your professional opinion?"

"He has no remorse or regret."

"Does Tina's cross have any religious significance?"

"Perhaps, but in my opinion he wanted a belonging to lay claim to his victim and remember the details of her death. Jewelry is personal and a convenient trophy." Katherine shivered. "A killer in a crime of passion doesn't take a souvenir."

"You believe," mused Jake, "he still has the jewelry?"

"I'm sure he considers them his most cherished possessions. I wouldn't be surprised if they're kept together in a special place." Katherine gazed mindlessly at the passing cars. "He wasn't as careful when Bethany died. What if she was the first murder? The grave was too shallow and not hidden well enough. If you want religious significance, examine the way he positioned his later victims—arms crossed, with a sense of repose, prayer even. He didn't simply dump them by the side of the road. They weren't mutilated. He took great care; his actions were respectful."

Jake snorted. "Murder is respectful?"

"He doesn't see it as murder." Her eyes widened. "I'm a good girl."

Jake gave her a cheeky grin. "Well, that's a crushing disappoint."

"I'm not," she sputtered. "I mean I am. I mean I'm not talking about me." Jake's grin widened, and she jabbed him in the arm. "Wipe that smirk off your face. The ghost used the phrase, only it didn't sound as if she meant herself—it could be what the killer said to her. If so, it adds to the pathology. Perhaps he thinks his actions save them."

"It's more to go on, anyway." Jake's lighthearted

manner vanished.

"You're worried," said Katherine.

"Yeah. Guys like him don't quit unless they're caught."

They pulled in front of Katherine's apartment building. She cleared her throat. "Why don't you come in? I'll make coffee."

Jake tensed. "Katherine, what I said before about Bethany…"

"When you're ready to talk more, I'm happy to listen. Meanwhile, we have murders to solve."

His stance relaxed. "Then coffee sounds good."

As they walked to her apartment, Jake placed his hand lightly on the small of her back, sending a pleasant tingle along Katherine's spine. They reached the second floor. Frantic meowing came from behind the door. Katherine turned the key in the lock with a puzzled frown. "Whiskers? What's the matter, sweetie—"

As soon as the door opened, a white blur bolted straight for the stairwell.

"Whiskers!" she cried. "Stop him."

Katherine and Jake took off at a run down the stairs to the lobby. One of the neighbors stood by the open front door. "Was that your cat?" he said with a stricken tone. "I-I'm so sorry. I didn't see him by the door."

Katherine dashed outside calling for Whiskers.

"There!" said Jake. The flash of a tail rounded the corner. "Get in the truck."

They jumped in, but by the time they reached the intersection, Whiskers was gone. Jake pulled to the curb.

Katherine scanned the street in rising panic. "I

don't see him anywhere. Where did he go?"

Jake grabbed her arm and pointed. At the end of the block, Whiskers sat placidly washing his paw.

As the truck approached, he scampered away. They followed down one street after another, Whiskers drawing them along.

"No cat treats tonight for you, young man," Katherine grumbled.

They turned a corner and Jake drew in a breath. "Katherine, check out where we are."

Katherine gaped at the street sign. "Culpepper Lane."

Whiskers darted along the sidewalk, making a beeline for Jake's house.

As soon as Jake parked in the driveway, Katherine jumped out and bounded up the front steps. Whiskers sat on the doormat, tail curled in front of his forepaws. She scooped him up. "You are a bad cat," she scolded. "What are you doing here?"

Whiskers purred.

"Don't try any sweet talk with me, young man. I'm still mad at you."

*Snick. Click.*

The deadbolt slid aside. Katherine and Jake stared in stunned disbelief as the front door swung open.

Jake leaned toward Katherine and whispered in her ear, "I guess my houseguest wants to say hi to all three of us."

Chapter 17

Jake placed an arm around Katherine's shoulders. "Ready?"

Katherine nodded, and they crossed the threshold. The door swung slowly shut behind them on silent hinges. The parlor door opened, and they exchanged an uneasy glance.

"Yeah, that's creepy," muttered Jake.

They entered the parlor, and Katherine put Whiskers on the floor. He padded softly across the room and sat below the mirror, gazing up in clear anticipation. Jake turned on the lamp and then went to Katherine's side.

Katherine cleared her throat. "Bethany, I know who you are now and why you're here. This man killed you and the others, and you want us to find him. Jake and I came from Tiffani's funeral. Thank you for showing me where he buried her. Tiffani's family has closure, at least." She glanced at Whiskers who continued to stare at the mirror. "Whiskers led us here. I-I don't understand how messages get across to him, but I believe this means you want to talk to us again."

The light flickered. A ghostly voice wafted through the parlor. *Tiffani wasn't the first.*

"Not his first victim…" Katherine's mouth went dry. "Were you?"

*No.*

A sick feeling settled in her stomach. "Was Tina?"

*He wanted her to be a good girl forever.*

Jake tugged at her sleeve. "What's she saying?"

"Tina was his first victim. Bethany was the second."

Jake swallowed hard. "Beth? I'm so sorry…" He drew a shuddering breath. "I-I should have been there for you. I swear to find this guy."

The temperature in the room dropped. *He knows.*

Katherine regarded Jake in confusion. "She says you know."

"I-I don't," he stammered. "Bethany, what do you mean?"

*He almost had him.*

Katherine turned back to the mirror. "Jake almost had him? I don't understand."

*See.*

The blotches in the mirror exploded into a patchy fog. Katherine squinted as shapes formed. "I see a room…" She stepped forward and placed her hands against the glass, straining to bring order from the chaos.

The blurry shapes regained focus. Katherine was in a bedroom. The furnishings were cheap and worn. Through an open door, she made out part of a living room. She tried to move, but her body refused to obey as if she had been pinned to the wall. Katherine looked down expecting to see arms and legs, but below was the top of a dresser. A wooden frame surrounded her.

*I'm in a mirror.*

A woman in her early twenties walked into the bedroom. She casually swept a hand at the door, closing it halfway. She wore heavy makeup and dressed in a lacy camisole shirt, short skirt, long zip-up high heel boots, and gold dangly earrings that nearly brushed her shoulders. She opened a purse, upended the contents on the bed, and fished a cell phone and business card from the jumbled pile. The woman studied the card in her hand, clear indecision on her face. After several seconds, her features hardened into determination and she dialed a number.

"It's Sapph—" She whipped the phone from her ear, glaring at the screen in irritation. A muffled man's voice came through the speaker, too faint for Katherine to make out words, but the flat monotone indicated a recorded greeting. A muted beep followed.

"Detective Sumner, it's Sapphire. You gave me your card. Call me when you get this. Delilah just told me…then I saw him… Anyway, he's the same one…" She blew her cheeks out in frustration. "Call me or come by—Fairfield Apartments, 12A." Sapphire left her number and tossed the phone on the bed. She sat next to it with her back to the door and unzipped her right boot.

One gloved hand eased around the door, quietly slipping it open. A man in dark clothing and a ski mask stood on the threshold, hands clenching and unclenching.

Katherine's heart hammered against her ribs. "Behind you!"

Sapphire tugged off the boot. With a sigh, she stretched out her foot, wiggled the toes, and then bent over to unlace the other one.

In mindless panic, Katherine pounded on the glass. "Sapphire, look in the mirror!" Jake called Katherine's name, but his voice sounded far away.

"He's coming for her," she shouted. "She doesn't see."

Sapphire kicked off the other boot and straightened her back. Her eyes went to the mirror and widened in horror.

The man lunged. His blow to Sapphire's head knocked her off the bed and sent her reeling to the floor before she uttered a sound. He jerked Sapphire onto her back and sat on her chest, blocking Katherine's view of the woman's face. His knees pinned her arms to the floor. His hands went to her throat.

"No!" Katherine screamed. "Get away from her!"

The man's arm muscles vibrated in intensity, squeezing hard. Sapphire made a gurgling sound. Her legs kicked in a frenzied attempt to shift the weight off her chest. The frantic thrashing subsided to mere twitches.

Two.

Then one.

Her legs quivered. All movement stopped.

"No." Tears streamed down Katherine's cheeks. A gentle arm pulled her close.

"I'm here, Kathy," Jake whispered. "What do you see?"

"It's him. He killed Sapphire."

The man slid off Sapphire's body, breathing hard. He removed his gloves and checked for a pulse. He gripped her ear and eased off one earring, then the other one. He stuffed the pair in his jacket pocket and put the gloves back on.

Bile rose in Katherine's throat. She swallowed hard. "H-he stole her earrings."

Sapphire's dead eyes stared at the ceiling. "You're

my good girl, now," the man whispered. He grasped one wrist, raising it from the floor as if to place it over her chest.

From the living room came the creak of a door opening. "Sapphire?" shouted a man. "It's Danny."

The man in the mask dropped Sapphire's wrist. He jumped to his feet, opened the nearest window, and vaulted outside.

"Sapphire? Damn girl, where you at? I know you're here. I seen your car outside." His voice grew louder. He strode into the bedroom. He wore a beat-up leather jacket and a gun tucked in his waistband. "I got weed to sell. Loan me your car and I'll make you a good deal—" His voice drifted away. He froze in place, gawking at the body in disbelief. "Sapphire?"

Danny's face turned the color of ashes. "Oh, Jesus," he moaned. "Oh, Jesus." He glanced around the room and then his eyes lit on the pile of items from her purse. He stuffed Sapphire's wallet and keys into his pocket. Next, he went to the bureau. He yanked open the drawer, tossed clothes on the floor, and seized a jewelry box.

The door to the outside opened again. "Sapphire," called Jake. "It's Detective Sumner. I got your message."

In wild-eyed panic, Danny whipped the gun from his waistband and fired. With the box under his arm, he bolted out the window.

Fog clouded the vision. Katherine staggered back from the mirror.

Jake's arms held her tight. "I've got you, Kathy. I'm here."

"It was awful." Her words came with a strangled

sob. "You were right. Sapphire's killer wasn't Danny. I saw the truth."

Jake stroked her hair. "I'm sorry... Let me take you home first."

"No." Katherine shot a glance at the mirror. The reflection of her pale face gazed back. "I'm not afraid of this place, and you need to hear the details while fresh in my mind."

They sat on the couch. Whiskers jumped into her lap as if eager to offer comfort. She stroked his head, tension easing.

"Take your time," said Jake. "If it gets to be too much, we'll stop."

"I'm okay now." With a shudder, Katherine described the murder scene, searching her memory for every last element. "The souvenir, the strangulation...it was all there."

Jake grip tightened. "I shot an innocent man."

"Who tried to kill you first," Katherine said sharply. "The shooting was justified, and his apparent guilt in Sapphire's murder was a natural mistake. He already killed a man."

"Doesn't make me feel any better," he grunted. "This same person murdered Bethany."

"And Tiffani a little over a year ago," said Katherine, "and then Sapphire less than two months ago, and Lacey a few weeks after that."

Jake's jaw tightened. "He's accelerating."

"If so, he'll kill again soon and we don't have a clue to his identity. A big help, I was," she added bitterly. "I didn't see his face. I heard only a whisper, and can't recognize the voice from that. His clothing was nondescript, nothing useful there either."

"That's not true," Jake mused. "He removed his gloves and touched Sapphire's skin with his hands."

Katherine regarded him with surprise. "You can get a fingerprint off a dead body?"

"DNA, too, but it depends on a lot of variables; moisture or lotion on the body, how firm the perp's grip, if the body had been dragged. Lots of things can obliterate forensic evidence. The ME checked Sapphire's remains and found several sets of prints, not surprising considering her line of work."

"Were the others ever identified?"

"Not that I recall. The case was so cut and dried no one brought them up again, and there was no trial, so the DA didn't need them to make a case." Jake rose to his feet. "I need to see her file again."

"Now?"

"It's Saturday afternoon. With luck, I can sneak in with no one any wiser. I'll run the plates on Parker's sedan, too. See if it popped up recently."

"I wonder what Delilah said," mused Katherine. "I got the impression Sapphire phoned you soon after speaking to her."

"I checked on the name Delilah with vice after Sapphire died, but came up empty. No arrests under that name. Working girls' aliases change, so she could have a different identity by now or even left the area. I'll make more inquiries, but run you and Whiskers home first. You've done enough for today."

They drove back to her apartment and parked in front. Jake hadn't said a word on the way over. "Are you okay?" Katherine asked kindly.

"Oh, I'm great," he grumbled, "for a man shacked up with a dead ex-girlfriend."

"Bethany didn't come seeking revenge, Jake. She came for help, and we're going to give it to her."

"First, I have to tie her murder to the others."

"We will. You're not in this alone."

Gratitude shined from his eyes. Jake walked Katherine upstairs. She unlocked the door and put Whiskers on the floor. He ambled inside without protest or a backward glance. "I guess he's done communing with the beyond," said Katherine lightly. She paused in the jamb and gazed at Jake. Heat rose to her cheeks. "Want to come in for a bit?"

His hand gently tucked a loose strand of hair behind her ear. "Yes, but I won't. You hide it well, but it doesn't take a shrink to see what happened today shook you badly. Get some rest."

Katherine rooted to the spot. Her breath quickened as she held his gaze. Jake's hand went from her cheek to the nape of Katherine's neck. She leaned toward him, heart pounding. He bent his head. His lips met hers, warm and welcoming. She placed her hand against his chest. His heartbeat thrummed in response increasing her desire.

Jake took her in his arms. She pressed tight against him, a perfect fit, two halves to a whole.

His kisses went up her face; the tip of her nose, each eyelid, her brow. His cheek rested lightly against the top of her head. His arms held her in a loving embrace. "Katherine," he whispered. "My life is a mess. You shouldn't get involved. Some men have ex-girlfriend issues, but I have a doozy."

"Big deal," she murmured. "I have a psychic cat. Sounds like we're made for each other."

"You should run from here," he said tenderly.

L. A. Kelley

"From me."

"Not a chance. I'm not afraid of you or Bethany's ghost. She's still my patient, and needs help." Katherine nestled against his chest. "You're not damaged goods Jake, only slightly irregular—nothing we can't straighten out together. It would be a damn shame not to try."

Jake's hand pushed lightly against her shoulder, easing her back. "I want us to start with a clean slate, no baggage, no history pulling us apart. Nothing to screw this up. That means I have to solve the murders first—put Sapphire and the others at rest. Including Bethany."

Katherine read the worry in his eyes. "I'm not going anywhere, so you better get to work."

**\*\*\*\***

Jake sat at the desk, running through paperwork. He pulled out the reports on Lacey, Sapphire, and Tiffani and then added the file on Tina Delaney. He threw one more file on top—Bethany Quinn.

A search through DMV records for Pratt's sedan yielded nothing recent; no speeding or parking tickets and no record of sale. Tags had expired, but not renewed. Jake tapped his pen on the desktop. Either the vehicle was abandoned after Tiffani's murder or it's out there with the killer.

His concentration flagged and Jake rubbed his eyes. Man, what a day. He was beat to the bone, but going home now was pointless, not to mention Bethany was in his house.

Bethany… Jake's heart gave a wistful tug. No matter Katherine's sympathetic words, guilt settled neatly on his shoulders. Bethany may not hold him responsible for her death, but that didn't stop him from blaming himself.

*If only I'd taken her call…if only…if only…if only.*

The one bright spot from today was Katherine. He hadn't meant to kiss her. It just happened. Just as he hadn't planned to mention Bethany, but the confession felt so right. Her lips against his sent a rush of sweet yearning. Her whispered assurance she wasn't going anywhere shed a ray of light on his gloom, but how long could he expect her to wait while he got his mess of a life straightened out? Was it fair to even ask?

"Watcha doing?"

Jake started. "Damn it, Ethan. Quit sneaking up on me. I thought you were meeting April?"

"I did. We had a nice time. I'm taking her to dinner next chance I get." He narrowed his eyes. "Interesting you have that information. Of course, April did say she met you at the funeral."

"I only accompanied Katherine."

"April said you spent a lot of time chatting up the other guests. You and Katherine were still there when she left. Then I come back to the precinct and, low and behold, find Detective Sumner perusing the files on the two dead women along with several others. What the hell's going on, Jake? And don't give me any crap that you're catching up on paperwork. Lt. Saldana will have a fit if she figures out you're investigating against her orders."

Jake leaned back in his seat with a sigh. "I have a hunch they're connected."

Ethan blinked in surprise. "All of these?"

"Yes, and I'm not obsessing." Jake cocked an eyebrow. "Believe me?"

Ethan shot a quick glance around the room as if to

confirm he wasn't watched and then pulled up a chair next to Jake's desk. His voice dropped. "What have you got?"

"More questions than answers. I learned Tiffani's necklace went missing with her. Lacey Calder had a dolphin pendant necklace that wasn't found with her effects." He shot a wary glance at Ethan. "I believe the killer took Sapphire's earrings. I noticed them when I gave her my card. The girl loved bling. She had big gaudy gold earrings that almost reached her shoulders. They weren't on the body."

Ethan sat back in his seat, skepticism all over his face. "Jake, I know how that case affected you, but wishful thinking won't turn it into an active murder investigation. Besides, Pierson is history. He couldn't have killed Lacey Calder."

"He didn't kill Sapphire, either." He held up his hand to stifle a protest and tossed over a file. "Read it yourself. Other than the bruising from the strangulation, prints were found on Sapphire's neck in the exact place a person checks for a pulse. Pierson would never do that. He couldn't have found his own ass with a set of written directions, let alone bother to check for a pulse. The autopsy also stated the same prints were found on Sapphire's ears. They weren't hers. What if they were left by the man who removed the earrings as a souvenir?"

Ethan regarded him with doubt. "They could have been left by any number of men. She made her living as a prostitute."

"Why were the strange prints only in those locations on the body? The ME's exam found no evidence Sapphire had sexual activity that day. Where were her earrings?"

"She could have taken them off," Ethan protested.

"Then why didn't we find them? Pierson stole her jewelry box. He had it on him when he died. Did you see earrings matching that description inside, or anywhere in her apartment?"

"No," Ethan grunted, "but there can be other reasons. You don't have a lot to go on—and nothing concrete to give to Saldana." He flipped through the file. "The prints weren't even identified."

"They're not in the system, so not Pierson's."

Ethan glanced at the desk. "Who are the others—" He stopped short. His eyes widened as he snatched up Bethany's file. "You can't be serious. Jake, you've got to get over this. You have nothing to tie her death to the other victims."

Jake's voice tightened. "Call it gut instinct. I'm telling you they're connected."

Ethan regarded him with sympathy. "Let's say I believe you. I'll tell you what Saldana will call it—six more months on Ingalls' couch. If you ever want to get fully reinstated, leave Bethany out of this."

"I can't," said Jake. He cleared his throat. "Even Katherine believes me."

"You shared police files with her?" Ethan shook his head. "If Saldana finds out, Ingalls will be the least of your problems. She'll fire you—" He eyed him with sudden curiosity. "What did Katherine say?"

"She believes the killer took the jewelry from his victims as a souvenir. The bent-arm position of the bodies showed he believed death moved them to a state of grace. They became good girls once more."

"Sapphire's body wasn't placed that way," Ethan

argued.

"What if Pierson interrupted him before he finished?"

"And Bethany?"

"Her body was found after heavy rains uncovered the shallow grave and washed the remains down a hillside. He could have originally placed her in the same position as the others. Bethany also owned a necklace—white gold with a diamond star pendant. It wasn't on the body, and I checked the investigator's report. The day Bethany disappeared witnesses said she had it on."

"Could have been washed away too. All I hear is lots of speculation." Ethan nodded to the last file. "Who's in that one?"

"It's an old missing person case, but I suspect a connection. Tina was an assault victim of the same man, but got away. She may still be alive and have a clue to his identity."

Ethan flipped through Tina's file. "This is a closed missing person case, nothing in here mentions an assault."

Jake pressed his lips together in a thin line.

"Jake, you're a good cop," Ethan snapped. "What the hell's the matter with you? You have all these conclusions drawn without any evidence. Nothing you told me connects Tina and Bethany to Sapphire, Tiffani or Lacey. Why are you so damn sure? Is this because of Bethany?"

"It's not that—"

"Don't pretend her death doesn't eat at you," he snapped. "Do you need closure so badly, the only way to get it is to create links where none exist? You're hunting ghosts, man."

Jake gave a rueful chuckle. "How right you are."

Ethan's tension visibly eased. "What's so funny?"

"Inside joke." Jake rubbed the back of his neck. "I'm not crazy. I'm not imagining things. I can't tell you how I know this stuff only that I do. As my friend and partner, I'm asking you to trust my instincts, but I can't give you any more than that. These cases are connected."

Ethan's scrutinized him sharply and then his voice softened. "This started when Katherine came into your life. She's become important to you."

"Yeah, she has."

"Have you told her this insane theory?"

His lips twitched in a smile. "We worked on the insanest parts together."

"Ah," Ethan said lightly, "she's feeding your fantasy. Not like Ingalls. Did you tell Katherine about Bethany?"

"Yes."

"Well, well, Jake Sumner letting a woman into his private pain. That's a first." Ethan shifted in his seat. "Did you ever discuss Bethany with Ingalls?"

"No."

"He's familiar with her case."

Jake's eyebrow rose. "How? Did you—"

Ethan raised his hands. "Come on, am I a rat? Lt. Saldana mentioned Ingalls brought up Bethany's case and asked if I talked to him about it. He's got connections in the department and must have dug into your background and found your name on the list of people questioned after her disappearance."

Jake stiffened. "What did she tell him?"

"Nothing. Saldana was pissed as Bethany's death had squat to do with Pierson's shooting. She asked if there was anything personal between you two as Ingalls seemed to be fishing for information." Ethan glanced around the squad room and then lowered his voice. "Saldana's losing patience with Ingalls. He hasn't given her a good reason to keep you from resuming duty. She suspects he's trying to milk the department for more money by extending the sessions. If the lieutenant had her way, she'd boot his access from the Sandy Shoals PD."

Jake snorted. "I won't shed a tear."

Chapter 18

As Katherine finished getting ready for work on Monday, she glanced out the window. A familiar truck was parked in front. The intercom buzzed and she answered with a smile. "Hey, Jake. Come on up."

Jake arrived holding a cardboard carryout container with two cups of coffee and a paper bag. "I stopped by to see how you were." He shook the bag. "Do you have time for bagels?"

"Always."

As they ate, Jake filled her in on his talk with Ethan. "I gave him a few details of our investigation."

Katherine shot him an innocent look. "Even the ghost?"

He chuckled. "I have a remnant of sanity left. Ethan isn't one hundred percent convinced of our theory of the murders. Even though he knows I'm holding back, he offered to help. For the moment, all I asked him to do was focus his attention the other way while I poke around, and I'll pass on any leads. Saldana will have a fit if she discovers Ethan wasting time on my wild goose chase. No point in having two of us in the doghouse."

"So what's next?"

His distaste was evident. "I have an appointment with Ingalls first thing this morning."

"You're snarling."

"Can't help it. After that, I'll take the rest of the day off and finish the demolition. I plan to imagine the wall as Ingalls' head." Jake's pushed back from his seat. "I should get going."

"Me, too. It's a nice day. I'll walk to the office."

"You want a ride?"

"Not if you snarl at me."

Jake's lips twitched in a faint smile. "How about two testy scowls?"

Katherine chuckled. "Nope. I demand only pleasant company."

"You're a tough one, Fleming."

"You've no idea." Katherine grabbed her purse, and they headed to the street. "You're still snarling," she said lightly as they got into his truck.

"What? Oh—it's not you. Meeting with Ingalls always puts me in a bad mood." Jake glanced at her. "Ingalls heard about Bethany. Ethan said he's been digging into my background." He turned the key. "He seems more determined to keep me from my job since you came on the scene."

Katherine's eyes widened. "You're blaming me."

"No, but maybe you said something unintentionally that gave him doubts about my fitness."

She bristled. "All I ever said to Jeremy was that Jake Sumner was ready to return to full duty."

"Hey, I'm sorry, but I'm grasping at straws, trying to find a reason for his actions. I need to get back to work, and Ingalls is the only thing standing in my way."

"Then take my advice. Agree with everything he says and for heaven's sake don't scowl."

"I'll try," Jake grunted, "but it's not easy." He pulled into the parking lot at the counseling center and parked the truck. "Want to have dinner tonight? I promise a better mood."

Katherine smiled. "I'd love to."

"Great. I'll pick you up at six."

****

*Tap-tap-tap.* Ingalls' pen beat a tattoo against his notebook. "You're not talkative today, Detective."

Jake sprawled in the chair. Only sheer force of will kept him from snatching the pen from Ingalls' hand and pitching both it and the owner out the window. "There's not much to say. We've gone over the shooting a hundred times."

"You don't find these sessions necessary, but I believe what occurred in the past continues to have a detrimental effect on current aspects of your life."

"I can't imagine how. My life is fine."

"And your relationship with Dr. Fleming?"

A sliver of unease crept up Jake's spine. "Relationship?"

"I saw you drive in together this morning."

What business was it of his? Jake's desire soared to shield his feelings for Katherine from Ingalls' prying eyes. "We're just friends," he lied smoothly. "I happened to see her on the street walking to work and offered a ride."

The tapping stopped. Ingalls scribbled in the notebook. "Have you discussed Pierson's shooting with her?"

"She knows I have to see you."

"That's not what I asked."

*Don't scowl. Don't scowl. Don't scowl.* "Yes. She was very sympathetic."

Ingalls looked up from the notebook. "I can see

there's an attraction between you two, Detective, but in my opinion this isn't a good time to pursue a new relationship."

Jake stifled a snarly response as Katherine's advice came back to him—agree with everything. He forced a smile. "I agree."

Ingalls blinked. "You do?"

*Ha! Didn't see that coming, did you?* "Yes. I have too much on my plate now. So does Katherine. Besides, she's not my type."

Ingalls leaned in. "How so?"

Jake shrugged. "Well, she's a nice person, but kind of quiet. A real intellectual. We don't have a lot in common."

"So you're saying you're not interested?"

"Exactly."

Ingalls glanced at his watch. "We're out of time for today. We're making excellent progress, Detective Sumner."

Jake rose to his feet, a subtle thaw evident to him in the frosty atmosphere. "Ready to sign off yet?"

"Not quite, but soon now. Perhaps the next session."

*Well how about that? It worked.* Jake stifled a display of triumph. *One small lie for Jake, one giant step closer to reinstatement.*

Ingalls showed him to the door. Jake walked down the hall. A burning sensation crawled up the back of his neck as if Ingalls watched every step. It took all his self-control not to turn around and glare.

Jake unlocked the truck and slid into the driver's seat. What was the deal with Ingalls? Why did a coworker's possible relationship with a cop get under his skin? Did he have a thing for Katherine or could it be an entirely different cause? Either way, it's clear now Ingalls wouldn't sign off if he suspected his attraction to her.

Jake arrived home still mulling over the session with Ingalls. He called Katherine. "Change of plans for tonight. We can't be seen together in public if there's a chance Ingalls will spot us."

****

Katherine hung up the phone with a puzzled frown. Jake's description of Jeremy's behavior unsettled her.

"Bad news?" Jeremy stood at the door.

Katherine heart raced. "You startled me. I thought you'd gone."

"Just got back." Jeremy walked into her office and motioned to the phone. "You seem bothered. Can I help?"

"No, it's nothing."

"Really?"

"Having to reschedule a dental cleaning doesn't qualify as a crisis." The lie slipped out easily with the smile.

"Okay." Jeremy's hand lightly rested on her shoulder. "I'm always available to talk. You're one of the good ones, Katherine. I'd hate to see that change."

The smile froze on her face. "Good ones?"

Jeremy cleared his throat. "Sorry, I didn't mean to come out and say that. It's an old-fashioned term. I meant people who do good for others. This job can be difficult. You come in contact with so much of the dark side of human nature it's easy to get jaded and burn out especially with no one to talk to."

"I appreciate the concern," said Katherine, "but

don't worry about me." His hand continued to rest on her shoulder. Her smile tightened, and she flinched under his touch. "I'm happy in my work."

Jeremy removed his hand. "I'm glad to hear that."

"I never asked why you decided to relocate back to Florida," she said.

"I came to visit my father who was in poor health. After he died, it seemed as if the time had come to make a permanent change."

"Didn't you once mention working at the women's correctional center for a while?"

Jeremy hesitated slightly before responding. "Yes. Why do you ask?"

"I was considering pro bono work, too. Helping young women in crisis always appealed to me."

"Me, too, but I wasn't pro bono. Social services had a grant, and I was only there for a few months until the money ran out."

"Oh, I see. How many patients did you have?"

"Quite a few, but in group therapy only. There were several counselors under the grant."

"You don't run group therapy sessions now."

"I discovered I prefer a personal connection," Jeremy said cheerfully. "I can accomplish so much more."

Jeremy said goodbye and Katherine's gaze followed him out the door. The sensation of weight still apparent on her shoulder as if his hand left an impression in the skin. She briskly rubbed the spot, and the feeling subsided.

Katherine eyed the computer. She rose from the desk and peered down the hall. Diana was on the phone at the reception desk. Katherine slipped into the ladies' room. She grabbed all the paper towels and tossed them in the trashcan. With a deep breath to steady her nerves, she ambled to the front and poured a cup of coffee from the pot in the waiting room kept for clients.

Diana hung up the phone and turned to Katherine with a smile. "Do we need a fresh pot yet?"

"No, we're good...by the way," she added offhandedly, "I just used the last of the paper towels in the ladies' room. Do we have any more?"

Diana blinked. "I swear the cleaning service filled the dispenser this morning. Watch the desk for me, will you? I have an extra package in the supply cabinet and will be back in a sec."

As soon as she disappeared from sight, Katherine slipped into the chair and ran a search of patient records.

She typed in one name...nothing.

Then another...nothing.

Katherine typed in a third. A box popped up: 1 File Found. Her mouth went dry.

The door down the hall shut. Katherine exited the screen and jumped from the seat a second before Diana appeared. "All done..." She regarded the monitor with a puzzled look. "Were you on my computer?"

She took a sip of coffee and tried to quell her shaking hands. "Checking my schedule for tomorrow."

"Stop messing with my stuff," Diana joshed. She pulled up the appointment calendar. "Your first patient is at 8:30. Do you need to reschedule?"

"No, it's fine." Katherine hurried to her office and shut the door. She leaned against it, comforted by the sense of support at her back. "One name in a patient file. Can't draw a conclusion from that."

The phone on her desk rang, and her heart skipped a beat. "Yes, Diana."

"Your next appointment is here," she said cheerfully.

Katherine rubbed her clammy hands along the sides of her skirt. "Send her in."

Chapter 19

After her last appointment, Katherine hurried home, her thoughts in a troubled whirl. One name hardly constituted proof of guilt, but her inner alarms clanged loudly with each step. She stopped twice to glance around. No one seemed to pay any attention to her, but an uneasy feeling of being watched crawled up her spine. She fished her cell from the purse and phoned Jake, but the call went to voicemail. "Get a grip," Katherine murmured. "You're on a crowded street in broad daylight. Nothing will happen." She rounded the corner to her apartment and picked up the pace.

Once inside with the deadbolt secured, Katherine relaxed. She changed into a t-shirt and jeans and fished the cell phone from her purse to call Jake again. Whiskers jumped to his favorite spot at the windowsill and peered intently at the street. Katherine leaned over him, but to her disappointment, Jake's truck wasn't there. The intercom buzzed, and her gaze went again to the recess. Jake stepped out and waved. Katherine greeted him at the door with a wide smile.

"I parked around back," said Jake. "I was on my way here when you called so didn't pick up. Hope you like Thai."

"We canceled plans for tonight. What brought on the change of heart?"

"Ingalls pissed me the hell off. He has no right to butt into my private life. I figured if we can't eat in public, I'll bring dinner to you." Jake set the takeout bag on the table and removed the cartons. He shot her a sharp look. "Does Ingalls have a thing for you?"

"Not a chance. He never made a pass and isn't exactly shy around women."

"He definitely discouraged any relationship between us. He warned me against seeing you."

Katherine suppressed a shiver. "He warned me about you, too."

"What did he say?"

"The gist was you have issues and you're not good for any woman."

Jake's eyes twinkled. "I already told you that." He put down the carton and peered at her with suspicion. "Something's wrong. What happened?"

Katherine cleared her throat. "I was about to call again when you arrived. I found Tiffani's name in the patient files at the clinic."

Jake sat up straight. "Holy shit, Katherine."

Katherine held up her hand. "I know what you're thinking, and this doesn't prove anything."

Jake's expression darkened. "Like hell. Ingalls treated her. They have a connection."

"So do lots of others. I only saw Tiffani's name and can't access the entire file without Jeremy or Diana discovering I've been snooping around. Even if I could, there may be nothing suspicious in it. When Jeremy first arrived in Sandy Shoals, he worked under a grant at the women's prison and held group therapy sessions. Connie told us Tiffani received counseling there."

Jake slammed a fist on the table. "I knew

something was off with this guy."

"We don't have anything, except a tenuous connection to one of the victims. Jeremy had already moved from Sandy Shoals when Tina was attacked and Bethany murdered."

"Yeah, but New York is only a plane ride away. You can't tell me you don't feel we're on the right track."

Katherine rubbed her forehead with a sigh. "Yes, I do especially after today, but feelings aren't proof he's a serial killer. Jeremy wasn't the only one who worked under that grant at the prison. Tiffani could have been seen by other counselors, too."

Jake glowered. "After Tiffani's name was made public, Ingalls didn't mention to anyone at the station he knew her."

"No." Katherine shuddered. "Not to me either."

"You can't go back there."

"I can't quit my job. Besides, we have nothing to tie Lacey or any of the others to Jeremy. Do the police have any grounds for an arrest or even to obtain a warrant to search his house?"

"No," sputtered Jake, "but we're talking about a serial killer."

"What do you expect me to do?" Katherine said, temper rising. "Leave town because of a hunch?"

"I expect you to listen to me!"

Her jaw tightened. "I won't turn away from Tiffani and the other women."

"Katherine, you're in over your head—"

"Stop shouting."

"I'm not shouting," Jake shouted. "I'm arguing loudly to try to force sense into your thick skull."

The tension slipped from her body. Katherine lips formed a weak smile. "It's not working."

"I hear that." Jake took her hand. "I couldn't live with the guilt if anything happened to you."

Her smile widened. "Nothing will. Would it help if I brought my suspicions to Lt. Saldana?"

"Not yet. We don't have solid evidence and Ingalls is a local boy with a lot of pull. His family has money and connections. Hell, he went to high school with most of the city council. Ethan told me, though, Saldana's getting fed up with him, too. When we have a story that doesn't sound crazy, she'll listen."

"We need proof." Katherine regarded him kindly. "Have you seen Bethany today?"

Jake shook his head. "I went into the parlor, but nothing. Not even the sense of a presence. It's almost as if she's waiting."

"For me?"

He shrugged. "You're her counselor. Could be she's more comfortable talking to you." A pained look crossed his face.

Katherine squeezed his hand. "You're afraid, Bethany hasn't forgiven you yet."

"Let's just say, it would be nice to hear her whisper, 'It's not your fault.' " His fingers entwined with hers. "We move carefully now. No more sneaking through the files, Katherine. Too much chance of getting caught. Ingalls is smart. The last thing we want to do is arouse his suspicions." His gaze drifted to their clasped hands. His voice tightened. "I don't want you to go back there. I can't think of any way to stop you."

Color rose to her cheeks. "I have patients depending on me, both alive and dead."

"Katherine—"

"If Jeremy gets an inkling we suspect him, he can get rid of the jewelry, cover his tracks. The best thing for us to do is to act normal."

"Normal?" His voice held a bitter edge. "So you continue to smile at him sweetly while I become a mindless bobble head at our sessions and nod enthusiastically at everything he says."

"Exactly."

Jake grimaced. "I'll try, but no guarantees." He released her hand and pushed back from the table.

"Where are you going?" said Katherine. "You didn't finish eating."

"I'm not hungry. I need to get to work, find out what I can about Ingalls—discreetly, of course."

Katherine swallowed her disappointment. "I'll walk you to the truck."

Jake had parked in an out-of-the-way spot next to the trash bin. "Well, goodnight." He tucked an errant strand of hair behind her ear. "I mean it, Katherine. Don't even think of trying to get into those files again. No attention."

"Sheesh, I heard you, Dad," she joshed. "Goodnight."

They gazed at each other. A smile twitched at Jake's lips. He leaned toward her. Katherine rose on her toes, meeting him halfway. Her hand slid up his chest. He wrapped his arms around her waist and drew her close.

Their lips met in a long kiss. Jake took a breath and nuzzled her ear sending a shiver of delight through Katherine. "Behind a garbage can reeking of old takeout," he murmured lightly, "is not exactly my top pick for a romantic rendezvous."

"You never thought to bring a woman here?" she joshed. "What's wrong with you?"

"Never found it so hard to say goodnight to one before this."

Katherine's face warmed. "You're welcome back inside. I'm sure it'll be fine with Whiskers."

Jake pulled her close, resting his cheek on the top of her head. "Damn, Katherine, you're a distraction. I keep telling myself this is a bad time to get involved, and then you start working your feminine wiles."

Katherine chuckled. "I have wiles? Good to know."

Jake's head rose. He squinted into the dark over Katherine's shoulder.

"What is it?" asked Katherine turning around.

"A car," he murmured. "Dark sedan. Didn't notice it before. Wait here. I'll check it out."

High beams winked on, catching them in a brilliant glare. With a squeal of rubber against asphalt, the car shot toward them.

"Look out!" yelled Jake. He yanked Katherine out of the way an instant before the car barreled past. The driver jerked the wheel and then sped off through the parking lot.

"Are you hurt?" barked Jake.

"I-I'm fine," Katherine stammered, pale and shaken. "Jake, you don't think…"

"Get back inside," he ordered, opening the driver's side door.

Katherine jumped into the passenger seat. "Not a chance."

"Katherine—"

"Yell later," she shouted. "The driver's getting

away."

With a stifled curse, Jake tore from the parking space. The sedan turned hard right into the street. Jake whipped out his phone. "Ethan, I'm in pursuit of a speeding car northbound on Magnolia Avenue...no, I'm not kidding...call it in...dark sedan...Florida plates, can't make out the numbers yet..."

A horned blared. Brakes squealed. Katherine held her breath as the sedan narrowly missed a car. She craned her neck. "I don't see him."

"I do...damn it...Ethan, he just made the turn onto Tenth Avenue. He may be headed for the interstate." Jake gunned the engine, weaving past cars. Avoiding an intersection, he cut through the parking lot of a strip mall and onto a cross street. Another sharp turn and they were back on the car's tail. As the truck inched closer, the sedan passed under a streetlight.

Katherine squinted. "I can make out the plate number...JMU-457."

The traffic light ahead changed to red. Cars in front of the sedan slowed to a stop. "Got you now, you sonuvabitch," Jake muttered.

The sedan veered hard right. The undercarriage hit the curb with a shower of sparks as the car bounced onto the sidewalk. Pedestrians scattered in terror.

Katherine gripped the armrest, her mouth dry. "He's running the red light."

As she spoke, the sedan rocketed through the intersection, the driver mindless of oncoming traffic.

"No!" Katherine flinched as a minivan making a turn swerved to avoid a collision. It ran into an SUV coming from the opposite lane. As they hit, both cars spun in a half-circle blocking traffic. The sedan tore down the street, turned a corner, and disappeared from view.

Jake pulled off into a parking lot. "Ethan, I'm at 10th and Oak. Accident with injuries…"

Katherine jumped from the truck and ran to the intersection. Broken glass littered the asphalt. Her stomach muscles clenched at the sound of a crying baby coming from the minivan. A woman in the driver's seat stared in a daze. The remnants of the deflated airbag hung limply from the steering wheel. Katherine jerked at the handle in the mangled chassis, but the door refused to budge. "Are you hurt?" she shouted.

"I-I don't think so. My…my baby…"

"I'll check on him. Don't worry. Help is on the way."

Katherine darted to the passenger side, breathing a sigh of relief when the door opened. She crawled into the backseat. "Shush," she crooned. "It's all right, sweetheart. I know, I know, that was a big scary noise, huh?" After a quick examination, her relief soared. The child was buckled snuggly into the car seat with no sign of injuries. Katherine gently stroked his forehead and his cries reduced to snuffling whimpers. "Everything will be okay. I'll check on your mom now."

The blare of multiple sirens neared. Katherine crawled into the front passenger seat and took the woman's hand. "My name is Katherine. I can't see any injuries on your son, but don't want to take him out of the car seat. Hear the sirens? The paramedics will be here soon. How are you feeling?"

"O-okay, I guess. My chest hurts. So does my face."

"You were whammed by the airbag and will

probably be sore for days. I'm going to unbuckle the seatbelt, but don't move yet. The paramedics will check and make sure nothing's broken. Is there someone I can call for you?"

"My husband. The phone's in my purse." Her voice caught in her throat. "That bastard... H-he could have killed us. What was he thinking?"

Hands trembling with rage, Katherine snatched the woman's purse from the floor of the van. "No clue, but I hope he gets what's coming to him."

\*\*\*\*

Jake stood in the middle of controlled chaos. Flashing lights from a bevy of ambulances, fire trucks, and police cruisers illuminated the intersection.

Ethan nodded toward a squad car. "Saldana's here. She's not wearing her happy face. Did she speak to you yet?"

"Just enough to get a preliminary report." Jake's gaze strayed to April standing next to Katherine. "Sorry I ruined your dinner date."

Ethan gave a wry chuckle. "Are you kidding? I offered April an exclusive on-site story of a car accident involving multiple vehicles. You scored me big bonus points, my man." He regarded him sharply. "So who was this guy?"

"I told you we didn't see his face."

"A random maniac who decides for no reason to run you two over?"

"Something like that."

"Damn it, Jake, you're my partner. Tell me what's going on."

*This is the same guy that killed at least four women and attacked Tina Delaney. The car he drove tonight once belonged to Tiffani, and he used it to dump their bodies. And I have no doubt who he is.* Jake said nothing and clenched his fists.

"Sumner!" Lt. Saldana stood by her squad car. "With me."

Jake caught Ethan's sympathetic look and his heart sank. *This can't be good.*

"What the hell were you thinking?" Saldana snapped. "You're on desk duty and had no authority to chase a suspect, especially through traffic. You're damn lucky all the injuries are minor."

Jake let out a protest. "I followed procedure, Lieutenant. I called it in. The driver of the sedan was the one who nearly killed those people. You've got their statements—"

"I'm not done, Sumner." Her face was dark with anger. "Your badge."

"Lieutenant—"

She held out her hand. "Now."

Jake's lips set in a thin tight line. He took the badge from his pocket and gave it to her.

"As of this moment, you're on suspension pending a full disciplinary hearing. I don't want you at the precinct." The lieutenant's harshness softened. "I'm sorry, Jake. I have no choice."

Jake's hands clenched. Everything he worked so hard for was slipping away. "I'm not the one at fault here."

"You think I don't know that? We've got a system in place. I've been trying to circumvent Ingalls and get you back on duty, but this incident doesn't make it any easier."

"Since I'm suspended, can I tell him to shove his

sessions up his ass?"

"Damn it, Jake, this isn't funny. What the hell is it between you two?" Her gaze drifted toward Katherine. "Is it personal?"

Jake sighed. "Nothing I can prove."

"But you have suspicions? Something doesn't sit right?"

Jake pressed his lips together. Saldana glanced down at the badge in her hand. "Go home. Stay away from the precinct and Ingalls. I'll call you when the hearing is scheduled. The chief is bound to contact Ingalls for his opinion on you."

Jake glowered. "I can imagine that conversation."

Saldana tucked his badge in her pocket and cleared her throat. "Don't forget you have friends on the force. When you're ready to talk, there are people who will listen. That's all I'll say on the matter."

The lieutenant got into her car. Jake watched her drive off, her last words ringing in his head. They almost sounded like an offer to help.

"Sorry, Lieutenant," he murmured. "I won't drag you or the department into my mess."

**\*\*\*\***

Katherine's heart sank as she watched from across the street. "The lieutenant took his badge."

"She had to," said Ethan kindly.

"I'm sure he'll get it back," said April.

Katherine turned to Ethan. "Is that true?"

He held her gaze for a moment and then glanced away.

"It's not fair," Katherine protested. "Nothing that happened is Jake's fault. He's only trying to help."

Jake walked over to them. His expression held no

emotion, but to Katherine the hurt poured out with each step. "Suspended," he said tersely.

"I'm sorry, man," said Ethan.

"I'll take you home, Katherine," said Jake.

"Wait." Her anger soared. "I won't let him get away with this."

Ethan jumped on her words. "You know who was in the car." He turned to Jake. His eyes narrowed. "So do you."

"Katherine." Jake's voice held a definite warning note. "Don't."

She motioned to April and Ethan. "They both have contacts and can gather information. Ethan can work from inside the force while the rest of us work from the outside. I'm sorry, Jake. It's time you realize, the solution to every problem doesn't rest on your shoulders. We both know who's responsible. I'm telling them." She turned to Ethan and April. "Jeremy Ingalls isn't the man he appears to be."

Chapter 20

April's eyes went wide. "Your boss?"

Katherine shuffled her feet. "I can't go into details because of client confidentiality, but I received information from a patient. Jeremy is a murderer, responsible for the deaths of Lacey Calder, Tiffani Nolan, and others. I also think he assaulted Tina years ago, and that was the real reason she left town."

April gasped. "Tell me this is a joke."

"I'm afraid not."

Ethan was clearly taken aback. "Katherine, if Ingalls committed a series of crimes and people are in imminent danger, you have a duty to report it, client confidentiality or not."

"She has no proof," said Jake quickly, "only hearsay."

"Did you see him in the car?"

"No," admitted Katherine with reluctance, "but Jeremy has my address." She described the incident in the parking lot. "The car tried to run us down right after he warned Jake and me to stay away from each other. It must have been Jeremy."

Ethan's eyes gleamed. "He threatened you? That's probable cause—"

Jake jumped in. "Nothing he said will stand up in court or get a judge to issue a warrant. Hell, the department can't even start an investigation. I've made my feelings about Ingalls public. Poking into his background now will sound like harassment."

"Not from me," said April with a cheeky grin. "I only come across as annoying. What have you got?"

Ethan glanced around the crowded intersection. "Not here."

"The studio is two blocks over," said April. "I have the keys. Ethan and I will meet you there."

"I'm in enough trouble," said Jake to Ethan. "I won't drag you down with me."

He clapped him on the shoulder. "Too late, besides, this is my choice."

"Mine, too," said April. "Tina was a friend."

Katherine walked to the truck with Jake. They got inside, the tension so thick it practically hovered between them like a dark cloud. "You're angry."

Jake turned the key, and then rammed the stick into drive. "Damn right, I'm angry. You had no right to involve them."

"April and Ethan are grown-ups. They can make their own decisions."

"What do you plan to tell them?

"Not that I got my information from your dead ex-girlfriend, that's for damn sure. We need them to believe us."

"They're not stupid. They won't buy that tip-from-a-patient jazz forever."

"The story only has to hold long enough to discover substantial evidence against Jeremy. Ethan can take it from there." Katherine shot a glance at him, but couldn't read his expression in the dark.

They arrived at GAB-TV, and Jake parked the truck. April and Ethan waited at the studio entrance with Parker and Connie.

"Oh, great," muttered Jake. "They must have been inside. Why not host an open house while we're at it?" He glared at Katherine. "You should have kept quiet."

Katherine bristled. "I couldn't. It hurts too much to see you shoulder unnecessary blame when others are willing to help. Besides, the Pratts have a right to hear about Tiffani." She slammed the truck door and stormed away. "You can lose the snotty attitude. We're on your side, Jake."

Jake ran after Katherine, grabbed her arm, and jerked her to a halt. "I'm on yours. Ingalls is a stone cold killer who has taken an unhealthy interest in you, Kathy. He almost killed you tonight…"

She read the agony in his eyes and her anger died. "This isn't your fault."

Parker walked up to them. "Is there a problem?"

"I'm trying to convince Katherine not to be pig-headed." Jake grunted. "It's not working."

"Young man," said Parker, eyes twinkling. "I've been married over thirty years. My advice is save your breath. When a woman is this passionate on a subject, it's best to simply agree and get on with it. Saves time all around." His voice softened. "You have information about Tiffani's murder?"

Jake sighed. "I give up. Let's go inside."

They sat at the table in the breakroom. Katherine and Jake took turns filling in the others with their suspicions.

Ethan shook his head after they finished. "You have a whole lot of nothing as far as evidence, my friend."

"Told you," said Jake. "It's a good story, but little

more."

"One I apparently can't tell to anyone else," said April with a wry tone. "You're killing me."

"Not a peep, April," said Katherine. "I can't back up any of these claims." She cleared her throat. "Client-patient privilege and all."

April raised an eyebrow. "Do I act as if I want to be sued by Ingalls for slander? He's loaded. I'm not. How can you even draw a connection to Tina and Bethany since Ingalls had already moved to New York?"

"Actually," said Parker, "he made frequent trips to town. I distinctly remember several times when I saw Jeremy at meetings of the Ingalls Trust with his father. I can find out the dates he attended. Want to bet they correspond with the attack on Tina and Bethany's murder?"

"It's still circumstantial," murmured Jake, "but at least it puts him in the area."

"Get me his financials," said Connie. "I'll find airline ticket purchases."

"Connie," said Katherine. "You told me Tiffani received counseling. Did she ever meet with Ingalls?"

"She only mentioned sessions the one time Parker and I visited her in prison and she didn't give us any names."

Parker's brow furrowed. "Didn't she also mention a halfway house?"

Jake and Ethan looked at each other. "Safe Harbor," they chorused.

"What's that?" asked Katherine.

"It's a privately funded nonprofit rehabilitation program," said Jake, "for female inmates after release from prison. Safe Harbor is a halfway house targeted toward nonviolent offenders on parole, specifically designed for those with substance abuse habits."

Katherine cocked her head. "Like prostitutes with drug convictions?"

"Exactly."

"Safe Harbor," murmured Connie. "That's Isabelle Addams' pet project. She's a member of Saint Anne's. Her daughter died of a drug overdose several years ago. After that, Isabelle founded Safe Harbor. The church has done several fundraisers. Why wouldn't she mention Tiffani's involvement to me? Oh." Connie's face paled. "At the prison, I made it clear to Tiffani not to contact us again unless she was clean for a year. She might have asked Isabelle not to say anything."

Parker squeezed her hand. "Don't blame yourself, Connie. At the time, we decided cutting Tiffani out of our lives was the best thing for both of us."

"I can talk to Mrs. Addams," offered Ethan, "and find out if any of the women at Safe Harbor were special friends of Tiffani."

April leaned in with an eager expression. "Can you get a warrant for Safe Harbor's files on what we have?"

Ethan shook his head. "It's not enough."

"The residents have criminal records," said Katherine. "They may not welcome talking to the police."

"I've found," murmured Parker, "most people have a basic need for their voices to be heard when they have a sympathetic ear like yours, Katherine. Women going through a recovery program will have more riveting tales than most." He turned to April with a twinkle in his eyes. "Know anyone with a cable access show?"

April wore an impish grin. "It just so happens, I do, and he always needs interesting guests." She sat back in the chair and gazed at the ceiling with a thoughtful expression. "What if I approach Mrs. Addams with the idea for a mini-documentary—a one-hour show on the lives of the women in Safe Harbor? Think she'd go for it?"

"An excellent suggestion," said Parker with growing excitement. "Programs such as that constantly need to develop new funding sources. Any publicity helps."

"What if Mrs. Addams says no?" chimed in Ethan.

"Seriously? To me *and* Parker?" April eyed him with such blatant disbelief, Katherine bit her lip to keep from smiling.

"Isabelle will agree," insisted Parker. "She's a smart woman and will realize a documentary can do a lot of good. By the way, she's firmly in favor of rehabilitation over incarceration."

"Sounds like a person I want to meet anyway," said Katherine. "I'd be happy to talk to her, too."

"That's settled," said Jake to Ethan, "so now I need a big favor."

"You got it."

He grinned. "Wait until I ask. Bring me what you can find on Ingalls without attracting attention. If you're caught, Saldana will probably skip suspension and go straight to instant dismissal from the force for both of us."

Ethan shrugged. "So I won't get caught."

"What do you hope to find?" Katherine asked.

"Ingalls left no clues, covered his tracks, and has everyone fooled. He's never been a suspect before—

never even questioned. He has a false sense of security, and somewhere, somehow he made a mistake." Jake glowered. "Ingalls is clever, but he's not smarter than all of us put together."

"He's dangerous though," said April softly. She reached out and squeezed Katherine's hand. "Don't go home. Stay at my place. Ingalls can't find you there. My landlady doesn't allow pets, but, screw it, we'll sneak in Whiskers when her back is turned."

"That's a good idea," chimed in Jake, "but Whiskers can stay with me." He shot Katherine a veiled look. "He's been to my house already and doesn't mind its quirks."

Katherine accepted with gratitude. In truth, the thought of spending the night alone left her cold. So did the disappointment that Jake didn't invite her to Culpepper Lane first.

Jake drove Katherine home. Her heart pounded as they reached the parking lot, but there was no sign of the sedan. Whiskers met them at the door with a welcoming purr. Jake ordered Katherine to step aside. He entered ahead of her and checked the apartment.

"You think Jeremy is hiding under the bed?" Katherine teased after he allowed her inside. "We're two flights up and he isn't a cat burglar. Besides, I have a funny feeling if Jeremy so much as poked his nose past the threshold, we'd have bloodstains on the floor. Whiskers would be curled on the couch with a self-satisfied smirk gnawing on a severed finger."

"Can't be too careful," Jake said. "Grab your stuff."

Ten minutes later, Katherine had a suitcase packed and ready to go. She and Jake gathered Whisker's things, and then once again, Jake led the way to the parking lot. Katherine held her breath as he stepped into the open. She let it out with a rush after he signaled all clear.

Jake placed the suitcase in her car and the cat carrier with Whiskers in the truck. He hadn't said much since they left the studio.

"Still mad at me for telling the others?" asked Katherine.

"A little," he grunted. "Okay, maybe not so much. Maybe even not at all, now."

"Ah, Jake Sumner accepts help at last," she said lightly. "That's a first. I see hope for you yet."

A faint smile twitched around his lips. "What can I say? I'm a work in progress. Get going. I'll follow you."

They drove to April's duplex a few blocks from the television station. April waited at the door and grabbed the suitcase from Katherine. "I've got this." Her voice dropped and she winked. "Go say goodbye already—to Whiskers, I mean."

Katherine and Jake walked to the truck. She stuck her hand in the window, poked a finger through a slat in the carrier and rubbed Whiskers' head. He closed his eyes and leaned into her. "I feel as if I'm abandoning him."

"He'll be fine." Jake cleared his throat. "I planned to ask you to my place, but April jumped the gun."

The heat rushed to Katherine's cheeks. "You were?"

"Yeah. It's probably better this way. April has a point. Ingalls won't find you here. I feel better someone is with you at night and my house…" He blew out his cheeks in exasperation. "Well, you know, dead ex-girlfriend hanging around. Not exactly the best way for this relationship to progress."

Katherine chuckled. "Don't forget. You're host to a psychic cat now, too."

"Wow, that makes me feel so much better. Fortunately, I also have a gun—my own, not my service weapon. I'm not defenseless. But you..." Jake brushed a hand against her cheek.

Katherine's heart skipped a beat. "I have my rapier sharp wit." She leaned down and whispered to Whiskers, "Jake is a bit of a pill, but take care of him for me."

Jake slipped an arm around Katherine's waist and pulled her into a long kiss. "Be careful, tomorrow. Ingalls..."

"Won't realize I suspect a thing."

Chapter 21

Katherine gripped the steering wheel, peering at the rear entrance of the Sandy Shoals Counseling Center. Her brave words made so much sense last night. All she had to do was face Jeremy without giving away any of her suspicions. Katherine licked her lips, mouth suddenly dry. *Deep breaths. Stay calm and composed.*

Her phone chimed with an incoming text from Jake. *Call from your office so I know you're safe.*

Katherine smiled. Five little words, *so I know you're safe*, could make all the difference in a person's attitude. Her gaze returned to the building. She squared her shoulders. *He won't suspect a thing.*

Jeremy's red sports car pulled into the parking lot with Diana right behind him. Katherine got out of her car and waited for them by the door. "Deep breaths," she murmured.

"Did you hear about the big accident on 10th and Oak last night?" asked Diana as she unlocked the door. "It was all over the news."

"That's not far from your place," said Jeremy.

Katherine caught and held his gaze. *Show no fear. No emotion.* "Practically around the corner. The news report sounded awful."

Diana shook her head as they stepped inside. "People should be more careful. Your whole life can change in an instant. One bad decision can lead a person down the wrong road, but I suppose if it didn't," she added lightly, "we'd all be out of work." She looked at Jeremy. "Think they'll catch the driver?"

"Perhaps, but there aren't any traffic cameras on that corner."

Katherine raised an eyebrow. "How do you know?"

For an instant, the mask slipped, and then Jeremy gave them a charming smile. "Friends on the force."

"Jeremy has a lead foot," chuckled Diana. "Don't ever get in a car with him. You'll take your life in your hands."

"Speaking of the police," said Jeremy. "I received an email from Lt. Saldana last night. It appears Detective Sumner has been suspended pending an investigation."

Diana sighed. "That doesn't sound good."

Jeremy's gaze went to Katherine. "I wonder what happened?"

"I'm sure Lt. Saldana will fill you in, if she thinks it's necessary."

"I'm not sure it is," said Jeremy coolly. "I have a feeling Detective Sumner won't be a police officer much longer. Certain people simply aren't cut out for law enforcement."

Katherine hurried to her office and called Jake.

He picked up on the first ring. "How'd it go?"

"Jeremy got word of your suspension. He said Saldana emailed him."

"Is that so? Interesting…did you mention nearly getting run down in the parking lot?"

"No, and Diana was the one who asked if I heard about the accident. Jeremy definitely knew it was close to my apartment though." Her voice hardened. "He had a smug tone when he said your name. Made me want to spit in his eye."

Jake chuckled. "Nice to know I continue to piss him off. Ingalls wanted Sapphire's murder forgotten by now and here we've brought to light two other victims. He must wonder if the police have anything to tie them together and doesn't dare show too much interest in how they're related or run the risk of raising suspicion." His voice was momentarily drowned out by the roar of traffic.

"Is that a bus?" asked Katherine. "Where are you?"

"Look out your window."

Katherine raised the blind. "I don't see…"

"Across the street. Alley next to the dry cleaner." Jake stepped from the shadows, grinned, and then disappeared out of sight again. "I'm keeping an eye on you, Fleming."

Warmth rushed through her. "You can't stay there the whole day."

"No, but I had to make sure you got in safe. As soon as we hang up, I'm on the way to meet Ethan. The license plate was a bust—it had been reported stolen. He pulled financials on Ingalls. Connie is also a CPA and offered to wade through the paperwork with me."

"Not so bad having help, is it?"

"Yeah, you're a bad influence." Jake paused. "Use your instincts, Kathy. If anything about Ingalls' actions sets off warning bells get out of the office immediately and head to the TV station."

"I promise. You be careful, too."

"I will. Until tonight then. Whiskers told me to say he misses you."

Katherine smiled. "That's nice to hear. I miss him, too. How did he settle in?"

"Just fine. I keep the parlor door open and put his bed under the mirror. He was napping when I left."

"Bethany?"

"Not a peep. I guess she likes cats."

****

Jake tossed another stack of papers on the pile. He leaned back in the chair, stretching his arms over his head to release the kink in his shoulder muscles. He and Connie had been sequestered in her office at the station for most of the day. "Ingalls sure likes to spend. How many credit cards does he have?"

"Five for personal use," said Connie, "and one for the business account, but I haven't examined that closely yet. The man enjoys living large," she murmured. "He has a multi-million-dollar home on the water and all the requisite toys."

"That's not out of the ordinary," said Jake. "He owns a successful practice."

"The practice isn't big enough yet to pay the bills," said Connie, "especially the way Jeremy loves the high life. Prentiss was a successful real estate developer, but left the bulk of his holdings in a charitable trust with a smaller amount in a separate trust set aside for his son. After his father's death, Jeremy started to receive regular monthly checks, but doesn't hold onto the money long. Most of the payout is gone by the end of the month and his savings are nearly nil. My guess is that's why he decided to expand the practice—to bring in extra cash."

"His father's death sure was fortunate," murmured Jake.

Connie leaned toward him. "Think there's more to that?"

"I have no idea, but am naturally suspicious of new money."

"Ingalls' business license is relatively new," added Connie. "I plan to dig deeper in the center's financials and might uncover something useful."

Jake's eyes gleamed. "Can the feds nail him on tax fraud?"

Connie chuckled. "How do you think they finally nabbed Al Capone?" She gazed at the piles of paperwork. "We'll find proof. We have to. I owe it to Tiffani. I couldn't help her when she was alive."

"You can't blame yourself for her death either," said Jake kindly.

"I don't. Tiffani made her own choices. So did Bethany." She jabbed him in the arm. "So stop eating yourself up. That's an order from one who's already been there, done that."

Jake grinned. "You sound like Katherine."

"She gives good advice. She's kind, too. She called a few times since the funeral to see how I was doing." Connie drew in a trembling breath. "Tiffani was no angel, but in those last few months tried to start fresh. I don't hold any illusions. She might have failed and returned to the streets, but Ingalls stole her chance. He needs to pay."

Jake gave her hand a squeeze. "This bastard will go down for all of them. I promise."

April bounded into the room with Parker. "We have an appointment to talk with Mrs. Addams." She gestured toward Parker. "He schmoozed her."

Parker's eyes gleamed. "It's what I do best. The

documentary definitely piqued her interest. April and I will meet Katherine at Isabelle's home at three o'clock." Parker glanced at his watch. "We should get going."

"I need to grab my purse," said April. "Oh, Jake, I just spoke to Ethan, and he asked me to pass on a message. He's got a lead on the guy Katherine saw at the bus stop that day with Lacey Calder."

\*\*\*\*

Katherine glanced at her phone—plenty of time. She locked the office and headed to the door.

Jeremy stood by Diana at the front desk. "Leaving?" he asked.

Katherine forced a cheerful response. "Yes, I just finished my last appointment and have errands to run."

"Five clients today," said Diana cheerfully, "and one of them is brand new. Your calendar is filling up, Katherine." She turned to Jeremy with a teasing grin. "You won't have to fire her, Jeremy."

"She does seem to be a good fit for the office." He glanced out the window. "The weather is warming. Why don't you two come to my house this Saturday and we can go out in the new speedboat? Lots of small islands dot the inlet past the reef. The whole area is secluded, accessible only to boaters. Why no one would ever suspect we were even there."

Goosebumps crawled up Katherine's arms. *He's toying with me.* "Sorry, I'm afraid I'm not a good sailor."

"Neither am I, Jeremy," said Diana with clear disappointment.

"That's a pity," he said. "How about dinner instead?"

"I already made plans."

"Next weekend?"

"I'll let you know. Gotta run." Katherine slung her purse over her shoulder and dashed out the door. Her hands shook as she gripped the steering wheel, the conversation ringing in her head. Surely, the invitation had been to gauge her reaction. *How do I keep him at arm's length because there's no way in hell I'm going to his house?*

Katherine sat up straight. What about Diana? Her attraction to Jeremy was obvious. She hung on every word. *Should I hint at my suspicions?*

Her gaze went to the building. She would surely take them straight to Jeremy. Katherine tapped her finger on the wheel. Diana was much older than any of the victims, near Jeremy's age. Even in his public life, he preferred hot young eye candy to decorate his arm. Her attitude toward him was more motherly. She tended his needs. He basked in her fussing. He wouldn't target Diana as a threat or a person in need of saving.

Katherine squirmed in the seat. Would he?

She brushed aside misgivings. No, Diana was safe. Katherine started the car and drove to a subdivision filled with large, well-kept homes. Parker and April waved to her from a driveway and Katherine parked behind them. "Waiting long?"

"Just got here," said April. She eyed the pleasant surroundings with approval. "Nice, huh? Didn't expect a woman who ran a program for ex-offenders to have such fancy digs."

"When Isabelle's daughter died of a drug overdose," said Parker, "no rehabilitation programs existed specifically geared for young women. Isabelle started the Safe Harbor Foundation and built the halfway house for newly-released convicts with drug convictions. Since then, the recidivism rate for those enrolled in the program dropped remarkably."

The front door opened and a middle-aged woman came out to greet them. Isabelle Addams had a firm handshake and a straight-forward demeanor. Katherine warmed to her immediately.

Isabelle led them to her office and poured cups of tea. "My condolences about Tiffani," she said to Parker. "I was out of town and didn't hear the news until I returned, so I missed the service. Tiffani was one of the first in the Safe Harbor program. I had high hopes for her. She worked hard on her recovery. As a matter of fact, I encouraged Tiffany to contact Connie when she moved to the halfway house, but Tiffani refused. She wouldn't even let me tell Connie she was in the program. Tiffany had relapsed so many times before she didn't want anyone to know until she was sure this time rehab would stick. After she left the halfway house, we lost touch."

"You assume she relapsed," said Katherine.

A wave of sadness seemed to flow from her. "We can't save them all."

"You didn't file a missing person report?"

"Tiffani completed the program. She was an adult, free to come and go as she chose. I wish now I had."

"Don't take it to heart," said Parker kindly. "No one suspected what had happened."

Katherine sipped her tea. "What kind of counseling do the women receive?"

"We use support groups at the correctional facility," said Isabelle. "Those that complete the program can apply to the halfway house in town. We only have ten beds and I'd love to expand, but don't have either the space or the funding."

A hard set came to Isabelle's jaw. "I'll let you in on a little secret. In this soulless political climate, it's much easier to get money for a new prison than convince people an expansion of social services programs is more effective and cheaper in the long run than locking people behind bars." She shot a coy look at Katherine. "I'm always hunting for volunteers to help draft funding proposals. A person with counseling experience would be particularly helpful."

Katherine chuckled. "I'd be happy to. I've only been in Sandy Shoals a few months and want to get more involved in the community." She cleared her throat. "I work with Dr. Jeremy Ingalls. He mentioned the correctional facility. Has he ever been involved with Safe Harbor?"

"Oh, yes. We can't afford him now, but he came to us in the early days of the program. County social services awarded Safe Harbor a grant to fund group therapy at the prison. We had several counselors, but the money has since run out. Now we rely on volunteers, but Dr. Ingalls began his new practice, and I couldn't talk him into returning."

"Do you happen to recall," said Katherine with an innocent tone, "if Tiffani was in his group?"

"Not offhand. Why?"

Katherine hesitated and Parker jumped in. "Connie and I want to thank him in person for trying to help."

"I can check." Isabelle leaned forward with an eager light in her eyes. "Now tell me more about this documentary."

**\*\*\*\***

Jake texted Katherine with an invitation to dinner at his house after the meeting. As soon as he opened the door, Whiskers wrapped himself around her legs. Katherine leaned over to scratch his ears and then motioned toward the parlor. "Any news from you-know-who?"

"Not even a single degree drop in temperature," said Jake. "Why don't we eat dinner first before we go inside?"

They went to the kitchen. Most of the cabinets had been removed. The refrigerator was still plugged in next to a folding table holding a hotplate, toaster oven and coffeemaker. As Jake dished out spaghetti from a pot on the hotplate, Katherine described the meeting with Isabelle Addams.

"What's your opinion of her?" asked Jake.

"I'm in awe. She built the whole program from nothing, plus she's gung-ho on the documentary. Not that I had any doubt with both April and Parker in the room. Between Parker's charm and April persistence, those two could convince the Pope to officiate at a gay wedding."

"So you're in?"

"Yup, and," Katherine added with a grin, "I want to help Isabelle get additional funding for Safe Harbor, so I don't feel guilty about taking advantage of her goodwill. Win-win. She's giving me a tour of the halfway house."

"When do you go?" Jake asked.

"Saturday morning." She took another bite of spaghetti. "This is really good."

Jake wore a look of pretended affront. "Why sound

so surprised I can cook?"

"Because your kitchen qualifies as a disaster zone. I keep expecting to see a FEMA trailer parked in the backyard."

"It's amazing what you can do on a hotplate."

"I could have brought dinner, but this is much nicer."

"Sawdust and all?"

"Sawdust and all."

Jake's cell rang, and he glanced at the display. "It's Ethan."

As he answered the call, Katherine rose to refill her glass with iced tea. When she sat back down, Whiskers jumped into her lap. She stroked him absentmindedly, regarding Jake with growing curiosity. The conversation certainly captured his interest. Ethan did most of the talking. Jake posed an occasional terse question. His expression remained thoughtful, but the gleam in his eyes hinted something was definitely up.

He ended the call, and Katherine raised an eyebrow. "Trouble?"

"No, but I have two pieces of interesting news. First, Ethan said Saldana didn't email Ingalls with news of my suspension. It's possible the chief slipped the information. Ingalls called Saldana to say he heard I'd been involved in a police chase and seemed to fish for details. She asked Ethan why Ingalls had it in for me. Ethan said I had suspicions Ingalls wasn't totally legit."

Katherine's excitement rose. "That's good, isn't it?"

"Yes, if Saldana already has doubts concerning Ingalls' behavior, it will be easier for us to convince her to open an investigation into him when we get solid evidence."

"You said there were two pieces of news."

"Ethan tracked down Lacey's boyfriend, Gavin, the guy from the bus stop. They had, let's say, a short, fairly vocal relationship."

"Let me take a wild guess," said Katherine, tongue in cheek. "No violence, but tons of drama?"

"You nailed it. Gavin worked for a local electric company. Remember the late season ice storm in Tennessee that caused all the damage? The company offered to send people from here to supplement the workforce on the downed lines. Gavin volunteered to go. That jumpstarted an argument as the dumb ass happened to mention his ex-girlfriend lived in the stricken area. A few days later, Lacey called him and left a message. According to our timeline, that was the last time anyone heard from Lacey Calder."

Katherine shook her head. "Why didn't he contact the police sooner?"

"Lacey had reason to be jealous. Gavin immediately hooked up again with his ex. He took a new job at an electric company in Tennessee and only returned to Sandy Shoals to empty his apartment and move his things. He didn't call Lacey back or learn she was dead. Fortunately, he listened to the message before deleting it."

Katherine leaned in. "What did it say?"

"Lots of people talking in the background, Gavin said it was hard to hear. Then Lacey shouts over the noise, 'Hope you're happy with the skank because I'm having much more fun without you. I have to go. My date is getting impatient.' "

Katherine drew in a breath. "A man was with her."

"And we both know who," said Jake. "Given Lacey's social habits, she was probably at a club. If we can track down the location, we might find a witness who saw Ingalls and Lacey together. That's solid evidence he hid their relationship. After Isabelle Addams confirms Ingalls knew Tiffani, too, we can take everything to the lieutenant. It'll be enough to open an investigation."

Katherine's fingers tapped a beat on the table. "There must be scores of places along the coast."

"Yeah, but it's a new lead." Jake placed his hand on top of hers, stilling the impatient beat.

His gentle grip held comforting warmth. "Optimism from Jake Sumner?"

"We're getting closer, Katherine. I feel it."

Katherine startled as Whiskers jumped from her lap. He scampered across the floor and then paused to peer over his shoulder as if to say, "Well? Aren't you coming?" She exchanged a wary glance with Jake and then in unison both rose from their seats and chased after Whiskers. He darted down the hall to the French doors. Without pausing, Whiskers bolted into the parlor.

Katherine drew Jake to a halt in the foyer and cocked her head. Muffled musical tones wafted around them, and her brow wrinkled in a puzzled frown. "Do you own a stereo?"

"It's packed in a box," Jake said. "Why?"

"I hear music coming from inside."

## Chapter 22

They entered the parlor. Whiskers sat in his basket under the mirror, gazing at them with an inscrutable feline air. Katherine eyed the rumpled blankets and pillows on the couch with unexpected irritation. Jake was sleeping here? *So what? Why should it bother me? Bethany's hardly a rival.*

Jake went directly to the center of the room. "I don't hear any music."

Katherine tore her gaze from the couch and strained to listen. The distant chords of a guitar faded in and out. "A guitar…a man singing, but I can't make out words."

As if an amp suddenly switched on high, the music's volume soared to deafening levels. Katherine grimaced. Man, it was loud. She could barely think with the racket. Jake turned to her, mouth moving, but none of his words were audible over the pounding beat.

Katherine touched the mirror. "Bethany?" she shouted. "I can't hear you."

The room was dark. Strobe lights in the ceiling cast dizzying flashes across the dance floor.

"The man over there wants to buy you a drink."

Lacey Calder sat on a stool as the bartender gestured toward the other end of the bar. She leaned forward, dolphin necklace dangling in front of her cleavage. Katherine craned her neck to see who captured Lacey's attention, but the room was too crowded. Lacey tossed back her hair, flashed a broad smile at someone, and then turned to the bartender. "I'll have a shot of your most expensive whiskey."

The lights spun in a maddening whirl. The music increased in pitch and tempo. People raced by in an indistinct blur as if something gave time an impatient shove ahead. As quickly as it began, the odd temporal disturbance ended. Blurs became distinct shapes once more, the focus sharpened until Katherine discerned individual people. A singer on the stage with a guitar wailed into a microphone. "You can lead me to the water, but can't wash my sins away…" He ended the song on a complex riff, and the audience roared approval.

"Thank you," said the singer. "This is an awesome crowd."

"Hope you're happy with the skank, because I'm having so much more fun without you." Lacey walked across the dance floor holding a cellphone to her ear. "I have to go. My date is getting impatient." With a smug smile, she dropped the phone in her purse and then pushed her way through the crowd. Katherine followed as she made a beeline for a side exit.

Jeremy stood outside the door. His face lit up with a wide smile. "There you are. I thought you changed your mind."

Lacey's smile mimicked his. "Not a chance. I just had to powder my nose. So where's this party?"

"No!" Katherine screamed. "Run!" She reached out to grab Lacey, but her hand went through the woman's shoulder. With a cry of pain, Katherine clutched her fingers to her chest. They stung with an icy chill.

Jeremy tucked Lacey's arm in the crook of his elbow. "Not far. My car is over here."

Katherine jumped in front of Lacey. "Don't go with him!" Lacey's stride didn't falter. She passed through Katherine like her body was vapor. Katherine staggered, gasping for air, as a blast of arctic cold tore the breath from her lungs.

Lacey and Jeremy went directly to a dark blue sedan on the outskirts of the crowded parking lot. He opened the passenger door and with a gracious sweep of the arm gestured her inside.

Katherine watched in helpless rage. The futility of her actions bore down like a crushing weight. Lacey Calder's life had been over for weeks. Nothing she did now could change the outcome.

*Kathy...* Her grandfather's voice whispered in her ear. For an instant, it almost felt as if a gentle hand rested on her shoulder. *Tell Jake what you see.*

Katherine staggered across the asphalt, legs moving as if strung with lead weights.

The engine turned over. Jeremy backed from the parking space and straightened the wheels.

*Hurry, Kathy.*

Katherine shambled to a halt in the middle of the lane. The vehicle accelerated straight at her. Illumination from a streetlight at the exit picked up Jeremy behind the wheel. He spoke to Lacey and brandished a charming smile. She fiddled with the dolphin pendant around her neck and laughed.

Katherine braced, gritting her teeth. The car bumper flew through her legs, and pain washed over her in a wave. Katherine's body floated by the front seat, the back, the trunk. Shards of icy cold plucked at her skin as if they were fingers made from glass. She gasped at an agonizing jolt. A shovel in the trunk with a rusty red blade went into the front of her knees and out the other side without leaving a mark.

Katherine turned around as the rear bumper sped by, the license plate now clearly visible, Florida tag KK7-29H.

Lights blurred, dimmed, and then sharpened into focus again. Katherine blinked. She was in a paneled room. On one side was a computer monitor. Attached to a wall were license plates from New York and Florida. From four, dangled a piece of jewelry; a silver cross, a diamond pendent, a filigree locket, and one pair of long, gaudy gold earrings.

The door opened. Jeremy entered with a hammer and a Florida license plate in hand, KK7-29H. He nailed it to the wall next to the others, and then reached inside a pocket to retrieve a necklace with a dolphin charm. Jeremy looped it over the plate and then stood back with a faint smile playing about his lips. He flicked the dolphin with a finger and it swung back and forth. "That's my good girl."

The lights went out.

****

"Kathy!"

Jake's voice came from very far away.

"Kathy, damn it, answer me!"

Comforting warmth surrounded her. Katherine opened her eyes. She was in the parlor again with Jake's arms holding tight, her head against his chest. She straightened with a gasp. "I saw him. I saw Jeremy with Lacey. Same car, but he switches license plates."

Jake led her to the sofa. "Sit before you fall."

Katherine sagged into the cushions. Whiskers jumped into her lap while Jake sat next to her and put an arm around her shoulders. "Tell me what you saw."

Katherine drew a steadying breath. She described the vision, straining to recall the tiniest detail. Words spilled out before they faded from memory. Finally, she leaned against Jake with a sigh and rubbed her temples. "That's all I remember."

"It's enough for now," said Jake. "Did you notice the name of the bar?"

"No."

"How about the band? I might be able to track them through local music venues."

"No, sorry." She swallowed back a lump in her throat. "Jake, there were so many license plates, at least a dozen, most from New York—only five pieces of jewelry though, including Lacey's."

"Let's hope that means he only upped his game to murder when he returned to Florida and didn't leave a trail of bodies up north." Jake rested his cheek on her head. "Ingalls' secret is out now."

"We still have no proof," she moaned, "and no way to stop him."

"We have more information. Ethan can run the plate numbers and may get a hit. We'll check with New York, get police reports. I'm willing to bet we also uncover a string of sexual assaults, maybe DNA evidence."

Katherine paled. "Or the women could be dead."

"You only saw five sets of jewelry."

"Five…" Katherine's voice trembled. "Until now, I believed we had a chance to find Tina alive."

"Unlike the others, we know Tina wasn't dead

when he took her necklace. Don't give up hope." Jake's voice softened. "Can you drive? You should go home and relax."

"I'm fine now." Katherine shivered. "It feels as if I was stuck for a time in a weird dream."

Jake called Ethan. He and April were at her place. Jake followed Katherine to the duplex in his truck. Ethan and April met them out front. Jake handed him the list of license plate numbers and Ethan eyed him askance. "Care to tell me how you got these?"

"No. You'll have to trust me they're legit."

Ethan tucked the paper in his pocket. "I do, but you don't make it easy."

"I'm sorry. Let's just say I'd rather not have you decide your partner is crazy."

"Too late. I already do." Ethan turned sharp eyes to Katherine. "I don't suppose…"

"Sorry." She cleared her throat. "Can't say any more at the moment. Client confidentiality."

"That excuse is wearing mighty thin." Ethan glanced at the list. "All these are related to crimes?"

"Ingalls keeps souvenirs," said Jake. "My guess is he switches license plates each time, in case his car is spotted with the victim. If so, they represent a different sexual assault or murder."

"The room only had jewelry from five women," said Katherine.

April's eyes widened. "You say that as if you saw them firsthand."

Katherine pressed her lips together and flushed.

Ethan jumped in. "If you've been in this room, it's enough for a search warrant, especially with a description of the jewelry. None of that was released to the press."

"I haven't been there," Katherine said in a rush. "It may be in his house, but I can't be sure."

"But someone you know has been in that room." He threw up both hands in disgust. "Wait, don't tell me. Client confidentiality. Can't you convince the witness to come forward? Women's lives are at stake."

Katherine and Jake exchange glances. "Sorry," she said. "Not possible."

Ethan scowled. "You met this person, but won't tell your own partner?"

"Nothing Katherine and I discovered," said Jake, "will stand up in court or get a warrant. All I can say is if you knew how we got the details, it would taint the whole investigation. No one would ever believe our story or that Ingalls is behind the killings, and if word gets back to him, Ingalls will destroy or move the evidence. We need a way to prove he's the killer without involving this witness."

"You're saying," said April, "he or she is unreliable."

Jake's lips twisted in a faint grin. "That's putting it mildly."

Ethan blew out his cheeks in disgust. "Fine, I'll run the plates, but this is getting damn annoying. I'll call when I find something."

\*\*\*\*

Katherine walked Jake to his truck, and then glanced back to the duplex with a grin. "I wouldn't be surprised if April asked Ethan to be an overnight guest soon. I'm starting to feel like mom crashing the kids' make-out session."

Jake tucked a loose strand of hair behind her ear.

"It's not safe to go home yet."

"I can't stay here forever. April's great, but I miss my place. I miss my stuff. I miss Whiskers." Her expression set in grim determination. "I'll stay with April until the weekend and then Whiskers and I will move back to the apartment."

Jake opened his mouth as if to issue a protest, but Katherine held up a hand. "Don't argue. I have good security and won't let Jeremy past the front door. I'm also rational. After Tina, Jeremy focused his attention only on certain types of women; prostitutes and party girls. They weren't picky about the men in their lives. I am."

"Oh," he teased, "and how many men are there?"

Katherine chuckled. "Only one who constantly reminds me of his issues."

Jake pulled her close. "It doesn't mean you aren't in danger. If Ingalls suspects…"

"If I disappear, many people will ask questions. Besides, you're the only one who makes him nervous." Jake made a disbelieving face. "I'm serious," Katherine insisted. "Jeremy considers you as a threat, not me. That's why he warned me away. He wants you isolated, alone, and off the force. It must have given him quite a shock to discover your relationship to Bethany."

She rubbed her forehead. "Jeremy's actions make so much sense now. Why didn't I see the connection before?"

"Don't blame yourself," Jake scolded gently. "No one did. Ingalls has charmed folks for a long time. He had everyone fooled until now."

"That's why he kept you on a short leash with the department," said Katherine. "He doesn't want you to poke into Bethany's death or draw a connection to any of the other murders. He's wary and knows you already believe Pierson didn't kill Sapphire. He was afraid you'd find a way to reopen the investigation. That's the last thing Jeremy needs. He also knows you won't stop until the truth is out."

Jake held her close. "What I know is if he lays a hand on you, he'll answer to me."

\*\*\*\*

Katherine stared at the ceiling. Sleep proved elusive tonight. The vision of Lacey leaving the club arm in arm with Jeremy played through her mind in a continuous loop. *Think, Katherine. There must be another detail you missed.*

An idea shot into her head. Katherine sat up straight and grabbed her phone. *Eleven p.m. Not too late. He may still be awake. I have no clients tomorrow afternoon. Plenty of time to meet.* She scrolled through her contact list and sent a text. A few minutes later, he responded in the affirmative. A smile twitched at her lips. Katherine rolled over and snuggled under the covers.

\*\*\*\*

The next morning, Jake picked a surveillance spot in the shadows across from the parking lot behind the Sandy Shoals Counseling Center. Ingalls arrived, but instead of entering the building, he lingered by his car. A few minutes later, Katherine drove to a parking spot. Ingalls walked toward her. Jake abandoned his position and casually strolled across the asphalt. He caught Katherine's quizzical gaze over Ingalls' shoulder.

"Good morning, Doctor Ingalls," said Jake in his most cheerful manner. He nodded to her. "Katherine."

Ingalls startled and turned around.

"Good morning, Jake," said Katherine brightly. "What are you doing here today?"

"Just passing by. I have a lot of time of my hands lately and thought I'd take a walk." Jake noted with pleasure the slight tensing of Ingalls' facial muscles before the composed mask slipped into place.

"You're on suspension," said Ingalls sharply, "and have no reason to be here." He turned away. "Katherine, we should get going."

"Hang on a second," said Jake. "I keep thinking of Sapphire." He scratched his head. "Weird, huh? I thought I left her death in the past, but now it's bugging me again, almost an obsession. Shouldn't I talk to someone? How about you, Dr. Ingalls? Will you take me on as a private client?" He gazed at him with an innocent air. "I sense we made a personal connection already."

"I'm sorry." Ingalls' voice was flat and cold. "My calendar is full."

Jake shook his head. "That's a damn shame. I could use your advice. I don't like it when a person I know gets hurt. I don't like it at all..." His voice dropped. "I get this itch to act, and nothing makes it go away." He gave them a friendly smile. "Well, I won't keep you two any longer. Have a nice day."

\*\*\*\*

Jeremy watched Jake amble across the parking lot. His sour expression caused Katherine a rush of amusement. "Is something the matter, Jeremy?" she said with an ingenuous look. "You seem angry."

"Angry?" He coughed. "No, not in the least. I must need another cup of coffee. I hope Diana has the pot

248

ready."

Diana stood near the coffeemaker, stirring milk into her mug. After a terse, "Good morning," Jeremy poured a cup, hurried to his office, and shut the door.

Diana worried gaze followed him down the hall. "What's with him?"

Katherine shrugged. "Beats me. We ran into Detective Sumner outside. He asked Jeremy to take him as a private client, but he refused. As a matter of fact, the request appeared to upset him. Any reason why it should?"

"No." The clipped answer came with a slight hesitation.

"But you can guess?" suggested Katherine.

Diana took a sip of her drink. "No. I can't."

Diana's intercom buzzed. "I need you," said Jeremy.

Diana put down the mug and hurried away. Katherine went directly to her office. She shut the door and called Jake. As soon as he answered, she let out a chuckle. "Was the ambush really necessary—or wise?"

"Nope, but it sure was fun. Ingalls understood I gave fair warning." Jake's tone harshened. "Messing with you means facing me—and that's a fight he'll lose. We're going to get this bastard, Katherine."

"He's worried, Jake. I can see it in his eyes... Diana had a look on her, too. I can't quite pin it down."

"Does she suspect Ingalls?"

"I'm not sure, but Diana handles the books and certainly has a lot of insight into both the business end and the clients. Whatever information she has though, isn't enough to frighten her away. She's been with Jeremy since he opened his practice and is loyal to a fault. She's always comfortable around him while I'm constantly fighting to keep a smile on my face."

"Interesting," Jake mused. "Diana might have come across something strange and chose to ignore it. I'll talk to Connie. She's still going through the clinic's financials. I'm helping Ethan compile a list of the local club scene, but dozens are downtown and at the beach. We'll have to knock on a lot of doors."

"Lacey didn't use her car. Her license was suspended."

"Yeah, so we're probably hunting for a cab, ride service, or a friend who dropped her off. I'll have Ethan check it out. By the way, all the Florida license plates you saw in the vision had been reported stolen. Ethan is waiting on the report from New York."

"I might have a way to narrow the search," said Katherine. "Last night, I called Andy Harrell to ask him to do a drawing of the singer. If we can't find the club right away, maybe we can find the band. I'm meeting him this afternoon."

"Great idea. We have the date Lacey disappeared, and the band's gig will tell us where. Call me when you're done."

Chapter 23

Katherine remained at her desk all day, purposely avoiding any casual encounter with Jeremy. After her last client's appointment, Diana rapped on the door and poked her head in the office. "Your calendar is clear. Jeremy has already gone. Want to catch an early dinner?"

"Thanks, but I have plans."

"A hot date? You are so mysterious about your social life."

Katherine regarded the slight lines around the corner of Diana's mouth. *That smile is definitely forced. Are you fishing for information?* "Nothing mysterious about me," said Katherine lightly. "Just hanging out with a few friends."

"That's a good way to stay out of trouble." Diana's gaze strayed to Jeremy's office.

Katherine tensed with a worrisome thought. "How about you? Plans this weekend? Not dining with Jeremy alone, are you?"

"No. Jeremy wants us to go together."

Katherine relaxed. "You've worked for him a while, haven't you?"

"Since he started his practice. Jeremy says he'd be lost without me, but he's the one who offered direction." Her gaze softened. "Before this job, I seemed to be drifting. Now, I'm anchored in place, as if the work I do here has great importance." She peered at Katherine with startling intensity. "People don't realize what a special man Jeremy is. He keeps that part of himself hidden."

Katherine's shoulders stiffened. "He certainly does."

Diana's brow wrinkled in a frown. "Did I say something wrong?"

"Not a thing." Katherine forced a smile and rose to her feet. "Have a nice weekend. See you Monday."

Since Andy's studio was over an hour away, he and Katherine decided to split the difference in mileage and meet at a shopping center between Bayou St. Pierre and Sandy Shoals. When Katherine arrived, Andy had already snagged a table outside a café and nursed an iced coffee.

Katherine slipped into a seat. "Thanks for coming." She ordered iced tea and a plate of pastry for them to share.

"No problem. Starving artists can always use a few extra bucks. So who is this guy?"

"I believe he witnessed a crime against my client."

"Why not go through the precinct?" said Andy. "The police will pay my fee for a sketch."

"I've seen the man, but not the actual crime and my client won't file a report. I thought if I showed the picture to Jake, he can track him down and ask discreet questions. It might convince my client to come forward."

Andy opened the sketchpad. "You've been through the procedure once before, so let's get started."

A little over an hour later, Katherine nodded her satisfaction. "That's him. Thanks, Andy, you're the best. How much do I owe you?"

"I charge the police $225." He winked. "The art show is tomorrow. Promise you'll come and buy one of my paintings and you can have it for free."

"It's a deal. I have plans in the morning, but I will definitely be there in the afternoon."

They said goodbye. The shopping center had an office supply store where Katherine made copies of the sketch. On her way to the car, she texted Jake. He sent an immediate reply, and they made plans to rendezvous at April's.

April was alone when Katherine reached the duplex. She changed out of business clothes and showed her the sketch. "I don't recognize him," April said, "but I'm not into the club scene."

Katherine eyes twinkled. "Perhaps you should consider it. I seem to recall not long ago you wanted a more active social life."

"It so happens," said April with a cheeky grin, "my social life has taken a recent turn for the better."

Jake and Ethan arrived. Ethan tossed his jacket over a chair. He had on his shoulder holster. Jake kept his jacket on.

Katherine handed each of them sketches. "Great," said Jake. "Ethan and I will split the list of clubs and call if we find anything."

"Excuse me," sputtered Katherine. "April and I are going, too."

"This is police work."

Katherine regarded him with a dubious air. "No, it isn't. You don't have an official case against Jeremy and, besides, you're on suspension. I have as much right to investigate as you. Actually, I have more considering I'm the one with the *special needs* client." Her voice dripped with meaning.

Ethan grinned. "Forget the argument, Jake. I already told you they'd never agree to stay behind." He held out his hand to April. "I'm too smart to waste time arguing and consider this a date—a very peculiar date, but a date nonetheless. Shall we go?"

April jumped up from her seat. "See you guys later."

Katherine turned to Jake with folded arms and tapped her toe. "Well? Are you planning to sit here all night?"

With a resigned sigh, Jake gestured toward the door. When they got to the truck, Katherine stopped him with a hand on his chest. She lifted one side of his jacket to reveal a gun in the shoulder holster.

"It's my own," said Jake. "Not police issue."

"Expecting trouble?"

"No, but it pays to be prepared." He placed his hand over hers. "I won't let anything happen to you, Katherine."

Her breath caught in her throat. "I know."

They visited six clubs with live music before calling it quits. Jake had also brought photos of Ingalls and Lacey from their driver's licenses. No one recognized them or the sketch of the band's singer. Katherine carefully considered the interior of each building and then scrutinized the parking lots. None of them matched her vision.

When they returned to April's apartment, Ethan's car was already parked outside. "I guess they didn't have any luck, either," said Katherine, discouraged.

Katherine opened the door. April and Ethan stood

close together in the kitchen. With a start, April stepped back. Slight pink tinted her cheeks. She ran her hand through her hair. "Find anything?"

"Nope," said Jake.

"Same here," said Ethan. "Maybe we'll have better luck tomorrow night. By the way, those New York license plates were stolen, too. I tracked down a detective in vice who heard rumors several years ago of a john who played rough—sex with his hands around a girl's throat. He got off as she gasped for air."

Jake's brow furrowed. "No deaths?"

"Nope, he quit in time. Just scared the hell out of them."

"Incident reports? Description?"

"No, but you know as well as I, not many prostitutes will file a police report. By the way, the rumors in New York stopped after Ingalls left for Sandy Shoals."

"I'm visiting Safe Harbor in the morning," said Katherine. "I might dig up new information there."

April jabbed Ethan playfully in the side. "I hadn't realized how much legwork was involved in an investigation. Now I know why they used to call detectives flatfoots."

Ethan grinned at her. April smiled back. The pink in her cheeks deepened.

Katherine cleared her throat. "April, you've been great, but it's time for me to move back to my place."

April yelped an immediate protest. "Don't go yet."

Katherine insisted, and April finally conceded. Jake's disapproval was all over his face. "You were supposed to stay until this weekend."

"I changed my mind," said Katherine. "I appreciate

all April's done for me, but miss my stuff. I'll pick up Whiskers, too." Jake's only response was a curt nod.

Katherine packed her suitcase and said goodnight to Ethan and April. She walked in silence with Jake to their two vehicles. He got in his truck and followed her to Culpepper Lane.

They walked up the steps to the porch. Katherine grabbed his arm. "You saw April and Ethan. They want to be alone, and I don't need to be there any longer."

Jake pulled her close. "Stay with me."

"Two women?" she teased. "Might get a little crowded in there."

"I'll manage."

Katherine's pulse sped up. "As much as I want to say yes, I'm not prepared to share you with Bethany."

"I'm over her," he protested. "Whatever we once had is long gone."

"The romantic ties are severed, but the psychological ones linger. You continue to assume responsibility for Bethany's death. You aren't ready for anyone else until you come to terms with what happened to her."

Jake's arms dropped to his side. "You have no idea how much I want to say you're wrong." Her heart gave a wistful tug at the pain reflected in his eyes.

Jake turned the key in the lock. Whiskers waited on the other side of the door as if expecting their arrival. She picked him up and rubbed her nose against his. "Eager to go home?" He responded with a purr.

"Give me your keys," said Jake. "I'll load the car."

As Jake gathered Whiskers' things, Katherine sauntered into the parlor and stood in front of the mirror. "Whiskers and I are leaving." Nothing but her reflection stared back. An unexplained wistfulness filled her. Funny how the space suddenly felt so empty. *Can a room be sad? Or is it Bethany?*

Despite no chill in the air, Katherine shivered.

\*\*\*\*.

Jake followed Katherine home and carried her suitcase upstairs. The door had no sign of forced entry, but he ordered Katherine to stay in the hall until he looked around. Practiced eyes carefully scanned the apartment for anything out of order before Jake allowed her past the threshold.

"I'm safe here," said Katherine. "Women like Lacey willingly went with Jeremy. I won't."

"Sapphire didn't."

"Her door was unlocked and she didn't expect trouble."

Jake's hand brushed her cheek. "You're worried. I can tell."

"Not about my safety." Katherine's sorrowful gaze drifted to the window. "Jeremy could kill again at any time. We have no way to know when he picks another victim. A woman may be out there at this moment with no clue she's headed for trouble."

"We'll find a way to stop him." Jake pulled Katherine close. He kissed her, yearning to erase every last bit of her pain. A burning ache filled him. The fire built, the taste of her lips flooding his senses. He wanted so much more than a goodnight kiss. Katherine wrapped her arms around him, melting into arms, her meaning clear. So did she.

Reluctantly, Jake let go of her and took a step back. "I'll see you tomorrow."

Her wistful smile tugged at his heart. "Right. See

L. A. Kelley

you tomorrow." She shut the door. He waited in the hallway until the deadbolt clicked and then tested the knob to make certain the lock was secure.

Jake drove straight home. The house was dark and quiet. Even after turning on the foyer light, the added illumination did nothing to ease the oppressively heavy atmosphere. He hadn't been this gloomy for several weeks—not since Katherine became an important part of his life.

He paused to take in the space around him. A ton of work left to be done, but plenty of potential. The first time he stepped over the threshold, a comforting sense of future gripped him. This house would be a good place to bring a wife, raise a family. Jake could almost hear kids running down the hall to greet him at the door. At the time, it seemed bizarre to make plans so far ahead. He never had before. He didn't want to. The new sensation was strange, but also fitting as if he belonged here. His life belonged here.

But now? When Katherine and Whiskers left, they also seemed to pack the essence of his future self and take it with them. The only person left behind was Jake-of-the-present. Jake-of-the-issues. Jake-of-the-ghostly-girlfriend in the parlor. None of them were good company.

Jake tugged at the parlor door handle, but it refused to open. "Bethany?" He rapped on the glass and rattled the knob, but the door remained shut. Jake pressed his hands against the glass pane. Did Bethany mourn their absence, too? Had she barred him entrance to await their return? "I asked Katherine to stay. She wouldn't."

*But you don't want her to, do you? Not until you forgive yourself. When will that happen?*

Jake scowled. Not tonight, that's for damn sure. Not with Ingalls breathing free air.

*Smug bastard.* Jake stepped back, his hands clenched. It would be so easy to end Ingalls the way he ended others. "What do you want from me, Bethany? Revenge?"

No sound came from the parlor. Jake was alone. With nothing but his dark thoughts for company, he stormed up the stairs.

Chapter 24

The halfway house was on the edge of downtown. Katherine pulled into the parking lot. Other than a small sign at the door that said Safe Harbor, the rambling structure resembled other older homes in the area converted to storefronts and offices.

A young woman answered her knock. "I'm Lisa Marx, resident manager. Isabelle couldn't make it, but she told me to expect you and give the tour."

Although the rooms had old, mismatched furniture, the house was spotless. Bright paintings on the walls and a corner filled with toys added homey warmth. Several women sat in the living room on the floor playing with a group of small children.

"We have ten residents here at the moment," said Lisa. "They rotate household duties and attend mandatory counseling sessions. We teach life skills such as job interview techniques and hold parenting classes. Many of the women have kids. Isabelle has an open-door policy for them to visit their moms. Programs such as this can make so much difference not only in their lives, but also their families."

"Has anyone been here from the beginning?" asked Katherine. "I'm trying to get an idea of the long-term success rate of the program."

With a cheeky grin, Lisa spread her arms and twirled in a circle. "Search no further."

Katherine's eyes widened. "You went through the program?"

"Yup. I was in the first group. When I finished, Isabelle hired me as resident manager. I'm working on a degree in social work now."

"You must have known Tiffani Nolan."

"Tiffani..." Lisa's voice held a wistful tone. "We all heard what happened. I would have gone to the service, but wasn't sure how the family would react if an ex-prostitute showed. I didn't want to cause them any embarrassment." She motioned toward the kids. "Why don't we grab a cup of coffee and talk in the kitchen? They don't need to listen to this."

They sat at the table and Lisa poured them each a cup. "Tiffani dropped out of sight so suddenly," she said with shiver. "Then Sapphire killed a year after that. It's a dangerous world out there when you walk the streets."

"You knew Sapphire, too?"

"Oh sure. All the girls had their own regular corner. You even keep an eye out for each other in a way. God knows no one else does."

Katherine sat back with a sudden thought. "By any chance, did you ever run into a woman named Delilah?"

Lisa stiffened. "She left here a long time ago."

Katherine laid a gentle hand on her wrist. "Lisa suits you better."

Lisa startled and then relaxed with a weak smile. "I think so, too. I haven't used Delilah in a while. I threw that life away when I finally got sober."

"Lisa, I'm consulting with Detective Sumner on Tiffani's case. We believe the same man is connected to her death and Sapphire's."

Lisa blinked. "Danny?"

"No. Another man."

"Makes sense," she murmured. "Danny was an ass wipe, but it floored me when the news reports said he killed Sapphire. A lot us went to him for drugs. We gave him sex, and he cut us a deal. Cheat him out of any money and he'd go ballistic, but he never roughed up any of the girls for fun. It was strictly business with him." Lisa paled. "A killer targeting prostitutes?"

"Not just them—other women, too." Katherine leaned toward her. "Did you talk to Sapphire the day she died?"

Lisa bit her lip. "I'm still on parole and not supposed to meet with ex-cons outside of this house. If my PO finds out…"

"He won't hear a word from me."

Lisa cast a nervous glance to the hall and her voice lowered. "Sapphire came up to me in the parking lot of Safe Harbor and wanted to talk. She seemed nervous, kept glancing around. One of her johns scared her bad. She'd been with him a couple of times—didn't get his name, but Sapphire called him Daddy Dearest because before they did it he always asked if she was a good girl. She thought it was a big joke and said, 'I'm not just good, honey, I'm great.' He always seemed flush with cash, so during their last hookup, she decided to try scoring a few extra bucks from him and said something like, 'Pay me a little more and I'll show you what a bad girl can do.' "

Katherine drew a breath. "What happened?"

"He backed Sapphire against the wall, hands around her neck, choking her. He kept saying she'd be his good girl forever. She kicked him with her stiletto heel and managed to get away. He scared her so much, she came to see me about rehab and getting off the streets. I said I'd try to find her a bed at one of the centers, but it could take a few days."

Katherine's excitement rose. "Did she give you a description of Daddy Dearest?"

"She only said he was a white dude, but then asked if I knew how to reach Tiffani."

"Why Tiffani?"

"Sapphire once saw Tiffani talking with Daddy Dearest on the street. She wanted to tell the cops about him before going into rehab and said Tiffani might know his real name."

"Why?"

"The way they acted. Tiffani had already been through the program and was clean. He shook her hand. That's not what a prostitute does with a john." Lisa cradled her cup. "This isn't a safe life. Girls drop out of sight, go missing. Another always takes her place."

Katherine squeezed her hand. "I'm sorry, Lisa."

She shrugged. "No big deal. You get used to nobody caring."

"I care." Her voice softened. "What did you tell Sapphire?"

"I never heard from Tiffani after she left Safe Harbor and figured she relapsed and went back to the life. Sapphire got this funny look on her face and said she hadn't seen her. Suddenly, she peered over my shoulder and froze. She said something under her breath that sounded like Danny Pierson. I thought she saw him across the street."

"Did you?"

"No. I turned around. Plenty of people were out, but I didn't spot Danny."

A sudden thought struck Katherine and she quivered with excitement. "Is it possible she said Daddy Dearest instead?"

Lisa blinked. "I-I suppose so. I turned back to Sapphire, but she already split without a goodbye. That was the last time I saw her."

**** 

Katherine called Jake as soon as she left Safe Harbor.

"Her message makes sense now," said Jake. "Sapphire didn't have information on Danny Pierson. She wanted to tell me about Daddy Dearest. She knew Tiffani hadn't gone back to the streets. She might have suspected he had something to do with her disappearance."

"Jeremy." Katherine spit out the name. "He must have spotted Sapphire while she spoke with Lisa and followed her home, but it still doesn't give any evidence to use against him."

"No, but we have a timeline now, and Sapphire may not have been the only prostitute who had a local run-in with Daddy Dearest. All we need is one woman to come forward and identify him. I'll pass the information to Ethan." He paused. "Want to come over?"

"I would, but I'm on my way to an art show in Bayou St. Pierre. I promised Andy Harrell I'd stop by. Do you want to come with me?" Her heart skipped a beat when he said yes without hesitation.

Jake was in the parking lot when Katherine arrived at her apartment and she hopped into his truck. As if in unconscious understanding, they steered the conversation from murder. She smiled as he described progress on the kitchen.

Jake raised an eyebrow. "What's so funny about ordering cabinets?"

"Nothing," she chuckled. "This is nice. I'd forgotten what normal people do when they're together." She leaned back in the seat. "I can get used to normal."

"Not too dull for you?"

"Dull might be good for a change."

The art show was at a park next to the pier. Jake bought fried shrimp po'boys from a food vendor for each of them. They ate the sandwiches at a picnic table and then strolled down the aisles checking the displays of pottery, paintings, drawings, and photography.

Katherine sighed. "Such lovely things. Too bad my budget isn't bigger. Let's find Andy's booth before I'm tempted to blow it all. I promised to buy one of his paintings."

Andy had a large canvas tent with the flaps pulled back to let in the breeze off the water. He stood behind an easel holding a pallet and brush. As Katherine and Jake entered, he put down his tools and came over to greet them.

Katherine's eyes roamed over a display of watercolors. Andy had seascapes, landscapes, even a few still lifes and portraits. Business must have been good. Bare spots dotted the walls.

"Andy, these are beautiful." Katherine's gaze fixed on a large rendering of the bayou with storm clouds in the distance. The setting rays of the sun cast amber streaks of light on the water. The whole painting seemed to glow. A blue ribbon with Best in Show hung from the frame along with a sold sign. "Congratulations. You deserved the win. This picture is gorgeous."

Andy beamed at the compliment. "Thanks. A local collector bought the original, but I did good business selling prints for twenty-five dollars. I only have one left."

"I'll take it, but I put aside money for an original Andy Harrell, too."

Andy searched through a stack of prints while Katherine wandered past the other pieces on display. She selected a small watercolor of a sandpiper with the ocean lapping at its feet. After paying for both, she motioned to the easel. "What are you working on?"

"It's a present for my wife. Go ahead. Take a peek."

Katherine gazed at a portrait in the early stages; a roughed-in figure on the beach with enough preliminary shading to define sand, sea, and sky. Clipped to the easel was the photograph of a young woman wearing cut-offs and gathering shells. She had long dark hair tossed by the wind, and a peaceful, almost serene expression on her face.

"I took the picture last fall," said Andy. "It's my favorite, so I decided to paint it."

"It's going to be beautiful." Katherine peered closely at the photograph. "Your wife seems familiar. I wonder if we've met."

Jake peered over Katherine's shoulder. His brow wrinkled in a puzzled frown. "You're right. She does."

"You can ask her." Andy gestured outside the tent. "Here she comes now."

A young woman toting two bottles of water edged through the crowd. She entered the tent and handed one to Andy. "I got them from the ice chest in the car. They're still cold. Now aren't you glad I made you pack the extras?"

Katherine stared at her. Andy's wife didn't wear glasses. She had the figure of a young woman instead of a girl. Even so, the resemblance to the photograph of a teenager in a school uniform was unmistakable. "Tina Delaney."

Chapter 25

Tina eyed her with a quizzical look. "Have we met?"

Katherine's surge of relief nearly knocked her flat. "No, but you have no idea how hard it is not to hug you now. I'm so happy you're alive. Contact lenses, am I right?"

"Um, yes," said Tina in a hesitant tone. "I'm sorry, but I don't remember you, and haven't used the name Delaney in a long time—a lifetime ago." Her voice had a faint quaver. Andy put down the water bottle and took her hand.

"We're strangers," Katherine blurted, "but Jake and I have been searching for you."

"Jake is a detective from the Sandy Shoals PD," said Andy. "Katherine is a psychologist. I did the sketch for her the other day." He turned to them. "What's this about?"

"We're involved in a murder investigation," said Jake. "I'm sorry to drag up bad memories, Tina, but we believe the same man who attacked you years ago is involved."

Tina paled. "He's back. H-how did you learn about me?"

Katherine's look softened. "I know this is difficult, but we need to talk."

"So many years…" Tina's lips twisted in a wry

grin. "I tried to put all the pain behind me, but I guess the past always catches up to bite you in the ass." She gazed at them with sorrowful eyes. "You think he killed others?"

"At least four," said Jake.

"I-I thought he'd kill me, too." Tina squared her shoulders and motioned to an empty picnic table behind the booth. "Let's sit over there."

"Give me a second," said Andy. "I'll close up early."

"No, you mind the booth. The show has another couple of hours to go."

"Screw the show." He held her tight. "You don't have to do this."

"It's time, Andy. Margaret Delaney couldn't discuss that day, but Tina Harrell can."

Andy kissed her. "I'm right here with you, babe."

She smiled gently. "You have been from the day we met."

Andy shut the tent flaps and they all sat at the table. "How did you learn about me?" Tina asked.

Katherine cleared her throat. "I have a client who suspected you'd been attacked, but couldn't give any details. For reasons Jake and I can't go into, we believe it's the same man who later committed several murders."

Andy placed an arm around Tina's shoulders. She gave him a grateful smile and then gazed off into the distance. "That summer is like a bad dream now. Life sucked. Mom was a drunk, never there when I needed her. We fought all the time. Soccer camp was my one escape. I delayed going home as long as possible. After practice, I always sat under the bleachers with a book and read to kill time until I figured Mom had passed out on the couch."

Tina swallowed hard. "I heard this sound in the bushes. Out of nowhere, I got this creepy vibe like a voice in my head, telling me to run." Katherine sat back in surprise. Tina regarded her with a puzzled look. "What is it?"

"Nothing." Katherine said in a rush. "Please go on."

"I got scared. When I tried to leave, a man in a ski mask grabbed me. He covered my mouth with his hand and slammed me to the ground. He sat on top of my chest and pinned my arms down with his legs. I could barely breathe. A hand ripped off my necklace. H-he called me a good girl."

Tina struggled to speak. "He put his hands around my neck and squeezed...told me I'd be his good girl forever. I began to black out, but then came that voice again, telling me to fight."

Her lips formed a faint smile. "I was tough—all that soccer practice. I managed to free an arm and punched him. He let go and I head-butted him hard in the face. His neck snapped back. Blood spurted from his mouth through the mask. I must have split his lip. He tried to grab me again, but I pushed him off, and then ran like hell and didn't look back. I didn't stop running until I got home."

Tina flushed with anger. "Not that I got any comfort there. Mom was drunk as usual. She wanted to know where I'd been. I stood in front of her with his blood on my hands and she didn't even notice. I ran into my room, wiped my hands on my shirt, and then tore off my clothes and threw them in the corner of the closet. I-I couldn't even wear my glasses anymore. They had drops of blood on them—his blood. I threw them in there, too. I took a long, hot shower, but couldn't stop shaking."

"You never saw his face," said Katherine.

"No. I'm sorry." Tina shuddered. "But he knew me."

Jake jumped on her words. "You're sure?"

"Yes. I dropped my backpack with my soccer gear, and it had my name and address inside. That night the phone rang. I answered and a man whispered, 'Good girl.' I couldn't eat. I couldn't sleep. He was out there watching, waiting for his next chance. My mother was useless, so I hopped a bus to my grandmother's house. She wasn't in good health, but took me in. I left my whole life behind, even changed my last name to Yancy, my grandmother's name. Now it's Harrell."

Tina gazed around the park. "I never planned to come back even this close to Sandy Shoals, but circumstances change." She smiled as her gaze went to Andy. "I found a great man and a great job, built a new life, a better one than I ever imagined."

Jake rubbed his chin. "You said you tossed your clothes and glasses into the closet. What happened to them?"

Tina shrugged. "Beats me. I didn't go in there again."

"I wonder…" Jake turned to Katherine. "Carlene said she didn't change a thing—shut the door and left the room exactly as it was."

Katherine blinked. "You think Tina's belongings are still there?"

"If so, the glasses and clothes have bloodstains. If

Carlene didn't wash them…"

Tina stiffened. "You've been to my mother's house."

"She never left the old place," said Katherine. "You're a different person now, Tina. Your mother changed, too. For one thing, Carlene is sober. She quit drinking in prison."

Tina's voice hardened. "I don't want to see her. Don't tell her where I am."

"I won't do anything without your permission." Katherine's voice softened. "I'd like to let her know you're alive and well."

"Suit yourself." Tina shrugged. "As if she cared."

"She does. She carries a lot of guilt."

"She should." Tina spit out the words. "I still have nightmares about that day."

Katherine took a card from her purse. She scribbled her cell phone number on the back. "Take this. Call me if you want to talk. Life is too short to carry the burden of unresolved issues and unnecessary pain."

Jake gazed at Katherine with a faint smile. "I second that."

Tina stared at the card. "I can't forgive her."

"Honestly," said Katherine, "I don't like the word forgive in cases of severe emotional trauma. On one level, it implies the perpetrator's actions weren't so bad. I'd never forgive the man who attacked you or killed all those women. I don't need to. Instead, I prefer acceptance. Accept Carlene's actions were beyond your control, and the harm done to you was terrible and unfair. Deal with the consequences. Break the chains of the past to forge a new relationship with her on your terms alone—or decide none at all is healthiest. Either way, nothing is left unresolved to hold you back."

Katherine leaned across the table. "I won't press you to mend fences with Carlene, but if you ever decide to take the next step and need a go-between—I'm here. Remember, control of the situation is in your hands. Tina Harrell isn't a helpless child anymore, and Carlene isn't a worthless drunk. Hearing her anguish and apology could do you good, but you choose the time and place."

Tina said nothing, but slipped the card in her pocket.

"Tina," said Jake, "will you come to the Sandy Shoals police department and make a statement? I'll be honest. Even when we find this guy, we can't prosecute him for the assault since the statute of limitations has passed, but your statement about the stolen necklace can add weight to the current case."

"I'm behind you, babe," said Andy. "Whatever you decide to do."

Tina rose to her feet. "I'll think it over."

"If you come," said Katherine, "call me first. I'll go to the station with you."

"Do you believe Tina will get in touch?" asked Jake as they drove from the park.

"Yes, I do." Katherine pulled out her phone. "I have Carlene's number. I'll ask if she ever went into the closet."

"Good." He glanced at her with a puzzled expression. "I saw you hand Carlene your card, but I don't remember she gave you a phone number."

Katherine flushed. "She called. I got her number then, and we've talked a few times."

He shot her a sly grin. "Giving away free advice is

no way to run a business, Fleming."

She harrumphed. "Especially when no one takes it. Want to go over your issues?"

"Nope—if Tina's clothes are there, I'll send Ethan to collect them. The evidence will seem tainted coming from me. Add that to my list of issues." His gaze strayed to the rearview mirror. He stiffened in his seat.

"What's wrong?" asked Katherine.

"A car has been back there since we left the art show. I noticed the same make and model on the way over."

Katherine's mouth went dry. "A dark sedan?"

"No. White compact. Only got a glimpse."

Katherine turned around in her seat. "I don't see anything, but Jeremy's car is red, sporty, and hard to miss."

"It's behind that truck." He pressed down on the accelerator. "Could be just a coincidence. Let's see how eager the driver is to follow." He drove through a yellow light just as it changed to red.

As they entered Sandy Shoals, Jake continued to shoot glances in the rearview mirror. "Nothing. Must have been my imagination."

When Katherine called Carlene and told her Tina was alive, the woman's tear-choked voice confirmed nothing in her daughter's room had changed. "I can't force her to speak with you," said Katherine.

"That's okay." Carlene swallowed hard. "I don't rate forgiveness. Knowing she's alive and well is enough for me."

Jake phoned Ethan and explained about the clothes. They exchanged a few more words before he hung up, clearly excited.

"What's gives?" said Katherine.

"Ethan will stop at Carlene's later, but right now he wants us to meet him at a bar. April traced the singer to a place called Maxie's on the night Lacey Calder disappeared."

Chapter 26

April waited in the parking lot with Ethan. "Maxie's is a bar, not a club, but I remembered they host live music on the weekends, so I dragged Ethan with me to check it out. No hits on Lacey, but a waitress working the night she disappeared definitely recognized the singer. His band played a gig here."

"I didn't find any credit card receipts for a ride service or cab the night Lacey disappeared," said Ethan, "but this place is only three blocks from her apartment. She must have walked." He ushered them into an office. "I had the manager pull up the security feeds from that night."

"How many cameras?" asked Jake.

"Two in the back, one in the front. One inside at the bar near the cash register. Not much field of view in that one, but if we're lucky, we'll catch sight of either Lacey or Ingalls."

"She was near the bar when she called," spouted Katherine without thinking. "We should watch that one first."

April regarded her with surprise. "How do you know?"

Katherine cleared her throat. "I don't. I simply made an assumption."

"Uh-huh." Ethan's tone dripped with skepticism, but he settled behind the monitor without further comment and started the feed. They watched for several minutes with no results. "Images of customers in the background aren't great," said Ethan. "The camera's range captures only the area directly in front of the cash register."

Jake squinted at the monitor. "Lighting sucks, too. Hard to make out facial features. Gavin said Lacey's call came in around 10:30 and we're just passed 10:15…wait!" He stabbed a finger at the screen where a young woman walked into frame. "Is that…?"

"Yes!" cried Katherine. "That's her." Lacey slid onto a barstool, and Katherine's excitement rose. "She's wearing a necklace. That's the same dolphin pendant I noticed at the bus stop."

"Nothing was found on the body," murmured Ethan. "You're right about the souvenirs."

"Hang on," said April. "The bartender spoke to her…she's checking out the other end of the bar…damn it, I can't tell if it's Ingalls. The angle is wrong."

"It must be someone interesting," muttered Jake. "She's smiling."

April made a face. "Definitely a dude then."

Lacey tossed back her drink. She jumped off the stool and ambled out of sight.

"No, no, no," sputtered April, "get over here. Bring him with you." They watched a few more minutes, without Lacey or Ingalls coming into view.

"They may have left," said Katherine. "Jeremy would want to get Lacey out of the bar quickly, less chance anyone noticed they were together."

"Ethan," said Jake, "pull up an outside camera."

"The one closest to the back door," chimed in Katherine. April and Ethan both gazed her with surprise. "I assume Jeremy parked in the rear lot in order not to attract attention."

"The club has two cameras there," said Ethan. "The one trained on the door doesn't move, the other makes regular sweeps across the parking lot. I'll pull up the one at the door first at 10:25."

Several minutes later, a man exited and lounged outside. "His back is to the camera," said Katherine with clear disappointment. "Great view of only the top of his head, but that's definitely Jeremy. I don't suppose you have enough for a warrant."

"No," said Ethan. "I can't see his face. Wait—here comes Lacey. I recognize her outfit."

She exited the bar and spoke to the man. He tucked her hand into the crook of his arm and they walked away from the door and out of range.

"Damn it," blurted Katherine. "He never turned toward the camera."

"No, but this is good," said Jake with rising excitement. "Ingalls didn't come into the bar through the rear exit. It's one way. He had to go through the main entrance. We saw what he's wearing now and may get a better shot of Ingalls from that angle and prove he was at Maxie's that night. First, let's see if we can spot his car. Ethan, bring up the other camera that sweeps the rear parking lot."

With a few clicks, the view changed. Figures moved across the asphalt, most headed to Maxie's, but two people walked in the opposite direction toward a dark sedan.

April's voice dropped to a shaky whisper. "Lacey is getting in the car, with no clue she'll be dead soon. God, I feel sick."

A moment later, the car started and backed from the space. "It's too dark to see the license plate," said Ethan.

The view changed as the camera swept to the far side of the parking lot.

"No, no, no," April yelled at the screen. "We need the other angle."

The camera stopped and reversed direction. The field of vision swung toward Ingalls' car.

"Move it," April moaned. "He's getting away."

Katherine gripped the edge of the desk. *Too slow. We'll miss them.*

Without warning, the picture jerked as if a hand gave an impatient shove. The dark sedan was now centered in the screen. April started. "Why the hell did the camera do that?"

"Who cares," said Ethan. "The view is better now."

Katherine held her breath. The car reached the spot where she had intercepted it. A streetlight shone on the sedan, and Ethan froze the screen. He zoomed in and cracked a grin. "Gotcha." Jeremy and Lacey were now clearly visible inside the car. "We've got blood on the clothes at Carlene's. This picture will be enough for a judge to compel a DNA sample, and a warrant for a search. Wanna bet we find a room with a bunch of license plates at his fancy house on the bay?" He sprang to his feet. "Come, on, April. I'll take you home and then stop at Carlene's for the clothes. Jake, meet me at the station. It's time the lieutenant is brought up to speed."

Jake dropped Katherine at her apartment, promising to call. As the hours ticked by, she fought the desire to run down to the precinct. After midnight, her phone finally rang and she pounced on it. "Well?"

Jake chuckled. "Not even a hello?"

"Hello—well?" she demanded impatiently.

"We have a camera shot at the entrance to Maxie's of Ingalls going inside two hours before Lacey. His clothes match the man exiting with her later. Although the plates were stolen, the car is the same make and model as the one Parker gave to Tiffani. The lab has the blood samples from Tina's glasses and clothing. With all that and the video of Lacey in the car, Lt. Saldana gave the order to expedite processing."

"What did she say to you?" asked Katherine with mounting excitement. "Back on duty?"

"Bawled me out for twenty straight minutes for investigating on my own and then lifted the suspension."

Katherine beamed at the triumphant tone in his voice. "Congratulations."

"I tried to keep your involvement out of it as much as I could," Jake warned, "but she may have questions for you."

"I'll stick with the client confidentiality excuse. It's worked so far. What's next?"

"Ethan and I are headed to Ingalls' house. We're going to park outside and watch until we hear from Saldana. She's with the DA now trying to locate a judge to sign search warrants for Ingalls' house and office. We're not waiting until morning to move on this guy."

"I have a set of keys for the counseling center," said Katherine. "I'll open the door and explain the patient filing system. Diana's computer is password protected though."

"No problem. We'll assign a computer tech with the search team. I'll send a squad car to pick you up."

"I don't suppose I can come with you instead and watch while you arrest Jeremy?"

"Nope, but I'll take a selfie for your scrapbook."

\*\*\*\*

"Ready?" asked Ethan.

"All set." Jake dropped the phone in his pocket. The familiar weight of the badge in its holder pressed against him. It felt good to be back in business.

They drove to Ingalls' residence and parked down the street out of sight.

Ethan let out a low whistle. "Must be nice to have money."

"Or come from it," said Jake. "Ingalls inherited from his father. Good thing the house is in one of the older neighborhoods or we would have to deal with a gated entry, too."

A light came on in a first floor window. "My, my, someone's up late," murmured Jake.

"Damn," said Ethan, "I hoped Ingalls was already in bed. I wanted to escort him on a perp walk through the neighborhood in his jammies."

Jake's phone chimed with a call from Saldana. "Warrants for the arrest of Ingalls and a search of the home and the clinic are signed," she said. "I'm on the way to his house. Wait for me. Dr. Fleming already let a team into the clinic. They're poring through the files as we speak."

"Roger that," said Jake. "Standing by for your arrival." He ended the call and the light on the first floor went out. "Strange timing," he murmured.

Ethan voice dropped. "What do you think?"

Jake opened the door. "Saldana will be here any minute, but nothing says we can't drop by for a friendly chat. Come on."

They strode to the front door and Jake rang the bell. "Maybe he's shy? Don't hear any footsteps hurrying to greet us."

"I'm hurt," said Ethan with a snort. "I'm beginning to get the impression he doesn't want to talk."

Jake pounded on the door. "Ingalls, it's Detectives Sumner and Reardon. Open up…" Jake cocked his head listening. "Nothing—let's head around back." As they rounded the corner of the house, a figure darted across the lawn toward the private dock. "Ingalls is rabbiting!" yelled Jake, pulling his gun. "Ingalls, stop!"

Ingalls jumped into the speedboat and unhitched a stern line from the cleat. He scrambled to the bowline.

"I said stop!" yelled Jake, setting foot on the dock.

Ingalls tossed the freed bowline aside. Moonlight reflected off a metallic glint in his hand.

"Gun!" shouted Jake.

Automatic weapon fire exploded through the air in a staccato of sound.

****

"Find anything?" asked Katherine.

"Patient files," said the officer, digging through Ingalls' desk. "Hang on…what are these?" He pulled out an unmarked folder containing newspaper obituary clippings.

Katherine peered over his shoulder, frowning, as he thumbed through the papers. "This is strange. I don't recognize the names of any of these people. They all seem to be from out of town and died before Jeremy opened the practice here. Wait, here's a local clipping of Prentiss Ingalls, Jeremy's father. He's the only one from Sandy Shoals."

"We'll check through them at the station. Thanks for your help, Doc." He signaled for the officers to haul away the file cabinet, along with the computer and items on the bookshelf and in the desk.

"Do you need to search my office, too?" asked Katherine.

"No, the warrant only covers Ingalls office, the front desk, and the common areas."

Katherine heaved a sigh. "That's good. Can I get into my patient files? I have client appointments on Monday."

"Sure, as soon as we're done. Although," he said with obvious sympathy, "I'm not sure how many will show once the news of Ingalls breaks."

"Yeah," said Katherine dryly, "I figured that, and I was just starting to build my clientele, too. I guess I need to start shopping for cheap office space to rent."

Katherine walked down the hall where an officer sat at Diana's computer. "Hear anything from Detective Sumner, yet?" she asked.

"No, but the lieutenant is on the way with the warrant. She should be there any minute. Take a seat, Doc, and we'll run you home as soon as we bag up the evidence here."

"What the hell is going on!" Diana stood at the front door, trying to push pass the officers, her face flush with anger. "This building is private. You're not allowed—" She caught sight of Katherine and her eyes narrowed. "Why are you here?"

"They have a warrant," said Katherine. "I let them in."

Her hand clenched and unclenched. "The police have no right—"

"Yes, they do. I'm sorry, Diana. Jeremy isn't who you think he is."

Diana drew herself up. "Don't tell me about Jeremy. I've been with him for years. He helps people. You don't know him at all."

An officer stepped forward with the folder containing the obituaries. "Do you recognize any of these names?"

The muscles around Diana's eyes tightened slightly as she leafed through the clippings.

An edgy sensation crept up Katherine's spine. *She knows something.*

"Prentiss Ingalls was Jeremy's father."

"You recognize the others," said Katherine.

Diana stiffened. "No."

"Please, Diana, you need to tell us the truth."

"Listen to her, Ms. Weller," said the officer. "Dr. Ingalls is in big trouble. He's a cold-blooded killer involved in multiple homicides. You don't want to get dragged down with him."

"I said, I don't know anything," Diana answered coolly. "You're so wrong about Jeremy. He's a wonderful man. He never murdered anyone. He helps people. We both do."

"I'd like you to come to the station and answer a few questions."

Diana glared at him. "Am I under arrest?"

"Shots fired!" An officer burst through the door. "We have a report of shots fired at Ingalls' house. Officer down."

*Jake.* An icy hand clutched at Katherine's heart as

people barked orders. Within seconds, the room cleared of everyone except the crime scene technicians and one patrol officer. Katherine watched the squad cars peel from the parking lot. As the sirens faded in the distance, she swallowed down the sick fear in the pit of her stomach.

"Do you want me to run you home, Dr. Fleming?" said an officer.

"Not yet. I'd like to wait for word."

He glanced around in confusion. "Where'd she go?"

During the commotion, Diana had slipped away.

\*\*\*\*

Ingalls jumped behind the controls, gunning the engine.

Jake returned fire, dropping to his knees beside his partner, heart hammering. "Ethan!"

Ethan wheezed, clawing at his chest. "Vest caught it—go!"

Jake tore down the dock, firing as the speedboat tore across the bay. He dialed and shouted into his phone. "Shot's fired. Officer down—" From behind came the sound of a smoke alarm. "What the hell...?" He ran from the dock.

Ethan struggled to sit up. "House is on fire."

"Call it in," yelled Jake. He raced across the deck and tried the sliding glass doors, but they were locked. He snatched a cast iron chiminea near a pair of lounge chairs. With a grunt, he hurled it through the glass.

The fire alarm shrieked. Smoke poured out the opening. Orange flames crackled from within the billowing gray clouds.

Jake grabbed a garden hose, turned the water on

full blast, and entered the kitchen. Ingalls had dumped paper and cushions in the center of the family room and set the pile ablaze. Flames shot high, already licking up the walls. Furniture near the makeshift bonfire smoldered sending acrid plumes into the air. Coughing, Jake sprayed the water, but the fire continued to grow. The smoke became thicker. Cinders swirled through the air and landed with a burning sting on his exposed skin. Each breath seared his lungs. The stream of water from the hose couldn't hold back the fire much longer.

"Jake!" cried Ethan.

"Here!"

Ethan staggered into the house, coughing as he clutched his ribs. He grabbed Jake's arm, pulling him from the flames. "Move it! I hear sirens. Fire department will be here any second."

They lurched outside, doubling over in a coughing fit. Ethan limped, leaving bloody shoe prints on the deck. "You're hit," said Jake.

Ethan gritted his teeth. "Grazed my leg. Be dancing in no time."

Jake draped Ethan's arm around his shoulder and helped him to the grass.

"Sumner! Reardon!" yelled Saldana.

"Here!" Jake croaked out.

Lt. Saldana and a dozen officers raced into the backyard followed by an ambulance and firetruck. EMTs rushed over to clap oxygen masks over their mouths and gently eased Ethan onto a gurney.

Jake sat on the ambulance bumper. He held the mask to his face, inhaling deeply as EMTs worked on Ethan. Another treated Jake's minor burns and abrasions. Firemen entered the house, dragging heavy hoses. Soon water gushed from the shattered doorway onto the deck and into the yard, turning the carefully manicured lawn into a sludgy mess.

The orange flames disappeared. Thick black smoke transformed into dull gray haze. An EMT handed Jake a bottle of water. He took a mouthful, swished it around to dull the caustic, burnt taste in his mouth, and then spit the water on the ground. He drank the rest in one long gulp.

Jake peered across the yard. Saldana stood to the side talking with the fire chief. Jake's eyes teared up again, and he blinked to clear his vision. The EMT had washed them out with saline, but they stung like hell. He grimaced. No doubt they would for a while.

The EMTs loaded Ethan into the ambulance. "I tell you I'm super good," Ethan grumbled with a slurred voice. "I don't need a hospital."

"Can it, Reardon," said Saldana walking up to them. "You're going and don't give me any lip. That leg needs stitches and you may have a broken rib. Good thing you had the vest or you wouldn't be here to bitch."

He cracked a loopy grin. "You're a nice lieutenant."

The EMT snickered. "Painkillers have kicked in. He'll be a happy camper the rest of the night."

Ethan grabbed Jake's sleeve. "Hey, call April. Tell her how manly I was."

"Yeah," he said dryly. "You hardly cried at all. She can come to the hospital and hold your hand."

"Okay." Ethan yawned and closed his eyes.

The ambulance pulled away. Saldana turned to Jake with a shake of the head. "Ingalls had no gun ownership on record, let alone an automatic."

"He sure didn't seem the type," said Jake. "Ingalls is more of a hands-on killer. Any word from Harbor Patrol?"

"Not yet. They'll scour the coast for the speedboat, and we issued the APB. Ingalls can't get far."

"Lieutenant," the fire chief called from the doorway. "Fire's out. Your people can go in. The flames were contained in that one room, but watch your step."

Saldana tossed Jake a flashlight. "You're lead on this, Detective."

Firefighters had cut the power when they arrived, so Jake shined the light around. The downstairs was a soggy shambles littered with broken glass and debris. They had chopped into the walls and ceiling searching for hidden embers. Jake slipped on a pair of evidence gloves and peered into each of the rooms. None on the first floor had any paneling and not a single license plate in sight.

With Jake in the lead, he and Saldana climbed the stairs and entered the master suite. The closet door was ajar.

Lt. Saldana grunted. "This is bigger than my whole damn bedroom. Who the hell needs this many shoes?"

Hung against the rear wall was a double row of designer men's suits. The light glinted off a round object. Jake pushed aside the clothing. "Hello…." He murmured. "What are you doing here?"

"What'd you find?" said Saldana.

"Hidden door," Jake said with rising excitement. "Funny thing to put in a closet." He grasped the knob. "It's locked."

Saldana edged beside him and ran her hand over the panel. "Crappy hollow core, cheap hinges, probably a DIY project. Ingalls should have ponied up for a professional if he didn't want anyone nosing around."

"Allow me, lieutenant." Saldana moved out of the way. One savage kick from Jake and the lock broke open. He entered the hidden room and played the beam back and forth. His expression lit up in triumph. "Gotcha, you sonuvabitch."

Chapter 27

The preliminary report on the shooting came in over the police radio, and the knot in Katherine's stomach finally eased. No one had been seriously injured, but her nerves didn't completely settle until Jake sent a quick text. *I'm safe. Ethan wounded, but no danger. Call April. Meet me at hospital.*

With the investigation at the counseling center concluded, a CSU tech offered a ride to the hospital on the way to the station. Katherine ran to the waiting room. Jake was slumped over in a chair, gazing blankly at the floor. She called his name. His head jerked up. He jumped to his feet, lines of exhaustion etched into his face. Katherine threw herself into his arms.

Jake nuzzled her hair. "Shouldn't get too close. I stink."

"Just like a giant s'more," she chuckled, "my favorite campfire treat. How's Ethan?"

"Cracked rib and stitches. He's sound asleep now. The doc's keeping him overnight for observation, but he'll be fine. April is with him. She holding his hand and has her phone on speaker relaying a report to the news station. I gave her an exclusive on Ingalls."

"That was sweet of you," said Katherine.

"I owed her. I owe all of you." Jake brushed his hand against her cheek. "We did it, Kathy."

"We did it." She touched his bandaged hand.

"You're hurt."

"A few cuts and minor burns." Jake rubbed the back of his neck. "It's been a long night."

Katherine motioned to the chair. "Sit. You look as if you're ready to drop. The officer who gave me a ride said they had no sighting of Jeremy yet, but Harbor Patrol located the speedboat ditched across the inlet. The deck had blood. You must have hit him."

"Ingalls won't get far on foot," said Jake. "APBs are out. We're watching roads, bus stations, and the airport."

"He might try to contact Diana. She's loyal and won't believe he's a killer."

"We have a patrol car watching her house now. The lieutenant will bring her in as a material witness. Would she help him escape?"

"Yes. She's not afraid of Jeremy. It'll be hard to convince her he's done anything wrong. What did you find in the hidden room?"

"Exactly like the vision—the license plates and five pieces of jewelry belonging to Tina, Bethany, Tiffani, Sapphire and Lacey." Jake snorted. "Tina must have really pissed him off. His first attempted murder victim got away."

"I'll fill her in," said Katherine. "She'll sleep easier now that the police have a name and are hunting for him."

"We found prints and fluids all over the jewelry," added Jake. "Apparently, he liked to uh…play with them."

Katherine wrinkled her nose. "Yuck. Spare me the details."

"We also found a black and gray jacket and boots.

The red shovel was in a tool shed, and the techs will do fiber and soil analyses." Jake shook his head. "This guy was a real freak. He had recording equipment tucked away in the hidden room and a secret camera over the bed. No telling what we'll find on those."

"What about the dark sedan?"

"Not in the garage. He must have stashed it at one of the vacant properties belonging to the Ingalls Trust. Being a member of the board, he had access to the addresses and could pick and choose." Jake stretched. "I need a shower and a few hours of sleep before I return to the station. I'll give you a lift to your apartment, see you get home safe."

Katherine leaned her head against his shoulder. "Jeremy won't come after me. Setting the house on fire was probably a panicked move to destroy evidence. As a matter of fact, I'm surprised he's not in handcuffs already. Nothing in Jeremy's ego suggested he considered the possibility of capture. My guess is he never planned an escape route and is hiding until the heat dies down."

"We have officers checking the properties controlled by the Ingalls Trust," said Jake. "They have quite a number, but Ingalls' face will be plastered all over the news by morning. Someone will spot him."

They stopped to see Ethan. He slept peacefully, April seated at his side. Jake slipped an arm around Katherine's waist as they walked to the exit. "This investigation will take a while to wrap up. I won't have a lot of free time until then, but when I do…" He pulled her close. "Things will change between us."

Katherine leaned into the kiss, reveling in the strength of his arms and taste of his mouth, smoke and all.

*Tell me what you see, Kathy,* prodded her grandfather's voice.

*I see my future. Jake Sumner has my heart and I'll never let him go.*

*Atta girl.* His approval rang in her head.

\*\*\*\*

Jake locked the front door and went to the parlor. He tried the handle, but it still refused to turn. He placed his palm flat against the glass. "It's over Bethany. Ingalls is on the run. We'll catch him, soon. Isn't that enough to bring you peace?" The door remained shut.

He backed away, disappointment mixed with sorrow. "Okay, I'll leave you alone."

Why wasn't Bethany at rest? What more could he do? What did she want from him? Fog penetrated Jake's brain, clouding his thoughts. Every muscle in his body ached. *No more thinking tonight.* He staggered upstairs to the bedroom.

\*\*\*\*

Katherine yawned and reached for the ringing cell phone. "Hello?"

"Sorry," said Tina. "Did I wake you?"

She sat up straight. "It's okay. Long night."

"I'll bet. I've been following the news since you called… It's really him?"

"Yes. They found your necklace. It's only a matter of time until Jeremy is brought to justice. How are you doing?"

"I'm not sure…a bit dazed. I stayed up for hours talking with Andy…"

Katherine drew in a breath. *Don't push her. She's*

*ready.*

"I've decided to make a statement to the police," said Tina. "Andy will drive me to Sandy Shoals."

"I'm proud of you, Tina. I realize this is hard."

"Thanks." Even across the phone the relief in her voice was evident. "Maybe you and I can talk about my mother, too."

Katherine suppressed a cheer. "I'd like that. Why don't you meet me at my apartment since the office is out of bounds at the moment? Besides, it's probably crawling with reporters by now. We'll all ride to the station together. Afterward, we can come back to my place. Does Andy like cats? He can play with Whiskers while we talk."

Tina chuckled. "Andy loves cats. Perhaps he'll even make a sketch or two while you and I hash out the issues I have with Mom."

"Great. I'll text my address."

Katherine showered quickly then dressed and called Jake. He picked up at once, no sign of fatigue in his voice. In the background was the din of multiple people speaking at once. "Are you at the police station already?" she scolded. "I thought you planned to sleep."

"I did. I also took a long, hot shower last night and another one this morning, so I no longer qualify as a s'more. Some people," he chided lightly, "have better things to do than sleep their lives away."

Katherine related her conversation with Tina. "That's good news," Jake said. "Still no word on Ingalls. Diana Weller never showed at her house. We're getting a search warrant now. Phone records show she called Ingalls yesterday around the time she arrived at the office."

Katherine's voice tightened. "She warned him the police were there. That's why he made a run for it."

"Yeah, and she must have picked him up. There's an APB on her car and we're watching for credit card usage. So far nothing, but Ingalls is wounded, and that has to slow them down. By the way, Connie called. She's going through Ingalls' financials. Guess who inherited a plot of land from his father, part of which was sold two years ago to Dr. Singh at the Westside Animal Clinic?"

Her eyes widened. "Jeremy."

"Yup. The noose around his neck keeps getting tighter. I'm also running through the obituaries you found."

Katherine shivered. "Let me guess...murder victims?"

"No. Funny thing, all the deaths are from natural causes. Each person was in a different hospital undergoing treatment for a serious illness when he or she suddenly succumbed to cardiac arrest. Because of preexisting health issues, staff didn't raise an eyebrow."

"Didn't the families have a clue?"

"Most were elderly. None had much of a support system."

Katherine gasped. "Are you saying Jeremy is also an Angel of Death?"

"It may have started that way. Why else have the list? A psychologist can have hospital privileges, and these patients all had serious illnesses. What if he simply hurried the process along?"

"How? Wander the halls, pick a random room, and stuff a pillow over a patient's head? One of the staff would have noticed." Katherine shuddered. "His father's name was on the list."

"That reason for his death may have been money instead of mercy. Prentiss wasn't in the hospital, but had a heart condition and high blood pressure."

Katherine shuddered, troubled by an antsy sensation. Something didn't sit well. "This doesn't fit Jeremy's profile. That list had elderly men and women's names. Jeremy only killed four young women."

"That we know of."

"Where are the souvenirs then?" she said. "He takes a token. There weren't any others at his house."

"Maybe he hid them elsewhere, or the collection started recently. Ingalls could have stashed them at one of his other properties. Have you considered the obituaries were his souvenirs?"

"They're not personal items from the victims, and why hide them separately from the jewelry and license plates? If Jeremy killed those people, why didn't Bethany mention it?"

"You got me. Maybe she's only in tune with the local spiritual plane," he said wryly. "The names on the list go back at least fifteen years and from around the country; Portland, LA, Dallas, Atlanta. The most recent was in New York."

"Jeremy's last address," Katherine murmured. "He never mentioned a practice anywhere except New York. Did you find any evidence he was in those other areas?"

"No, but I've only started digging. As soon as I get off the phone, I'll check with the hospitals' human resources offices."

"You sense it, too." Katherine's uneasiness increased. "Jake, something stinks about all this. We need to speak to Bethany again."

"She hasn't exactly been welcoming lately." His voice held a bitter note. "I tried to talk to her last night—tell her about Ingalls, but the door is locked. I can't get in."

"After Tina leaves, we can go back to the house together."

"Fine with me, but don't get your hopes up. Bethany's information can be a little vague."

"Even so, I want to try. See you soon."

\*\*\*\*

Jake drummed his finger on the list of names, his brow furrowed in a frown.

"Can I help?" Ethan limped to his desk.

"What the hell are you doing here?" Jake barked. "You're supposed to be resting. Does Saldana even know you're out of the hospital?"

"Nope. I checked out early and April gave me a ride on her way to the local TV station. The news director wants a report from her firsthand on the hunt for Ingalls."

Jake eyed him with mock severity. "She's enabling your lousy decision-making."

Ethan's mouth split in a broad grin. "I know. Isn't she great? She's even happy I was raised Episcopalian. She calls it Catholic Lite." He leaned against the desk with a grimace. "What can I do that doesn't involve a lot of walking?"

"Check with the team at Weller's house. The search warrant should be signed by now. See if they found anything."

"Will do. What was recorded on the feed from the hidden camera?"

"Sex tapes with lots of grunting and groaning. None of the women match Weller and all left the bedroom on their own. Techs found Ingalls' little black book on his computer. He noted the names and dates of his sexual exploits and we're checking to see which women match those on the tapes. So far, all are alive, although highly humiliated, and probably rethinking the wisdom of one-night stands in their future. None caught a glimpse of Ingalls' darker side."

Ethan went to his desk, and Jake returned to the list. Katherine made a good point. These names didn't add up with the rest of Ingalls' MO. He phoned the hospitals. None of them had ever heard of Dr. Jeremy Ingalls. Frustrated, he tossed the list aside and dialed Connie Pratt.

"I was just about to call you," she said. "Parker verified Jeremy was in town to attend board meetings at the same time Tina was attacked and Bethany murdered. We also got a call from Isabelle. Tiffani attended group therapy at the prison with Ingalls. So, any leads on the slimy bastard's location yet?"

"No, but I passed on your report of Ingalls' investment properties in the city. We have officers searching each one, but so far he's a no-show. With the amount of blood found in the speedboat, he didn't get far without medical attention, so he must be hiding with Weller, the office manager. She's gone, too."

"I'll check the paperwork again," said Connie. "Speaking of Weller, did you find any other financial records in the office?"

"Not sure. We haven't finished sifting through all the material in the computers and filing cabinets. Why?"

"I can't find any record Ingalls paid payroll taxes for a person named Diana Weller. In fact, I didn't find any employment data at all. No social security number, no health insurance payments, nada. I found records linking to Katherine, but you wouldn't realize from examining the files Ingalls had a second employee. The funny thing is doctors usually don't handle stuff like that in-house and contract an HR and payroll firm. Ingalls didn't. The copies of Katherine's paperwork are in order. I assumed they were put together by Weller, but only Ingalls' signatures are on the documents. No trace of Weller at all. The IRS will have a field day."

Jake hung up the phone. He leaned back in his chair, staring mindlessly at the computer screen. Niggling worry poked at the back of his mind. Why no records of Weller? Was Ingalls hiding funds or did he have a more sinister motive? Katherine's words floated back... Killing those patients wasn't Ingalls style. It didn't fit his profile. Jake picked up the sheet of paper and gazed at the names. *Ingalls' profile...*

Jake sat up straight, slamming his feet to the floor.

*What about Weller's profile?*

Ethan peered at him. "What's up?"

"A hunch," Jake shouted. "Back in a minute." He dashed out of the room, raced to the crime lab, and burst through the entrance. "Did you finish processing the fingerprints in Ingalls' bedroom?"

The tech regarded him in disbelief. "Seriously? Do you know how many there are? He was a very busy boy. I got a hit in the hidden room though—only one other pair. They're all over the place. A second person liked to watch the sex tapes with him and play with his toys."

Jake sucked in a breath. "A woman named Diana Weller?"

"Weller? No, Diana Petrovich."

"Arrest record?"

"No. Petrovich is a nurse. She worked at a few VA hospitals, and her fingerprints are in the system since it's an employment requirement. Cops in New York would like to talk to her though." The tech motioned to a computer monitor.

Jake peered at the screen. Underneath Diana Weller's face was a notification from the NYPD. Diana Petrovich was wanted for questioning in the death of an elderly heart patient.

Chapter 28

Jake tore from the lab. Lt. Saldana waited by Ethan's desk as he spoke on the phone. Jake pulled up the file on his computer. "Ingalls isn't the Angel of Death. It's Weller—or rather, Diana Petrovich."

Saldana's eyes gleamed as she read over his shoulder. "According to this, at Weller's last hospital in New York, the death of a patient under her care raised a few red flags. What about the other hospitals?"

"I'll check, but I'll bet Weller worked at each one on that list. Three of them were VA which is why her fingerprints are in the system. She must have met Ingalls in New York."

Ethan slammed down the phone. "They found the dark blue sedan in Weller's garage. Plates are gone. I've extended the APB to her car, too, but she may be using stolen plates. Prentiss Ingalls died at home," murmured Ethan. "I wonder if his loving son brought back a private nurse to care for dear old dad?"

"Well, why the hell are you asking me?" barked Saldana. "Find out."

As Jake ticked off each hospital, his excitement grew. He called Katherine and filled her in. "Diana Petrovich worked at each place at the same time and on the same floor as a deceased patient from the list. At her last job in New York, Ingalls was at a clinic next to the hospital that employed Petrovich."

"That's where their paths crossed," said Katherine. "No one suspected her?"

"She moved around too much and only picked victims in poor health with no family nearby. The intern who treated the last patient in New York was the first one to find a death suspicious. She raised concerns with hospital authorities. The police were called in to question Diana, but by then she had disappeared. A few days later, Ingalls resigned and relocated to Sandy Shoals citing a family emergency."

Jake didn't need to see Katherine's face. Her anger practically crackled through the phone line. "No wonder he wanted her name off the books. I knew Diana's feelings ran deep for Jeremy, but I didn't suspect this."

Ethan waved Jake to his desk "Gotta go," said Jake. "I'll call you soon."

"Weller definitely came to Florida with Ingalls," said Ethan. "I spoke to Prentiss Ingalls' old housekeeper. His heart condition took a sharp turn for the worse soon after Ingalls Junior returned home. His son had hired a private nurse—a seemingly devoted woman named Diana. The housekeeper was dismissed, and Diana tended to all his needs. He died a few weeks later."

Jake's brows knit together in a frown. "No one was suspicious?"

"Nope. Senior had a well-documented health condition, but it makes you wonder if Nurse Diana and Junior helped speed the natural process."

Jake's cell phone rang. He brightened at the name on the display. "Good timing, Katherine, I've got news about Weller—"

"Something's wrong!"

\*\*\*\*

Whiskers sat at the window, flicking his tail back forth. Katherine leaned over and peered at the street. "No one yet? Don't worry, Andy and Tina will be here soon. Put your best paw forward now and you may be immortalized for posterity in one of Andy's watercolors."

Her phone chimed with an incoming text. "See? I told you. It's from Tina. They're a block away. I'll meet them in the parking lot—"

Whiskers jumped from the sill and ran to the door. His back arched and he uttered a throaty growl. Every hair stood straight up from the ears to the tip of his tail.

Katherine's breath caught in her throat. "Whiskers?"

Her heart jumped as the phone rang. "We're here," said Tina, "parking the car now—"

Whiskers' eyes narrowed. He glared at the door and hissed, muzzle drawn back to expose his teeth.

Katherine's heart pounded. "Change of plans, Tina. Don't get out of the car. Go directly to the police station..." The call cut off. "Tina?" Her pulse raced. "Tina, can you hear me?"

She whipped open the door and bolted down the hall, phone in hand. Taking the stairs two at a time, she thumbed Jake's number. "Something's wrong! Whiskers is acting funny. Tina called from the parking lot, and then the phone went dead."

"Stay in the apartment," he ordered. "I'll be right there."

Katherine shot out the back exit. "Too late, I'm already here."

"Get back inside, now! I'm on the way."

"Oh, no…"

"Katherine?"

Katherine knelt beside a crumpled figure on the asphalt and checked for a pulse. Relief swept over her at the steady beat.

"Katherine, answer me!" Jake breathed hard as if he was running. "Kathy!"

"I-I'm not hurt. It's Andy. He's unconscious. I think he was tased."

Jake shouted to someone to send an ambulance to her address.

Katherine scanned the parking lot and swallowed hard. "Tina's gone."

"I'll be there in minutes. Damn it, Katherine, get back inside and lock the door."

Katherine's heart drummed wildly against her ribs. "No one's here, but I see Diana's car." Her blood ran cold. "Oh my God, I didn't make the connection… Jake, she drives a white sedan. They must have followed us to the art show and found out Tina was alive. Jeremy has Tina—she's the one that got away. He's going to kill her."

"I'll put out an APB on Andy's car. We'll find her."

Minutes crawled by like hours. The blare of multiple sirens approached. Jake arrived with the ambulance and several squad cars. Katherine backed away from Andy as the EMTs scrambled to his side. Jake gathered Katherine into his arms. "You okay?"

"Just shaken." Her voice broke. "How will we find her? They could be anywhere."

Soft fur brushed against her ankle. Whiskers rose

on his hind legs. He placed one paw on her and another on Jake, peering at them with ferocious intensity. Katherine picked him up. "I forgot I left the door open. He followed me outside—"

Whiskers uttered a low growl. His body stiffened as if in preparation for a fight.

Katherine inhaled a sharp breath and whispered out of the corner of her mouth, "You don't think…"

Jake's eyes widened with understanding and he pulled Ethan aside. "Katherine and I have to leave."

Ethan gaped at him. "Now? Why? Where are you going?"

"I can't tell you."

"Damn it, Jake." His expression hardened.

"I can't. Trust me, Ethan," he pleaded. "Ingalls plans to kill Tina. Each second counts and I don't have time to argue."

"Please," begged Katherine. "If we don't move fast, she's dead."

Indecision danced across his face for an instant and then disappeared. "Saldana's on the way. I'll make up something to tell her. You must really love being on suspension."

"Thanks, man," said Jake. "Let's go, Kathy." Cradling Whiskers in her arms, Katherine ran with him to a squad car.

"You owe me big time, Jake," yelled Ethan.

Jake mashed the accelerator. The squad car peeled from the parking lot. They tore through red lights, siren screaming, until the brakes screeched to a halt on Culpepper Lane. As soon as Katherine opened the door, Whiskers bounded from her lap, ran up the steps and sat on the mat, staring at Jake's house in anticipation. He let out a keening yowl.

The handle turned. The door opened.

Katherine and Jake raced to the foyer. The French doors to the parlor swung wide. Whiskers dashed inside and paced below the mirror growling. The fur on his back stood straight up.

Blotches in the mirror spun in a dizzying whirlwind. Katherine slammed her palms flat on the glass. "Ingalls has Tina. Help us, Bethany."

No flickering lights this time. No sudden drop in temperature. As if Bethany had been poised, waiting for the three of them to arrive, the parlor disappeared. Mist surrounded Katherine and then the smooth walls of the Culpepper house transformed into dirty chipped paint mottled with cracked lath and plaster. Faded wallpaper curled at the seams. In the corner, a shotgun was propped against a table. Blurry figures became people.

Jeremy and Diana hovered over a rusty metal cot. Tina lay on the mattress, her eyes closed. She had a large bruise on the side of her temple and her hands and feet were tied. Relief flooded through Katherine at the slow rise and fall of Tina's chest. Jeremy's left pants leg was cut away. A wound had been expertly bandaged although slight blood seepage caused a rusty stain. He carried a gun in a shoulder holster.

"Katherine!" Jake's voice was far away. "What do you see?"

She tore her gaze from Tina and took in her surroundings at a glance. "I'm in the room of an old house. Tina is here. She's alive, but unconscious. Diana and Jeremy are both armed." Katherine wrinkled her nose. "Musty smell in the air. I don't think anyone has lived here in years."

"Can you see outside?" said Jake.

Katherine turned her head toward a window. Glass shards littered the floor underneath a broken pane. "Lots of trees. Old pecans mixed with pine and hawthorn bushes, too." She craned her neck. "Parked outside is an SUV with the rear gate open. Must be Andy's car. I can't see any other buildings. This might be a cabin in the middle of the woods."

Katherine turned her attention back to the bed. "Tina has a bruise on her head, but her breathing is regular. She may have been tased, too, and knocked out when she fell. Jeremy doesn't look too good, either. His face is pale and he has a bloody bandage on his leg."

Her eyes narrowed. Katherine aimed a savage kick at the bandage. Her foot passed through Jeremy, and he grimaced.

*Well, well. Felt something, didn't you?*

Katherine kicked harder. He winced, but remained on his feet.

*Dammit.*

"Painkillers wearing off already?" asked Diana. Her oozing sympathy sickened Katherine.

"Just a twinge," said Jeremy. "I'm fine." His gaze remained fixed on Tina. His fists clenched and unclenched. "Now?"

"She's not awake yet." Diana tsked. "You're so impatient."

"Only with Sapphire," he griped with a petulant tone. "She saw me following. I had to finish her quickly."

"Would it have killed you to wait a few minutes? I was on the way. You promised I could watch." Diana moistened her lips. "I like to watch them at the end."

"I'm sorry." Jeremy took her hand. "Don't be mad. It won't happen again."

"You'd never have found her if I hadn't suggested we follow Detective Sumner and Katherine."

"I know. I'm grateful for everything you've done for me." Jeremy turned to Diana with a pleading look. "Can't you wake her?"

"No." Diana patted his arm. "Be patient. You waited for this one a long time. A few minutes more won't matter. Once we're done with her, we'll leave. I have the papers with new identities and another car hidden close by. It's amazing what money buys with no questions asked. In a short time, we'll be in a new country and can start again." She let out a contented sigh. "They're always so peaceful in the end, aren't they?"

Jeremy smiled. "My good girls forever."

Tina stirred and moaned.

"Soon now," murmured Diana, "she'll set foot on the path to eternal peace."

Jeremy's breath quickened. "When it's done, I want her wedding ring for my new collection."

Diana smiled and moved a chair behind him. "Of course. Now sit. Rest for a bit. God's work starts soon."

****

The vision faded. As if yanked by a tight cord, Katherine stumbled back from the mirror and fell into Jake's arms.

"Are you okay?" he asked.

Katherine nodded, gasping for breath. "Yes. Tina is alive for now." Her face paled. "Jake, how will we find her? I didn't notice any roads, any markers."

Jake whipped out his phone. "I'm calling Connie."

He put her on speaker. "Ingalls has Tina Delaney. We believe they're in a heavily wooded area. On that list of properties owned by the trust is there a place with a structure on it—an old hunting cabin? It has to be secluded, away from any main roads."

"Hang on—I remember seeing something..." Papers rustled in the background. "The Ingalls Trust owns several parcels at the north edge of the county. All are good sized and had been farmed at one point. We're talking over a hundred acres in total, but according to the tax assessor none of the land has generated income for years."

Katherine's heart sank. "She could be on any of them."

Parker's voice came on the line. "Jake, I'm here with Connie. One of the farms is listed on property rolls as Tisdale Acres. Ingalls' mother was a Tisdale. She grew up on the farm and inherited the land when her parents died. No one has lived there for years, I have the survey..." Papers rustled again. "There's an old farmhouse on a dirt road off County Road 438. Texting directions..."

Jake's phone chimed. "Got them. Thanks, Parker." He hung up and peered at Katherine. "My gut says go. If it's a bust..."

He didn't have to say it. *Tina's running out of time.*

Whiskers padded to a stop in front of the French doors. He turned his head toward them, right paw suspended mid-step. A loud *mew* issued from his throat.

Katherine grinned at Jake. "My psychic cat agrees. That's good enough for me."

They raced to the squad car. Whiskers settled in Katherine's lap. She held him close even though he stared out the window displaying no inclination to move. They tore through town, heart hammering in Katherine's chest. Although traffic was light, time raced against them. It took nearly half an hour before she spotted the sign for County Road 438.

"It's gravel," Jake muttered. "Got to slow down." He turned off the siren and onto the road. Stones kicked up by the tires clattered against the car.

Movement seemed to slow to a crawl. Katherine's mental alarm beat a frenzied warning. *No time...no time...no time.*

"Should be nearby..." said Jake. He slammed on the brakes and motioned. "Over there." To the left was a rutted country lane. "What do you think?"

"Go."

Jake made the turn. The car bumped along for several hundred yards. Katherine jumped at a crack of thunder. A lightning flash lit up steel-gray clouds billowing overhead. The scent of rain hung heavy in the air.

Katherine peered at the surroundings in growing panic. "All this overgrown brush...there's no sign of a car. Did we guess wrong?"

Without warning, Whiskers sat up, pawing frantically at the glass. Jake shot Katherine a glance. "Whiskers says otherwise." Katherine jerked against the seatbelt as Jake braked to a sudden halt. He motioned off the road. "Tire tracks that way. I'll call it in. We'll have a chopper with searchers up here in minutes."

"That'll take too long." Katherine opened the door. Whiskers jumped from the car and ran into the brush. Katherine bolted after him.

"Katherine, stop!" yelled Jake.

Ignoring his shout, Katherine dashed into the woods.

\*\*\*\*

As Katherine disappeared behind the trees, Jake stifled an oath. He contacted Ethan, requesting medical assistance and immediate backup.

"Hold your position," cried Ethan. "I'll be there soon."

"Can't wait." Jake cut the connection and ran. He pushed through the brush searching for any sign of Katherine, but her trail vanished. "Where the hell are you?" he muttered. Everywhere he moved thick foliage surrounded him. He could be walking in circles. "Think, damn it. She can't be far."

Jake leaned against a longleaf pine and peered at the sky. "Bethany," he whispered, throat tight, "if you're watching, I need a little help."

The wind shrieked through the branches. The spindly tree bent toward the east. Without a second thought, Jake raced away. Another breeze gusted. Another sapling swayed. He ran; eyes on the treetops. This way. Then that way.

Jake pushed through the brush into a grove of old pecan trees. In the distance was a ramshackle farmhouse surrounded by more trees and overgrown hawthorn bushes. He pulled his gun and crept forward.

A gunshot blast ripped the air.

*Katherine!*

Heart pounding against his ribs, Jake broke into a run.

Chapter 29

Katherine skidded to a halt. Whiskers had vanished. "Which way, which way..." she muttered in dismay. The wind gusted, swirling eddies of dead leaves. As the storm inched closer, even branches heavily laden with new leafy growth bent in the stiff breeze.

White fur darted through the underbrush. "Whiskers?" Katherine eased through a clump of bushes and halted. Up ahead was a dilapidated farmhouse with a sagging porch surrounded by old pecan trees and hawthorn. The front door hung open on a broken hinge. The wind shoved her forward as if to hurry her along. In a crouch, she darted ahead and placed a tentative foot on the porch. A rotten floorboard squeaked under her weight.

Katherine froze, mouth dry, listening hard for any response from inside. No footsteps headed her way, but nearby was faint rhythmic scratching. Hugging the wall, she followed the sound to the rear, and peeked around the corner of the house. Tina wasn't in sight, but Jeremy and Diana stood near an SUV. Jeremy wore a gun. The shotgun was propped against the car within arm's reach of Diana. They each used a shovel to dig a rectangular outline in the soil roughly measuring six feet by three feet.

Jeremy leaned against the handle and swiped a

hand across his sweaty brow. "Isn't this deep enough? She'll wake any minute."

"A few more inches will do it. A forever home needs to be perfect. You don't want her to end up like your first one—the grave washed away in heavy rains, the body exposed."

Jeremy shuddered. "No. I wish I had you with me then. You'd have made it right."

The bliss on Diana's face made Katherine's stomach heave. She crept from the corner and returned to the front porch. Since her vison had shown the SUV in plain sight through a window, Diana and Jeremy must be digging outside the room where Tina was captive. She glanced around searching desperately for any sign of Jake, but to no avail.

*You can't wait for him.*

Skirting rotting floorboards, Katherine edged across the porch and into the house. She tiptoed by a central stairway and down a hall past several rooms until entering a kitchen in the rear. Immediately, she dropped low. Jeremy and Diana were only a few feet away from a large window over the sink. The panes were cracked and broken. Too much noise from her would bring them to investigate.

At the other end of the kitchen was a closed door. Any window inside that room surely had a view of the yard to match the vision. Katherine inched across the floor. The surface was covered with a mixture of moldy leaf debris and an assortment of rodent droppings. Each step wafted an acrid smell into the air. She clapped a hand on her mouth to stifle a gag.

Katherine reached the door and paused to listen. The digging continued uninterrupted, with no sign either Diana or Jeremy suspected an intruder in the house. Her hand grasped the knob. It turned freely and she gave the door a push.

*Creeeak.* Rusty hinges shrieked a protest.

The digging stopped. "What's that?" said Jeremy.

Katherine froze. Blood roared through her eardrums.

"I didn't hear anything," said Diana. "Don't stop now. It'll be dark soon. We're almost finished and need to be on our way." The digging began once again.

Staying under the window, Katherine snatched a piece of glass off the floor and crawled to the bed. She sawed at the bindings on Tina's hands. Tina squirmed on the mattress and moaned.

"Shhh." Katherine clapped a hand over Tina's mouth. "It's Katherine. I'm going to get you out of here."

Tina's eyes fluttered open. She gazed at Katherine with dawning recognition.

"Keep quiet," whispered Katherine. "Jeremy and Diana are both outside. Understand?"

Tina nodded. Eyes wide, her gaze darted back and forth across the room. She licked her lips. "Where am I?"

Katherine removed her hand. She slashed through the last of the rope on Tina's wrists and cast it aside. "Farmhouse in the woods. You were attacked."

"I-I remember. Andy and I got out of the car. A woman approached." She struggled to sit up, panicked etched in her features. "Andy—"

"He's fine. He was tased. You, too. The woman's name is Diana, Jeremy's accomplice. The police are on the way, but we have to get out of here now."

"How did you find me?"

"No time to explain." Katherine freed Tina ankles. "Can you walk?"

"I-I'll try."

Katherine helped Tina to a sitting position and then motioned to the window. "Stay low. Don't make a sound."

The digging stopped. An object thunked to the ground as if a shovel had been tossed carelessly aside. "Perfect," said Jeremy. "We're finished here."

Katherine paled. "We're out of time." She yanked Tina off the cot. "We have to run."

Tina swayed on her feet. Katherine grabbed her arm, pushing her out the door. As they ran past the kitchen window, Jeremy and Diana turned their way. In an instant, the emotion on Jeremy's face went from stunned disbelief to rage. He pulled the gun and fired.

Katherine and Tina ran to the porch. Diana stepped around the corner of the house, shotgun to her shoulder, a crazed light in her eyes. "Where do you think you're going?"

Shots fired from across the field hit the siding and splintered the wood. Diana stumbled back.

Jake stepped into the open. "Kathy, run! I'll cover you."

Katherine bolted toward the trees. Tina lumbered alongside; each inhaled breath came in a ragged pant. Automatic gunfire filled the air.

They passed a pecan tree, a spray of bullets blasted slivers of bark from the trunk. Katherine dragged Tina deeper into the woods. Her gaze darted back and forth in panic. *Jake? Where is Jake? Where did we leave the car?*

Leaves rustled. Katherine shoved Tina behind a bush and signaled for quiet. She dropped to her knees and peeked through the foliage. Diana entered the clearing toting the shotgun. "I know you're near," she purred in a sing-song voice. "My stepfather took me hunting all the time. Kill the game quickly, he always said to me or else you'll get a beating. Don't let them suffer."

Stock to the shoulder, Diana's gaze swept the clearing. "I'm an excellent tracker. I even found my stepfather once when he tried to hide. He didn't suffer, either." A smile twitched her lips. "He was never a happy man, but peace came to him at last after it was over. I knew then I found God's true calling. I'll help you find peace too, Katherine, safe from the ugliness of the world, but Tina must go to Jeremy first. It's for the best. She'll be a good girl forever."

Diana moved out of sight. Katherine swallowed hard to ease the tightness in her bone-dry mouth. "Tina," she whispered, "we have to go—"

Tina was motionless, her eyes closed.

Katherine reached a shaking hand to Tina's neck to check for a pulse. She bit her lip to prevent a cry of relief at the steady beat. Still alive, but not able to walk any farther for now.

A branch snapped a dozen feet away. "Katherine," called Diana, "there's no point in running. Show yourself."

A few more steps and Diana would stand in front of them. Katherine scoured the earth for anything to use as a weapon, but found nothing at hand except twigs and dirt.

"I say your trail stops here." Diana's amusement

tinged her voice. "Shall we see if I'm correct?"

Katherine started as a shotgun blast rang out. Pellets ripped a gaping hole through the foliage ten feet to the left.

"Not quite," said Diana lightly, "but I'm close, aren't I?"

Adrenaline flooded Katherine's veins. *Think! Find a way! She's toying with you. Jake must have heard the blast. What do you see in her?*

Katherine pressed her lips together in a thin tight line. The shaking stopped. *Overconfidence. Diana chooses victims who can't fight back. She expects a quick chase and an easy victory. Gonna give it to her?*

Katherine scooped up a handful of pebbles. *Hell no.*

"Come out, come out, wherever you are," Diana crooned. "The fight is over, Katherine. Detective Sumner is dead. Jeremy isn't much of a marksman, but I showed him how to use an automatic weapon. All one has to do is point and shoot."

*Jake dead?* White hot rage surged through Katherine.

Diana stepped in front of the bushes. "You can't keep me from God's work any longer."

Katherine sprung to her feet, and flung the pebbles at Diana's face. She fell back with a cry. Katherine tackled her, and the shotgun discharged.

\*\*\*\*

Jake fired, sending Diana scurrying for cover. "Kathy, run!" he shouted. "I'll cover you."

The discharge from an automatic weapon raked the woods. Jake threw himself to the ground and rolled as bullets kicked up the dirt around him. He crawled behind a tree. "Give it up, Ingalls," he yelled. "You're not getting out of here."

"Sorry, Detective, but Diana and I must finish what we started. After that, we'll rest easy together. Just like Bethany."

Jake's grip tightened on his gun. "You're a murdering bastard, Ingalls. Not a saint."

"I saved her. I saved all of them. I don't expect you to understand. No one does except Diana. She understood the urges. She showed me the way."

Bullets spit through the air as Jeremy and Diana made a break for the woods. With a curse, Jake scampered to his feet and followed. He lost sight of them in the thick undergrowth until a round from Diana's shotgun broke the silence. Jake veered off in the direction of the blast. Another round fired, even closer than before.

*Katherine.* Jake's heart sank as he raced ahead. *Which way?*

Leaves rustled. The shape of a white cat flitted through the bushes and without hesitation Jake followed.

****

The shower of stones peppered Diana's face. She cried out in shock and took a stumbling step backward. Katherine barreled into her, wrestling for the weapon. The shotgun's explosive discharge reduced a sapling to splintery bits.

Seething hate fueled Katherine's savage kick. Her shoe smashed into Diana's knee with a satisfying thud. As Diana dropped to the ground, Katherine yanked the shotgun from her hands.

Diana scrambled to her knees with a sly smile.

"You can't kill me. You're not one of God's chosen servants. The stain of my death will be on your soul forever."

"No argument from me," Katherine panted, gulping a breath. "I'm no murderer." In one swift move, she swung the barrel, clocking Diana on the side of the head. She dropped to her rear end with a grunt. Katherine loomed over Diana and jabbed her in the ribs with the toe of a shoe. "But I'll beat you unconscious without a shred of remorse, so don't move."

A cold cylindrical object pressed against Katherine's spine. "I can't let you do that, Katherine." Jeremy reached around, tore the shotgun from her grip, and tossed it aside.

Blood pounded in Katherine's ears. "Jeremy, you don't want to hurt me."

"No, I don't." His voice held a hint of indecision.

Diana staggered upright, swaying on her feet. "Jeremy, Katherine is in our way—in God's way. You see that, don't you?"

"I'm sorry, Katherine. Diana is right. Diana is always right. I'd never have gotten this far without her." He grabbed Katherine's arm and shoved her around the bushes next to Tina.

"Jeremy," Katherine said, "It's over. The police are wise to you—"

A faint thrumming came from overhead.

Katherine stifled a cheer. "That's a police helicopter. They'll discover the car any minute now. Your escape route is gone."

Jeremy anxiously scanned the overcast sky. "What do we do, Diana?"

Diana picked up the shotgun and placed the barrel

L. A. Kelley

against Tina's head. She cocked the trigger. "We end them now. They'll find the four of us here." Her eyes held a dreamy gaze. "God's servants will be called to paradise together."

Jeremy grabbed Katherine and held her tight. She flinched as cold steel pressed against her skin. "Jeremy, don't."

"One move and you're dead, Ingalls."

Jake ran into the clearing, his gun pointed at Jeremy's head. "Drop it."

Whiskers padded into view. He sat at Jake's feet, eyes half-lidded, head tilted to the side as if listening to a private message.

"An interesting dilemma, Detective," said Ingalls. "My gun has a hair trigger. One twitch and Katherine is gone, and if by any chance you kill me, Diana will finish off Tina before you take a second shot."

An enraptured smile transformed Diana's face. "Jeremy, I see the truth of God's plan now. Detective Sumner can't kill us both in time to save Katherine and Tina. He has to choose."

"It doesn't have to end this way," cried Jake, his voice tight. "We can all walk out of here."

"Our work is done," said Diana. Her finger tightened on the trigger. "The honor is yours, Detective Sumner. God wants you to decide which one comes home to him."

Jake held Katherine's gaze, anguish in his eyes.

"Only one," whispered Jeremy.

The muscles in Jeremy's gun hand twitched. The muzzle trembled against Katherine's head.

"Don't do it," yelled Jake.

"My good girl forever," Jeremy murmured.

320

*Murderers. Murderers. Murderers.*

Katherine's eyes widened as the unearthly whisper echoed through the trees. From the shock on Jake's face, he clearly heard it, too.

Jeremy's grip on Katherine eased. The gun barrel shifted a fraction of an inch. "Diana?" His voice was tight and strained. "Did you say that?" She shook her head, face pale.

The wind gusted, spinning a pile of dead leaves. The swirling eddy rooted in place sucking in more vegetation. The column grew in height, rotating faster and faster.

A blast of air rocked Jeremy on his feet and he let go of Katherine. Treetops swayed and bent.

*Crack-crack-crack.*

A roaring gale ripped through the forest, splitting trees in half with explosive retorts that reverberated through the woods. Jeremy and Diana gawked in horror as spidery branches on a cluster of old pecans snaked together, weaving and twisting into rope-like projections.

From the center of the vortex of spiraling leaves came a woman's shout.

"Murderers!"

A ferocious gust knocked Katherine across the forest floor. Jake rammed his gun in the holster. He snagged her with one hand, with his other scooped up Whiskers. They huddled over Tina.

Thunder rumbled from the sky and the trees reached to the ground.

Diana screamed, firing the shotgun mindlessly overhead. The barrels emptied, but the branches kept coming. Knotted limbs lashed out, snaring Diana and pinning her arms to the side. She struggled helplessly in their grip. "Jeremy," she shrieked, "save me!"

Jeremy staggered back, mouth open, face gray. He dropped the gun and ran. A jumble of twigs snagged his legs. More branches wrapped around until only his head was visible. Cocooned in place, he was jerked upright next to Diana, inches from the swirling vortex.

The spinning slowed to a stop. Suspended in air, the leaves melded into the shape of a young woman.

"Bethany," whispered Jake.

Jeremy and Diana screamed in terror, as the branches lifted them high overhead.

Bethany's face twisted in rage. "I'm not your good girl any longer!"

With a deafening *boom!* a bolt of lightning struck the tree. The screaming stopped. The knotted wooden fingers relaxed their grip. Two lifeless bodies fell from the sky and thudded to the ground.

Trees snapped back into shape. The wind disappeared. Katherine and Jake staggered to their feet as soft rain began to fall. The image of Bethany turned to face them.

Jake's voice broke. "Forgive me. I didn't save you."

"There is nothing to forgive," said Bethany. "My death wasn't your fault. No one could save me. I led a selfish life and brought pain to many others."

A jumbled flurry of sensations flew from Bethany to Katherine; contrition, absolution, resolve, gratitude, and, finally, peace. Their intensity rocked her to the core.

Bethany nodded with a smile. "Katherine sees now. She understands the truth."

A hopeful look came to Jake's eyes. "What truth?"

Katherine blinked back tears. "The haunting wasn't your penance. It was Bethany's. She caused your guilt and it chained her here."

"All these years, Jake," said Bethany, "I watched you suffer. I shouted to let go, but my voice alone wasn't strong enough for you to hear. Then Whiskers came and you brought Katherine to me and I knew what to do. I needed the three of you to help me stop them from killing again. Only then could we both be free of the past."

As if a spark had been lit, the leaves glowed from within. Bethany's visage transformed with joy. "It's done." The light became brighter. Leaves drifted from Bethany's shape and fluttered to the ground. "Take care of them. Be happy…"

Jake swallowed hard, his voice barely above a whisper. "I will."

Whiskers let out a plaintive mew. Bethany bent her head toward him with a smile. "You, too."

The light disappeared. The remainder of the floating leaves collapsed in a pile on the forest floor.

Jake reached for Katherine's hand.

Kelley

Chapter 30

The EMT tossed Jake a blanket, and he wrapped it gently around Katherine's shoulders. "Cold?"

She stroked Whiskers as they huddled on the porch. "Better now."

April dashed through the rain with Ethan at her side. "Lieutenant Saldana gave me a statement," she said with a grin. "I phoned it in and the news manager at the local TV station wants to see me tomorrow."

"You got the job," crowed Katherine.

"I think so." April shot her a sharp look. "Anything you want to add to the report? Wait, don't tell me. Patient confidentiality."

Katherine's eyes twinkled. "Sorry, I'm bound by oath."

April turned a piercing glare on Jake. "And you?"

He gazed at the sky with an innocent expression. "All statements from the police must come from official channels."

April blew out her cheeks in frustration. "They're hiding the truth, Ethan."

"No kidding," he said with a snicker. "Didn't you hear Jake and Katherine's cockamamie story? Jeremy and Diana climbed a tree to ambush them and got hit by lightning. And nothing they said justifies why they brought a cat on a rescue operation. Seriously, I don't get how either of them kept a straight face."

Katherine nudged Jake. "It's an excellent story. I believe it one hundred percent."

Jake grinned. "So do I."

"So does the lieutenant," added Ethan. "At least, she didn't press you hard. Even the EMTs said the deaths appeared to be from a lightning strike. I suspect the ME will agree. Case closed. Nobody will care Mother Nature saved the city the cost of a trial."

Ethan gestured toward an ambulance with flashing lights. "Tina's demanding to say goodbye before they take her to the hospital. Lucky for you two, she only has a few blurry memories. After the goodbyes, I suggest certain people get the hell out of here before Saldana has second thoughts about what really went on in those woods."

Katherine handed Whiskers to Jake and crawled into the back of the ambulance. Tina lay on a gurney with an IV and a bandaged head, and greeted them with a weary smile. "I borrowed one of the EMT's phones to call Andy. He's already released and waiting for me at the hospital, but I had to thank you before I left."

Katherine patted her gently on the arm. "Feeling better?"

"I'm sore all over, but grateful to be alive. I don't remember much except waking up in the farmhouse and then running with you through the woods."

Katherine shot Jake a glance. "I'd say that's for the best."

"Me, too. Funny thing," she mused, "considering I was kidnapped today, I'm completely and totally at peace. For years, I had a shadow darkening my life. Now, all of a sudden, it's gone." She chuckled. "Or my new attitude is due to the damn good drugs they pumped into me."

A wistfulness in her features caught Katherine's eye. "Something else on your mind?"

Tina's gaze drifted out the back of the ambulance. "All that emotional baggage with my mother... I'm ready to let it go."

Katherine's voice softened. "I'm glad to hear that. Want me to tell her?"

"No. I-I want to hear her voice. I'll call from the hospital." Her eyes twinkled. "Are you available for a counseling session?"

"Anytime," Katherine chuckled. "Although it might be in a coffee shop. I don't have an office any longer."

As the ambulance drove away, an officer returned with Jake's squad car. "Let's get out of here," said Jake, "before I have to field any more questions from Saldana." He opened the car door and Katherine placed Whiskers inside. The rain stopped. Jake pulled Katherine close. She wrapped her arms around his neck and peered at his face. No shadows hid in the depths of his eyes. No wariness colored his features. Eager lips met hers.

"Kathy," Jake nuzzled her ear. "Can I interest you in a man with a slightly used heart?"

"Most definitely, yes." She nestled happily against his chest. "He has tons of potential, but I'll only be able to give a proper diagnosis after a few one-on-one sessions."

"I'm almost ready to begin." Jake kissed her again, "but first we'll drop off Whiskers. I have one last place to go before we start those sessions, and I want you to come with me."

\*\*\*\*

"Thank you, Jake." Mrs. Calder brushed back a tear and clasped her husband's hand. "It was good of you and Dr. Fleming to come and tell us Bethany's murderer had been found."

Mr. Calder swallowed hard. "It's been so hard all these years not knowing who killed our daughter."

"He and his accomplice are dead," said Jake. "They can't hurt anyone again."

"We're so sorry for your loss," said Katherine, "but you deserved to hear first before the story hit the newspapers."

"It's so strange…" Mrs. Calder motioned to a box at the door. "Those belonged to Bethany. None are important, they have no sentimental value, but I couldn't bear to part with them until now. Then this afternoon a weight lifted from me as if Bethany whispered in my ear, 'Let it go.' The time suddenly seemed right to donate them to the animal shelter. I can't even say why I hung onto this stuff all these years. We don't own a cat and the woman who took him only wanted the pet carrier."

Jake exchanged a bemused glance with Katherine. They lifted the flaps and peered inside at a food dish, a small pet bed, and several cat toys. Jake cleared his throat. "When did Bethany get a cat?"

"A few weeks before she died," said Mrs. Calder. "A cute little white kitten, but Paul and I couldn't keep him. He's highly allergic."

"We posted an ad," said Mr. Calder, "and a woman came by. Kind of an oddball as I recall. She said I had a transcendent aura."

Jake muttered an aside to Katherine. "You don't

think…"

She whispered back, "I rather not."

****

Katherine inhaled deeply. "The barbeque smells delicious, Connie. Thanks for having us over."

"Yeah," said Jake with a grin. "Katherine is tired of my hotplate cooking. She'd make a lousy pioneer."

Katherine shot him a dirty look. "Even Whiskers agrees a full kitchen is a necessity for civilized dining."

"I second that," said Parker.

"Hey, we're almost there. Floors are done. The cabinets and countertops are installed and the new appliances arrive tomorrow. Then we can invite everyone over to our house for a party."

"Sound good to me," said April.

"Since when do you have time to party?" joshed Ethan. "You're a hotshot reporter now. Hey, did you all see her segment last night on the city council meeting? April even made the zoning committee's report riveting. I almost stayed awake through the whole thing." April punched him in the arm.

"And you, Katherine?" said Parker. "Keeping busy?"

She stared down at the table. "Not so much. Most clients canceled after the news about Jeremy broke. The building housing the clinic was one of the properties owned by Prentiss Ingalls. With Jeremy's death, it reverted to the trust. They were kind enough to allow me to stay to the end of the month, but my remaining clients always managed to turn the conversation to Jeremy and Diana. They became distracted from their own healing. I finally referred the last of them to other counselors." Katherine raised her head and forced a weak smile. "Time to start the job hunt again."

Jake placed a comforting arm around her shoulder. "You'll find another position soon."

"I hope so." *What if I don't? What if Jeremy's taint lingers and the only option is to start over again far from here?* She swallowed hard.

Parker shot his wife a veiled look. "New opportunities can come when you least expect them."

Katherine narrowed her eyes. "What's going on? You invited us here for a celebration, but have been awfully secretive."

"We'll explain when our last guest arrives," said Connie airily.

"Is it about the documentary on Safe Harbor?" said April.

"Not exactly, although we decided on an airdate in two weeks. You and Parker did an excellent job, April. We had a preview showing, and it garnered rave reviews."

April's mouth dropped open. "With whom?" she cried in dismay. "Why wasn't I invited?"

"I apologize," said Parker. "There was no time to call, so I made a last minute decision… Ah, here she is now."

Isabelle Addams walked into the backyard. "Sorry, I'm late. The meeting ran longer than expected."

Parker pulled up a chair for her. "I take it everything went well."

Isabelle beamed and took a seat. "Better than you can imagine."

"Don't keep us in suspense, then." Parker turned to the others. "As you know, Connie and I are acquainted with several board members of the Ingalls Trust."

"At the moment," chimed in Connie with wicked glee, "they're struggling with a severe public relations image. Jeremy was an active member of the board. Diana even attended meetings with him. Many in town believe the members should have suspected them."

Katherine gave a derisive snort. "I can say for a fact, Jeremy and Diana hid their secret lives well."

"Don't stand up for the board," said Parker with a twinkle in his eye. "Their embarrassment serves the greater good."

Isabelle laughed. "Connie and Parker showed them the documentary at the last meeting. Afterward, they suggested a large donation to an organization that helps victimized women will work wonders to improve the trust's tarnished reputation."

Katherine's eyes lit up. "They gave to Safe Harbor. Congratulations."

Isabelle grinned. "Thanks. We'll be able to move to a larger facility and triple the enrollment at the halfway house, but that's not all." She fidgeted in her seat as if barely able to contain the news. "The Ingalls Trust also offered the old farmhouse and funds to transform it into a place to help abused and troubled girls so they don't turn to the streets. I can also expand counseling services for victims of sexual assault like Tina who had no family support."

Isabelle leaned toward Katherine with a sly look. "This is a lot of work for one person. I need an assistant director to help set up and run the programs. A counseling background is a must. Can you think of anyone who would be interested?"

Katherine jumped from her seat and threw her arms around Isabelle's neck. "Hell, yes! I have so many ideas—"

"Me, too," gushed April. "I can get the station involved and do a series of stories on the expansion."

"I'll talk to Saldana," said Jake. "The police department supports several charities. I'm sure they could add one more. Besides, it's good community relations."

"A walk-a-thon to raise awareness and more funding?" added Ethan.

"You can always count on GAB-TV for free publicity," said Connie.

Katherine's eyes glowed. "When do we get started?"

Isabelle laughed. "Can I eat first?"

\*\*\*\*

When Katherine and Jake returned that evening to Culpepper Lane, Whiskers met them at the door with a purr.

Katherine picked him up. "He's saying, 'Welcome home.' "

Jake slipped an arm around her waist. "Welcome home."

As if in unspoken agreement, they entered the parlor and Katherine gazed at the surroundings with a smile. "Such a beautiful room…the details, the woodwork. Funny how I didn't notice before."

"We got distracted." Jake pulled her close. "I'll redo the parlor next. You need an office now. This will be perfect."

"Don't make it too nice," she joshed. "I'll never leave."

Jake's grip tightened. "That's the idea. I love you, Kathy."

Katherine gazed at the antique mirror. Nothing but a wavy image of the three of them together reflected from the glass. Just as it should be. "I love you, too."

## A word from the author...

I live in Florida where the heat and humidity have driven everyone slightly mad. I write fantasy/scifi adventures with humor, romance, and a touch of sass. In my spare time I call in Bigfoot sightings to the Florida Department of Fish and Wildlife. They are heartily sick of hearing from me.

If you enjoyed *Good Bones*, please take a moment to leave a review. No essay is necessary. A few kind words makes any author's day. Want to connect? Visit my lurking spots or drop me a line. I love hearing from readers.

http://www.facebook.com/l.a.kelley.author
Blog: http://lakelleythenaughtylist.blogspot.com
Twitter @AuthorLAKelley
l.a.kelley.author@gmail.com
~*~
Other L. A. Kelley titles
available from The Wild Rose Press, Inc.:
*THE NAUGHTY LIST*
*ONE ENCHANTED EVENING*
*SECOND CHANCE CITY*
*SPIRIT RIDGE*

Thank you for purchasing
this publication of The Wild Rose Press, Inc.

If you enjoyed the story, we would appreciate your
letting others know by leaving a review.

For other wonderful stories,
please visit our on-line bookstore at
www.thewildrosepress.com.

For questions or more information
contact us at
info@thewildrosepress.com.

The Wild Rose Press, Inc.
www.thewildrosepress.com

Stay current with The Wild Rose Press, Inc.

Like us on Facebook

https://www.facebook.com/TheWildRosePress

And Follow us on Twitter
https://twitter.com/WildRosePress